Their ... snow, twelve ragged figures emerged from their hiding places in the trees

Each man was dressed in the thick layers that the frozen climate demanded and each one held a weapon, which included semiautomatic pistols and a pair of Kalashnikov AK-47s with their stocks removed. At the back of the group, Ryan saw Jak, held tightly by a man dressed in rags with a pair of night-vision goggles visible above his scarf. Jak stood limply, as if dazed.

"You want to try it?" the man with the goggles snarled. "Be my guest. All the more food for us after we've chilled you."

As the man spoke, two more figures clambered down the slope from the copse of trees, carrying the slumped forms of Krysty and the girl in their arms.

Outnumbered and with his colleagues' lives in danger, Ryan ordered his team to stand down.

Ricky looked agitated, shooting Ryan a furious look. "We can take them," he whispered.

Ryan shook his head no. His people were at risk, too much so for him to start a firefight at such close quarters. For now, they would stand down.

And wait for a better opportunity to arise.

**Other titles in the
Deathlands saga:**

JAMES AXLER

DEATHLANDS®

Chrono Spasm

A GOLD EAGLE BOOK FROM

WORLDWIDE®

TORONTO • NEW YORK • LONDON
AMSTERDAM • PARIS • SYDNEY • HAMBURG
STOCKHOLM • ATHENS • TOKYO • MILAN
MADRID • WARSAW • BUDAPEST • AUCKLAND

Recycling programs
for this product may
not exist in your area.

First edition March 2013

ISBN-13: 978-0-373-62619-9

CHRONO SPASM

Copyright © 2013 by Worldwide Library

Printed in U.S.A.

Time...is motionless, and without beginning or end. That it has motion and is the cause of change is an illusion.

—H.P. Lovecraft &
E. Hoffman Price,
*Through the Gates of the
Silver Key,* 1932

THE DEATHLANDS SAGA

This world is their legacy, a world born in the violent nuclear spasm of 2001 that was the bitter outcome of a struggle for global dominance.

There is no real escape from this shockscape where life always hangs in the balance, vulnerable to newly demonic nature, barbarism, lawlessness.

But they are the warrior survivalists, and they endure—in the way of the lion, the hawk and the tiger, true to nature's heart despite its ruination.

Ryan Cawdor: The privileged son of an East Coast baron. Acquainted with betrayal from a tender age, he is a master of the hard realities.

Krysty Wroth: Harmony ville's own Titian-haired beauty, a woman with the strength of tempered steel. Her premonitions and Gaia powers have been fostered by her Mother Sonja.

J. B. Dix, the Armorer: Weapons master and Ryan's close ally, he, too, honed his skills traversing the Deathlands with the legendary Trader.

Doctor Theophilus Tanner: Torn from his family and a gentler life in 1896, Doc has been thrown into a future he couldn't have imagined.

Dr. Mildred Wyeth: Her father was killed by the Ku Klux Klan, but her fate is not much lighter. Restored from pre-dark cryogenic suspension, she brings twentieth-century healing skills to a nightmare.

Jak Lauren: A true child of the wastelands, reared on adversity, loss and danger, the albino teenager is a fierce fighter and loyal friend.

Dean Cawdor: Ryan's young son by Sharona accepts the only world he knows, and yet he is the seedling bearing the promise of tomorrow.

In a world where all was lost, they are humanity's last hope....

Prologue

This much he knew for certain: traveling through time always came with a cost.

Don Nectar knew all too well the cost of sailing passage on time's stream. He had lost so much to get here. He had lost everything he had ever been.

He had been a family man once, with a wife and children, a house that was more than just walls; a house that was also a home. He recalled these things only vaguely now, they seemed so distant to him that it was as if he was recollecting only a story he had been told, and he could no longer put the faces in place.

This much he knew for certain: his wife had been beautiful and he had loved her very much.

But the details—it was like trying to discern a painting through the fog. The details, the subject matter, all of it lost in the blur, nothing now but an abstract pattern of darkness and light. That was an apt description of his whole life—no details remained.

He couldn't remember how the journey through time had begun, nor where. He suspected that he had been forced on the journey, for why would a man give up so much—his whole life—for so little reward, simply to visit Hell? Perhaps it had been a punishment, he pondered, perhaps a sentence for some great ill he had been responsible for somewhere in the great forgotten past.

Perhaps he had killed a man.

How would he know? How could he remember? Even if he was told, would the details stick in his memory or would they simply fade away as everything had faded away, a broken thing that no longer made sense, a watch that could no longer tell the right time no matter how many times one wound it.

Don Nectar looked at the equipment before him, as he had a thousand times before. The days became weeks, and, conversely, the weeks days. The time machine would take him home, would fix the things he had lost from his Swiss-cheese memory.

This much he knew for certain: each time he engaged the machine, it sliced another chunk of his fractured soul away.

He would cry sometimes, when he realized how far he still had to go, when the futility of the whole exercise seemed to bear down on him with too much weight, some bastardized Atlas struggling beneath the weight of all of muddled, muddy time. Each attempt that he ran the time machine it spit debris into the atmosphere, shards of ruined time that clung to the surrounds in craters, like pockets of some gas that was heavier than air.

Things had stepped through the time window, too, things that should never have been, things that lived and fed and consumed. Things that made no sense outside the sense of the distilled time he had captured and purified. Don Nectar had studied the things. He was a man of learning, an authority on several disciplines of science; though he could no longer remember where he had obtained such knowledge, where he had studied. The creatures lived as parasites who fed on time, consuming the frayed edges where his bold experiments had caused pockets of chronal collapse, where the chrono spasm wouldn't cease.

The facility had been built to survive that, of course. When Nectar had arrived, the place had almost burned down, its walls alight from the trauma of his time shunt. He had survived, running out into the snow. And, later, he had damped down those fires with the snow, finally putting out flames that had raged for days. He felt unable to leave then, so he turned his attention to the machinery, employing all of his extensive knowledge to repair it, all the while struggling to remember just who he had really been. He felt like a shadow, a thing without true substance, just a mockery of a man. He had lost so much.

Once repaired, the machinery could open windows into other eras, provide smooth passage through the time stream, navigating its ebbs and its flows. The colossal generators towered before him, their low humming shaking his body within the radiation suit, feeling like a young colt yearning to break free of its reins. He gave the wrench another quarter turn, watched as the displays ran through their start-up sequence again, the towering generators shuddering against the thick gloves of his radiation-wear. The dials whirred in slow rotation, each one following the proscribed path that would assure the traveler a clear window into the past. It hadn't worked yet. But it had to, *it had to.*

This much he knew for certain: to return through time was the only goal he could have. To have any other would be to dilute his purpose, and without that determination the project would never be completed and he would die here in the Deathlands, having never seen his wife again. His mind was already too altered to allow himself the luxury of being distracted. He needed to focus to survive and to succeed in his escape through time.

Each endeavor, each time he got closer, it brought a little more disruption, turning the region all around him into a pockmarked mass of broken ages, of time spilled from the stream. To think…that time was a physical thing, to be molded and shaped. *And dumped.*

The voice called to him through time, his wife calling him home for dinner, as it had called every day since he had arrived in this place all those years-weeks-seconds ago. But there was another voice this time, one that spoke with the fractured resonance of the time displaced, just like him. He couldn't mistake that sound, it was the sound of his own voice when he caught himself cursing aloud the time machinery. The words seemed to filter to him from a distance, weaving through the air and into his skull, a poisoned arrow targeted straight for his brain.

For a moment, the lost time traveler known as Don Nectar cocked his head, trying to hear through the protective layer of his radiation suit. The words were lost. It was like trying to comprehend someone through the taffeta layers of a dream. But the sense of the speaker was clear in his mind's eye. It was the missing piece of the puzzle, the thing that would turn the machine on its axis. He felt sure of it.

This much he knew for certain.

Chapter One

It felt like a gut punch, the kind that the bullies would hammer into Ricky's stomach when they had cornered him in the back alleys of his hometown of Nuestra Señora. He slumped to the floor, grimacing against the pain, his arms clutched to his sides. J. B. Dix had told him that it could be bad, but he hadn't realized how bad it would be. Ricky Morales was sixteen and, unlike his six traveling companions, still a newbie when it came to journeying via a mat-trans.

"The kid gonna be okay?" Ryan Cawdor asked as he reentered the mat-trans unit, checking the safety on his SIG-Sauer blaster. He was a tall and imposing man with broad shoulders and a mane of curly black hair that fell to his collar. His bronzed face bore a long scar down the right-hand side, white and hairless, that ran from the corner of his eye all the way down to his mouth. His missing eye was masked by a black leather patch, the thread fraying a little along its stitching. He wore a heavy fur coat over a dirt-smeared shirt and dark undershirt, combat pants and scuffed boots, more durable than stylish. Ryan wore one other item, too, an item he had carried with him since the companions jumped to a redoubt in Canada called a Diefenbunker. There Ryan had traded his beloved Steyr-SSG scoped rifle for a Steyr Scout tactical model which was now slung across his back.

The son of a benevolent baron on the East Coast of the Deathlands, Ryan had grown up in luxury, only to have that life cruelly snatched away when his psychotic brother, Harvey, had tried to expunge the bloodline so that he could take the barony of Front Royal as his own. In the resulting struggle, Ryan had lost his left eye to Harvey's blade, and he had been set on a path to travel the Deathlands, eventually finding a home with Trader and his war wags.

Over the years since, Ryan had amassed his own family of sorts, one whose ties ran deeper than blood and who traveled together searching the Deathlands for a better tomorrow. Ricky Morales, a handsome Puerto Rican kid from the port of Nuestra Señora, was the newest addition to Ryan's companions, and the only one of them who hadn't become accustomed—yet— to the devastating effects of mat-trans travel on human physiology.

"I vouch that the young gentleman will be fine," Doc Tanner opined as he stood protectively over the youth's clenching body. Doc was a tall man, scarecrow-thin with a shock of gray-white hair on his aged head. His face was lined, and his penetrating blue eyes spoke of years of wisdom. His clothes, like his manner, were throwbacks to another era, a gentler time when life ran at a slower pace. He wore a black frock coat, a white shirt that was stained with grime and sweat, narrow breeches that clung to his rangy legs and black knee boots.

Though he appeared to be at least sixty years old, Doc Tanner's history was far more complicated than that. Dr. Theophilus Algernon Tanner had been born in South Strafford, Vermont, on Valentine's Day, 1868. He had married his beloved Emily in 1891 and they had lived in wedded bliss for five years, raising two children—Rachel and Jolyon—before Doc's life changed forever. In 1896 he was time trawled from his own era by the twentieth-century whitecoats of Operation Chronos. Proving to be a difficult subject, Doc was hurled forward in time to the Deathlands. The effect of this forced time travel on Doc had been twofold—firstly, it had prematurely aged him, transforming his body into that of an old man; and second, it had fractured his mind, leaving him with a sometimes tenuous grip on his sanity. Over time, and with the patient help of Ryan and his other companions, Doc had managed to regain much of his sanity—or at least, as much of it as any man who had lost so much could—and become an invaluable asset to the survivalist band.

Inside the green-and-yellow-striped armaglass-walled mat-trans chamber, Doc was leaning on his ebony swordstick, peering at Ricky as he shuddered on the floor. "The lad's strong, my dear Ryan," Doc assured the one-eyed man with a knowing smile. "He has the constitution of youth of his side."

Ryan nodded, pushing the magazine of 9 mm Parabellum bullets into the housing of his SIG-Sauer P-226 blaster. "Lot of good it'll do him if he can't stand up."

"I…can stand…fine," Ricky mumbled, struggling to pull himself up off the floor.

Doc reached down, taking the youth's arm in his strong grip. "Slowly, son," he advised. "There is no need to rush."

Ryan watched as the handsome young man brought himself to his feet. He was struggling to stand up straight, sucking at his teeth as he drew each breath. Mat-trans jumps were bastard-hard on a man's constitution, Ryan knew, plucking at the guts and cross-wiring the brain's synapses so that a person was beset with a deluge of nightmarish visions. The other companions had become either used to or resigned to it by now, after dozens of trips. While jump nightmares and nausea were nothing to get complacent about, Ryan and his companions knew that they would pass in time. Ricky, however, wasn't as experienced. Ryan stepped over, placing one arm around the youth's back to keep him on his feet.

"I've got him," Ryan told Doc.

The teenaged Ricky Morales had traveled with Ryan's group for only a few weeks. Ryan was still adjusting to having the kid on his team, another person to worry about when the bullets started flying or muties came sniffing for blood. Ryan had lost companions before, and the most heart-wrenching loss had been that of his own son, Dean, who had been a few years younger than Ricky when he had been spirited away by his mother, Sharona. A recent encounter with Dean had ended badly.

Ryan's other companions had been less affected by the trauma of the mat-trans jump. Jak Lauren, who had vomited, as usual, had already exited the chamber along with Ryan's lover, Krysty Wroth, and his most-trusted ally, J.B. When the one-eyed man had given the all-clear, they had gone in search of supplies on this floor of the military redoubt.

The remaining member of the group, Dr. Mildred Wyeth, was sitting just outside the door of the mat-trans, running an inventory of the medical supplies she carried in the satchel at her hip. She wore camou pants and a drab olive shirt, and her hardy jacket hung from the back of her seat. "If you all need a proper doctor," she called through the open door, "you just shout. I'm doing a two-fer-one flu jab this week, special offer, friends only. Get 'em while they're hot."

Doc smiled at her as he stepped from the mat-trans chamber. "You're in a chipper mood, my good Doctor," he observed.

Mildred shrugged, her beaded plaits clacking against one another. "What can I say? No one likes a grump."

Doc nodded, accepting her point.

Like the old man, Mildred was a time traveler of sorts, albeit one who had spent a full century in the sleep-induced coma of cryogenic freezing. In the twentieth century, Mildred had been a medical doctor who had been researching cryogenics. She had also been an expert shot, whose skill with a pistol had earned her a silver medal at the last ever Olympic Games. What should have been a routine surgical procedure in December 2000 had turned problematic, and the decision was made to place Mildred in suspended animation until a solution could be applied. A few days later, the world Mildred knew came to a dramatic end when the escalating hostilities between the United States of America and the United Soviet Socialist Republic had reached their peak, resulting in a nuclear war that had unutterably changed the face of Earth forever.

Stuck in suspended animation for a hundred years, Mildred had been awakened by Ryan and his companions to a world recovering from nuclear holocaust, where humankind had been culled to just one-tenth of what it had been before the war, where society had broken down entirely and where mutants with genetically manipulated bioweapons roamed the lands. It was, not to put to fine a point on it, a rather rude awakening.

Ryan followed Doc, assisting Ricky through the door. "Deep breaths," Ryan told him. "Take it slow."

"I'm all right now," Ricky said, wincing. "It was nothing." The young man respected Ryan a lot, thought he was the kind of man he would like to grow up to be. He didn't like Ryan to see him in pain like this; it made him look weak.

Ryan smiled, recognizing the lad's false bravado. It reminded him of his early days with Jak, the group's second youngest companion, who had become a man at fourteen without ever knowing a childhood. In those nascent days, Jak had been so reticent to show emotion that he seemed more like an animal than a boy. In some ways, that was mebbe still true now, Ryan reflected.

He walked Ricky over to a chair that had been placed to the right of the chamber door. "Sit and take deep breaths," he said again. "In and out."

With that, Ryan left the youth in the recovery position, head ducked low between his knees, while Doc took up a position nearby to keep watch on the lad.

The room outside the mat-trans chamber was as familiar to Ryan as the chamber itself, despite having not visited here before. Located in a military redoubt hidden behind thick walls of concrete and steel, the mat-trans was contained in a purpose-built chamber surrounded by armaglass. Outside its hexagonal walls lay the familiar anteroom, then the control room, computer monitoring desks arrayed in rows. At the far end of the control room was a set of steel-reinforced doors that led into the long-abandoned military complex. The doors were propped open, their steel plating shimmering beneath the flickering fluorescent lights overhead that had come on automatically with the operation of the mat-trans. The system of redoubts dated back to the twentieth century, before the nukecaust, and was largely automated, which meant that it still operated despite the fact that these redoubts hadn't been accessed in over a hundred years. The level of automation sometimes gave Ryan the sense he was walking in a dream, as if a kind of hidden hand was bringing things back to life.

Mildred sat at one of the desks closest to the center of the room. The contents of her medical kit were spread out across two desks as she took stock of and reordered her meager supplies, rationalizing them into less space and discarding the used packaging. The arrayed contents consisted of recovered drugs, ointments and a selection of wicked-looking scalpels, their blades honed to razor-sharpness. Mildred also had a blaster on the desk, uncocked and within reach of her right hand should anyone happen to rush into the control room. The weapon was a Czech-made ZKR 551 target pistol, a neat, matte-black .38 caliber with plenty of punch. She glanced up as Ryan approached.

"You want me to look him over?" Mildred whispered, her eyes flicking to their new companion where he sat doubled over in his seat.

"Not necessary," Ryan told her quietly, shaking his head. "Doc's right—the kid's strong. He just got caught unawares by the jump."

As they spoke, their remaining companions returned, entering the control room through the double doors.

Leading the group was John Barrymore Dix, a compact man much like the weapons he favored. Also known as the Armorer, J.B. was the group's weaponsmith and an expert with just about any firearm or detonation device. What he didn't know about blasters wasn't worth knowing. He and Ryan owed their companionship to their time spent with the Trader, a legendary survivalist and trader who traveled the Deathlands with his own band, each an expert in his or her own field. J.B. and Ryan had formed a close bond over the years, so close that they often seemed to know what the other was thinking.

Despite being inside the warm redoubt, J.B. wore his usual battered brown fedora and a leather jacket. A pair of wire-rimmed glasses was perched on the bridge of his nose, through which his eyes assessed everything he saw.

Though J.B. appeared squat, that was in fact an illusion created by the shape of his jacket, whose voluminous pockets had become bulked out with various weapons and devices he carried out of necessity. The Armorer was happy to maintain this illusion, preferring that potential enemies underestimate him on first glance for it often ensured they never had the chance to realize their mistake. You only needed to chill a man once to survive, J.B. would insist.

"Place is all cleaned out," he announced, throwing Ryan a new magazine for his SIG-Sauer. "Plenty of ammo, but not much we can use."

Ryan snatched the magazine from the air and pocketed it. "What about food?" he asked.

The beautiful red-haired woman who followed J.B. through the doors shook her head regretfully. "There's been an interruption in the power supply at some point, lover," she told Ryan. "Refrigerator's open and everything's spoiled with mold all over. I wouldn't touch it."

"We might have to," J.B. added, scratching at the day-old stubble that lined his jowls.

"Let's hope not," Ryan said. "Mebbe this time we landed in a nice field full of tomatoes and strawberries."

J.B. laughed at that. "'Cept knowing our luck they'll be the kind of strawberries that got themselves irradi-ated and have taken to eating folks who come to pick 'em."

The redhead shot the Armorer a mock-serious look as she joined Ryan. "If you've jinxed us, J.B., I won't ever forgive you," she chastised as Ryan ran a hand over her back. Krysty was the one-eyed man's lover. A striking woman, tall and svelte, Krysty's red hair drew the eye. The hair seemed almost alive in the bright fluorescent light of the control room; and in truth it was— Krysty was a mutie, with prehensile hair that reflected her emotional state. She had other abilities, too, that sat outside the realm of the average human—some precognition and the ability to tap an incredible well of superhuman strength that came from calling upon the Earth Mother, the goddess Gaia. These bouts of incredible strength lasted only moments and left Krysty drained and as weak as a newborn. Dressed in a red shirt, jeans and blue cowboy boots with silver pointed toes, Krysty had a Smith & Wesson .38 revolver secured at her hip, its burnished silver finish worn from years of service.

Krysty kissed Ryan on the lips, then mouthed a promise of "later" before hurrying across the room to fetch the coat she had left on a seat behind a comp desk.

Doc placed his hand to his brow as Krysty passed, tipping an imaginary hat. Beside him, Ricky was bringing his breathing back to a more normal level, his teeth still gritted in pain. The Latino eyed Krysty for a moment before her eyes met with his, and then he turned away with embarrassment. Ricky thought Krysty was the most beautiful woman in the world.

The last member of Ryan's crew was waiting in the doorway, his red eyes almost flashing in the flickering lights. "Don't like pisshole," he spit. "Stinks." Jak Lauren, a man not yet twenty years old with the white skin and hair of an albino, and the thin body of a teenager. Jak's eyes were twin orbs of a cruel, ruby red, and his face was a series of scarred white planes like some brutal sculpture carved by a careless knife. Jak's chalk-white hair brushed past his shoulders, sweeping against the glistening razor-sharp slivers of glass and metal that he wore sewn into his camou coat—especially the collar and shoulders—to ward off any would-be attacker.

Though he followed Ryan, Jak was very much his own man. Semiferal, Jak had grown up in the swamps of Louisiana, where a cruel dictator called Baron Tourment had demanded absolute fealty. Jak's father had rebelled against Tourment's rule and it had cost him his life. At fourteen, Jak had assumed his father's place, leading a revolution against the sadistic baron and overthrowing him with the help of Ryan and his companions. Other than the time Jak had spent with his now deceased wife, the albino had remained with Ryan ever since, and his exceptional tracking skill and his deadly use of a knife had proved invaluable. Jak saw the world in terms of black and white, but he was a good man to have at your side. Ryan had trusted Jak with his life more times than he could count.

Ryan nodded, agreeing with Jak's assessment. "Okay, people," he said, glancing around the control room. "Let's check out what the local area has to offer."

Doc helped Ricky get to his feet while the other companions grabbed their belongings and prepared to leave. Up ahead, the redoubt's lights burned brightly, each concrete-walled corridor brutal and soulless beneath the unforgiving fluorescent glow. Ryan led the way, his companions following him through the familiar corridors to the redoubt's exit.

It was always like this. The companions would travel

from location to location, hopping across the Death-lands via the hidden mat-trans network, unable to pro-gram the system and so shooting randomly from point to point. Sometimes they would find a little oasis where kindness reigned and the locals welcomed their visit; more often they would walk slap-bang into yet another level of Hell, where the final remnants of humankind fought tooth and nail simply to see another sunrise, an-other day; where the weather patterns included acid rain that could strip a person to the bone, and where irradi-ated muties waited in ambush to tear a person apart. It was a life that knew little joy, but Ryan's group carried on, always hoping for a better tomorrow, for a reprieve from this Hell on Earth.

They reached the main doors to the redoubt inside of four minutes. It was a small complex, just a dozen rooms in all, sealed since before the first nuclear strike had impacted on mainland American soil a century ear-lier. In the years that followed, whatever had remained had rotted or spoiled or simply disintegrated to dust, little seams of powder lining the rooms like sawdust where once there had been perishable goods. The re-doubt had been understocked, "probably a real haven of last resort," according to J.B. Perhaps it would have saved someone's life if they had got here in time; it looked like no one had ever had the chance to find out.

Ricky struggled a little to keep up, hefting his DeLisle carbine in one hand.

Doc strode along with the youth, thrusting his sword-stick out with a flourish. "How are you feeling now?" he asked as they neared the redoubt's external doors.

"Like I ate something real bad," Ricky admitted. "Is it always going be like that?"

"Probably not," Doc replied. "But who knows?

Maybe that was our last jump and we are about to step out into paradise, right behind that door."

J.B. was at the door, punching the keypad with the numbers that would open it. After a moment, the door made a loud clunking sound before it started to ponderously slide open.

The companions waited at a safe distance, their weapons poised on the emerging gap before them as the door creaked open. The first thing that they noticed as the door drew back was the cold. It struck them like a wall of ice, taking their breath away even as it fluttered like mist in the air.

"If this is paradise," Ricky told Doc, "then it sure is colder than I expected."

But before anyone could say another word, a woman's face, emaciated with dark circles under the eyes and ragged tangles of long hair, appeared in the open doorway of the redoubt. The dirt-smeared face was accompanied by a blaster, its dull metal glinting beneath the glow of the fluorescent lights.

"Pomoshch," she hissed, bringing the nose of the blaster up to J.B.'s startled face.

Chapter Two

J.B.'s hand snapped up, grabbing the blaster before the pale-faced woman realized what he was doing.

"Makarov," J.B. said emotionlessly, his eyes fixing on the young woman's. "Neat little blaster for what it is but has a lousy double-action pull."

The young woman glared at him, straining to bring up the blaster as he forced her hand to point at the ground. J.B. had overpowered her in a second.

"Yours, incidentally," the Armorer finished as he revealed his own weapon, a Smith & Wesson M-4000 shotgun, "is all out of ammo. Thought you'd like to know."

The woman looked at J.B. fearfully as he casually turned his shotgun on her, cocking the trigger. Behind him, she saw now, were a half dozen other people, each one training his or her own blaster on her.

"P-pomoshch," the woman repeated, her voice coming through clenched teeth. *"Pomoshch moi!"* She was a thin young woman, with sharp, narrow features and straw-colored hair that snaked down to the small of her back in a series of twisting spirals. Her face was streaked with dirt, and she had dark circles under her eyes. She wore a ragged old dress that ended just below her upper thighs, leaving her legs bare. She was barefoot and beneath the hemline of her dress, her legs were

turning blue from the cold. *"Pomoshch!"* she cried desperately.

"Who or what is *pomoshch?*" J.B. asked, still holding the woman in his grip. He eased it a little, pressing the muzzle of his shotgun against her side.

"Pomoshch," the woman repeated, seeing the blank expressions that J.B. and the others wore. "Help me!" she pleaded. "They're coming. They're just behind me. Hide me, please!"

As she spoke, the companions became aware of hoofbeats from a little way to their right, which were accompanied by shouts coming from very close nearby.

"This way," a man's voice called. It sounded angry. "Don't lose her."

"I'm comin'," another voice insisted and the hoofbeats drummed faster.

"Someone out there," Jak hissed, eyeing the door. "Close."

Outside the redoubt it was night, the clear sky above a rich shade of blue-black, like writing ink. The redoubt entrance was surrounded by an overgrown tangle of bushes, and in the illumination cast by the open doorway they could see a few bloated flakes of snow drifting languorously to the ground. The ground itself was a scrubby patchwork of green and frost, snow settling in clumps and clinging to the bushes tiny leaves.

J.B.'s brows knitted as he glared at the emaciated woman in the doorway. "You point a blaster in my face and come asking for help," he drawled as he twisted her wrist in his grip. She squeaked in pain, dropping the Makarov to the concrete floor with a clatter. "Real friendly, sister."

Then J.B. stepped back, pulling the young woman inside the corridor of the redoubt where his friends were waiting. Beyond the door, they heard more shouts, the words sounding muffled by the falling snow.

"She came through here," a man said. "Maybe she jumped the fence."

The young woman looked plaintively at J.B., her haunted expression speaking an encyclopedia volume of fear. "Help me," she whimpered.

Around J.B., Ryan and the other companions had fanned out to cover the wide doorway into the redoubt.

Jak sidled up to the door, pressing his back to the wall, his trusted Colt Python blaster clutched in a two-handed grip. It looked massive in his relatively small hands.

On the opposite side of the doorway, Krysty had adopted a similar pose, pressing her back to the wall and drawing her Smith & Wesson .38, its muzzle aimed out into the open air. She was wearing her coat now, its shaggy fur design like something that had just been killed. She prowled like a cat toward the open door, footstep over silent footstep, her breath hanging in the air in cloudy puffs of mist.

Mildred and Doc had also moved forward, and the physician had dropped her satchel silently to the floor as soon as the shouting started. Doc had something of a unique weapon in his possession, a reproduction LeMat percussion pistol styled from the turn of the nineteenth century, its .44-caliber barrel augmented with a second shotgun-style barrel that could unleash an incredible burst of shrapnel capable of punching a good-size hole in a wall—or a human torso.

Ricky remained at the rear of the group. An experienced fighter despite his young age, he yearned to be on the front line in any combat situation. But his constitution following the mat-trans jump had left him compromised, and he was wise enough to know that trying to lead while unfit only served as a hindrance to his allies—and a potentially lethal one.

The final member of the group, Ryan trusted his colleagues to keep the door covered. He had his SIG-Sauer poised not on the open door but on the young woman in J.B.'s arms.

"Who followed you?" Ryan growled. "Quickly, tell me."

The young woman looked at him fearfully, still struggling in J.B.'s grip.

"Quit struggling and answer him," J.B. urged.

"Mytante," the girl responded with her strange accent. *"Mytante groupa."*

"Fireblast!" Ryan growled. "Muties."

As the words left Ryan's mouth, two muscular steeds came crashing through the tangled briars at the front of the redoubt, tossing broken branches aside and snow in their wake. The steeds looked almost black in the unforgiving illumination spilling from the doorway. Each was shorter than a horse but more bulky, with sturdy bodies like great walls of muscle and a curling set of thick horns branching out from their wide, triangular heads. A honking noise issued from each creature's snout, accompanied by a cloud of warm breath, and each steed carried a rider bareback.

The riders were dressed from head to toe in strips of material and fur, with hoods covering their heads and dirt-streaked scarves bunched over their mouths and noses. The two riders wore goggles over their eyes, the familiar green tint of night-vision lenses recognizable to the companions straightaway.

"Caribou," Mildred said, startled. "They look like caribou."

THE FIRST RIDER leaped from his steed, wielding a vicious-looking pike with a cruel blade attached to one end, a second spiked arm running in parallel beneath it for added penetration.

"What the hell is this place?" he asked his comrades. "You ever see this before?"

Astride his own mutie caribou, the man shook his head. "Maybe she went inside," he called as he unstrapped a blaster from its leather sheath at the side of his boot. The weapon was some kind of abbreviated carbine, its barrel sawn so short that it could only possibly be effective at close range.

The first rider clomped over the snow-brushed scrub, holding his pike at a horizontal in line with his waist. "Come on out, sweetie," he cooed. "Your little game's all over now."

"Pomoshch," the frightened woman in J.B.'s arms whispered. "Please."

As the first rider reached the doors, Krysty emerged from her position behind the door frame, bringing her blaster up to the man's temple with a click of the cocked safety. "You want to drop the stick and reach for the sky?" she suggested.

The man reacted far quicker than anyone expected, whipping the pike around and swiping at Krysty with the long haft. The redhead grunted as the rounded metal pole struck her across the rib cage, and she stumbled forward with a lurch.

"Bad choice," J.B. stated as the other companions began firing, peppering the figure framed in the doorway before he knew what was happening. The mysterious figure stumbled back as a half-dozen bullets struck him. In Deathlands the best rule was to shoot first, and the companions hadn't lived as long as they had by taking chances.

As the figure went caroming to the ground, the second rider brought up his abbreviated carbine—the chop-shop remains of a Simonov SKS—and began blasting. A stream of vicious 7.62 mm bullets came singing from the weapon's stubby nose, drilling through the doorway like the expulsion of a shotgun rather than a rifle.

Krysty skipped back, her boot heels scraping across the hard floor as chunks of concrete were kicked up from the walls and floor under that deadly assault.

"Back," Jak barked, targeting the rider in the sights of his Colt Python and pulling the trigger. The weapon coughed, blasting the first of three .357 Magnum bullets at the rider. But Jak's angle was wrong. His bullets struck the thick head of the mutie caribou. The creature reared up, snarling with a low rumble as three bullets skipped across its hide.

Atop the beast, the rider was working the carbine one-handed, resting its grip on his leg as he reached into his ragged cloak for something else. Nearer the door, both Krysty and Jak saw just what it was in the second it appeared—a round metal pineapple no bigger than a man's palm. A grenade.

In a single instant, the rider on the horned caribou tossed the bomb at the open doorway of the redoubt, where his partner lay in a bloody heap.

"Gren!" Krysty shouted, leaping back from the doorway with her arms outstretched.

"Protect yourselves!" Doc gasped, dropping back against the nearest wall.

The other companions backed away as the grenade landed inside the open doorway, striking the floor with the low tink of metal on concrete. Jak, however, leaped through the doorway and out into the snow.

The gren went off, sending a shock wave through the air with a great clap of noise. Nearby trees and bushes trembled, tossing snow from their branches as the wave of pressure rolled over them. Jak ignored it, using its power to drive him forward toward the riderless caribou that waited twenty feet in front of the redoubt. His breath came harsh in the cold air, each inhalation burning against his nostrils and throat like ice.

The remaining rider had turned his head as the gren exploded, sending bloody chunks of his own partner through the air in a spray of mangled flesh and bone. He looked back in dismay as Jak raced across the powdered snow, his white skin and hair so pale it seemed almost as if an empty set of clothes was running across the snowy ground.

Jak tossed his Colt Python aside, brushing it from his mind as it sunk into the powdery snow. It was no use against these creatures and their thick hides. To deal with them he needed to get up close and personal—just the way he liked it. The albino sprinted, pulling back his jacket and reaching inside with both hands in a practiced movement, drawing loose two leaf-bladed throwing knives.

First one hand then the other whipped forward, throwing the vicious little blades ahead of him as he ran toward the nearer of the beasts. The first blade struck the creature's black hide and bounced off it to no effect. The second blade fared a little better, clipping the mutated caribou just above its lip and carving a rent through its right nostril.

Jak was a master of the throwing knife, expert at judging the weight of the metal. The creature reared in pain, its breath puffing out in a damp cloud of water vapor.

Then Jak was on it, jumping into the air, another twin set of blades already materialized in his chalk-white hands. He carried countless blades about his person, hidden in wrist and ankle sleeves, strapped to his torso and stitched into every accessible tuck of his jacket's lining.

Jak leaped at the caribou, plunging one of his drawn knives into its face as his feet struck the animal's flank. The creature huffed in pain as Jak's knife grazed its eyeball, tearing a great gob of flesh from its flat nose. Above its triangular head, Jak twisted, kicking out at the startled rider and knocking him from his mount. The rider shrieked in surprise as much as pain, his carbine going off again as he sank from the creature's side.

Jak was astride the creature now, and with a quick shift of his weight he kicked his heels against its flanks and drove both of the blades he held into its back, where the head met with its stubby, armored neck. The monster growled deep in its throat, the sound like a goose's honk as it began to charge wildly ahead. The second of the monstrous caribou was just a few feet away, and Jak dug his heel in once more to aim the panicked creature at the other. The mutie caribou reacted instinctively, ducking its horned head low as it spotted the other charging it. Between them, the fallen rider struggled to roll free of the destined clash, but he was too late. Suddenly, he found himself trampled by his own steed, leg bones and ribs shattering as the mighty caribou stomped over him.

Jak leaped free as the two-horned monstrosities butted heads together in a thunder crack of bone, blood still spurting from the first creature's knife wounds.

Beneath them, the mutie rider was screaming in agony, his body a mangled and bloody mess as the angered creatures crashed together in a contest of supremacy.

Inside the redoubt entrance, the companions were just recovering from the shock wave that had struck the redoubt's door. Positioned at the rear of the group, Ryan and Ricky were the first to recover. Ricky had one hand up against his ear, trying to stop it from ringing. Ryan looked about, scanning the entrance to the redoubt and checking that his friends were all accounted for.

"Everyone okay?" Ryan asked. "Where's Jak?"

"I believe our pale-skinned companion decided to take the fight outside," Doc said, dabbing cement dust from his brow with a blue handkerchief.

"Sounds about right," Ryan grumbled. "Everyone else okay?"

They were shaken by the blast but otherwise unharmed. Ryan hurried over to check on Krysty, but she confirmed that she had gotten clear of the blast with seconds to spare. "Well, maybe one second," she admitted when Ryan gave her a dubious look.

"The entry took most of the impact, by the looks of it," Mildred said as she made her way to the doorway. A blackened crater marred the floor where the grenade had gone off.

Doc was at the doorway now with Mildred at his side, scanning the bleak landscape for Jak. Two mutated caribous were butting heads in a smear of blood and pulp, while Jak, with considerable aplomb, crouched in the snow to pick up his discarded Colt Python while still watching the fight. The albino looked like a kid who had snuck into a prize fight.

Back inside the redoubt, J.B. was just bringing himself up off the floor. He had been very near to the explosion when it had gone off, and it had only been his quick thinking that had moved him and the mysterious young woman out of harm's way.

"Dark night, that was close," J.B. said as he struggled back to his feet. He had reacted instantly at Krysty's warning, shoving himself and the young woman to the floor at the speed of thought. The blonde was sprawled on the hard concrete floor, sobbing quietly, tears streaming down her cheeks.

"It's okay," J.B. told her. "We're still alive."

The young woman looked at him with a tentative smile. "They are gone?" she asked.

"Two of them—both chilled," the Armorer confirmed.

"Nyet," she said, shaking her head rapidly. "There were more of them. More than…twelve, maybe fifteen." She was fretting immediately, and J.B. had to hold her arm to steady her as she tried to run deeper into the redoubt. "They're after my father."

"Hear that, Ryan?" he called.

Ryan nodded grimly. "Then we'd better get moving," he said.

A moment later, the seven companions and their mysterious new charge exited the redoubt, Ryan tapping in the coded sequence that sealed the door before they made their way out into the snow-speckled night, past the riled-up mutie caribou. The caribou ignored them, their horns locked, too busy engaged in their own squabble to worry themselves with the trifling affairs of the humans.

Chapter Three

"Alaska," J.B. said, lowering the tiny folding minisextant and putting it into one of his deep pockets. "That's my best guess, anyways."

Standing amid the fallen branches, Ryan looked at him. "Best guess?" he probed.

The Armorer shrugged. "Stars are in the right place for sure," he explained, "but by my calculations we're farther north than the maps go."

"The maps could be wrong," Doc opined, tugging his collar closer to his neck. While the others were well-equipped for cold weather, the old man only had his light frock coat to keep him warm and, ironically, he was the one who felt the cold most. "A lot of changes were wrought unto the landscape with the outbreak of the nukecaust."

"Doc has a point," Mildred added, not looking up from where she was examining the blonde. "We know that tectonic plates have been shunted out of their old positions in other parts of the world. No reason it didn't happen here, wherever here is."

"Might be Nome," J.B. said with marked indifference, scanning the vinyl-covered predark map that he had produced from one of his jacket's capacious pockets.

Krysty laughed. "Sounds more like a creature than a place," she said. "Gnomes and pixies and little elflings. My mother told me all about them back in Harmonyville."

"Well, wherever we are, it's here," Ryan said with his usual pragmatism. He scanned their surroundings for a moment, eyeing the patchy snow clumping indifferently against the frozen tundra. Having locked the redoubt, the companions had made their way through the thorny bushes that surrounded the entrance, following the path that the tired-looking young woman led them through. She was clearly distraught, mumbling in a language that Ryan couldn't make sense of. She led them up a frost-carpeted slope to a cluster of trees, well hidden in the moonless night while providing an ideal vantage point of the immediate area.

Ryan had put Jak and Ricky on sentry detail, the latter assuring the one-eyed man that he had finally recovered from the effects of the mat-trans jump. Ryan peered through the trees at the snow-dappled ground all around them. Visibility was poor, but that meant that anyone sneaking up on them would have just as much chance of missing the companions as they did them. Anyway, Ryan figured, there wasn't much to see. All there was was another pest-hole full of chillers.

"The girl's calmed down," Mildred said as Ryan surveyed the area. Beside him, J.B. carefully stowed away his battered map. A chill breeze cut through the trees, tossing the falling snowflakes on the air like dancers at a predark ball.

Ryan nodded, pacing across to where the young woman sat with her back propped against the trunk of a tree. She looked frozen, hugging herself as she tried to keep warm. Mildred had given her a blanket from their supplies and had handed over her spare socks in place of her missing shoes. It wasn't much, and Mildred felt it was even odds that the young woman might lose a foot before the night was over unless they got her somewhere warmer.

"You okay now?" Ryan asked the shivering woman as he stood before her.

She looked at him, and Ryan eyed her closely for the first time. Behind the smudges of dirt and the messy tangle of hair she was young and quite beautiful. He estimated she was no more than nineteen, but it was hard to tell, given how thin she looked. Probably not much food going spare if the weather's always like this up here, Ryan realized.

The teenager was staring at Ryan's eye patch, as if unable to look away. She began to say something, but it was unintelligible to Ryan.

"I think she wants to know why you wear your patch," Doc suggested.

Ryan nodded solemnly. "You want to know how I got this?" he asked, and the young woman nodded once. "Fight with my brother. You have a brother? Or a sister mebbe?"

She nodded. *"Tri,"* she said. *"Dve sestry*...end brother."

"They around?" Ryan asked.

She averted her eyes, looking at the ground as she shook her head.

"I'm Ryan," he told her. "You have a name?"

"Nyarla," she said timidly after a moment's consideration.

Ryan held his empty hands out to her. "You're okay now," he told her. "You're safe."

Nyarla nodded again, taking his hands for just a moment in gratitude. After that, Ryan stepped back to confer with his companions.

"Any sign from Jak or Ricky?" Ryan asked.

J.B. shook his head. "They're out there, we'll know if they spot anything."

JAK STALKED through the icy undergrowth with Ricky a few steps behind him. They held their bodies low to create smaller targets. Jak was a natural loner, used to operating alone even while playing his role in Ryan's hodgepodge team. Having Ricky at his side was new. He liked the kid, had seen and admired the way he handled a blaster when all hell was breaking loose. But it still took some getting used to having the kid at his side like this.

Jak brushed at his collar, smiled momentarily at the snow that had settled across the line of his shoulders, clinging to the sharp shards of glass and metal that were sewn there. In this environment the snow was good— it provided camouflage, helping him and Ricky blend into the surroundings.

Jak was an expert tracker, blessed with enhanced senses far superior to an average person's. Right now, as the two of them made a circuit around the copse of trees, Jak smelled something. He sniffed again, scenting the air. It was blood, and even with the wind whipping around the trees the way it was, he could tell it wasn't coming from the direction of the bloodbath at the redoubt. Something else had lost blood out here this night, and Jak wanted to know what.

Ricky saw Jak slow. "What is it, Jak?" he whispered from behind him, hunkering low to the ground. He had never seen weather like this, never felt cold like this. Alaska was a hell of a long way from his home on Monster Island.

Jak's nose wrinkled, his keen eyes searching the

woods. The trees were sprinkled with snow, not thick but enough to line their branches, ice crystals making their leaves glisten in the faint starlight. Little patches of snow littered the ground, too, dotted here and there like some unfinished mosaic, the green shoots of grass clumping between the tiny oases of white.

Jak said nothing, merely gestured to Ricky to indicate that they would keep searching. He hurried on, weaving swiftly between the trees, the Latino youth following in his wake. The smell was getting stronger, a smell like raw meat.

The trees were less dense here, and Jak could see now almost the whole way down the slope on the opposite side to the path they had taken to reach the copse. Down there, where the ground leveled off, he saw a dark shape splayed across the snow. It looked like a snow angel.

Jak stopped suddenly, motioning with one hand for Ricky to do the same. "There," he said, pointing to the snow angel.

"What is it?" Ricky whispered, narrowing his eyes to see. His hand was automatically reaching for his Webley Mk VI revolver, instinct kicking in.

Jak glanced at the boy's hand and shook his head. Not yet. He didn't want any shooting unless necessary, bad enough they had had to chill the two mutie riders at the redoubt's doors. Why draw more attention unnecessarily?

Jak held his hand up, his pale flesh ghostly in the faint glimmer of distant stars. He motioned toward a snow-sprinkled ridge that ran down between the trees. The ridge was shallow enough to climb down. "Safe way."

Ricky nodded, following Jak down the slope, his

hand still close to the butt of his holstered revolver. In silence, they hurried down the slope, ever alert to the presence of other people or wild animals.

There was a subtle change in the acoustics at the bottom of the slope, one that Ricky noted just momentarily, while Jak seemed much more concerned with it. The snow was light in the air, but it was enough to muffle noise, sufficient that they might be crept up on without noticing.

"Careful," Jak warned his companion.

Ricky nodded, and then Jak was away, legs and arms pumping as he darted out beyond the edge of the line of trees, keeping his body low as he sprinted to the figure lying in the distance. Ricky followed, his heart pounding at his chest as he hurried to keep up. Ahead of him, Jak was a white blur, the blush of snow across his shoulders and back.

The two stopped. It was a man, naked and nailed down with his stomach opened to the elements. The flesh of his stomach had been pinned back, trails of guts and intestines pulled out from it in bloody coils that turned the snow red.

Ricky gulped, tamping down his urge to throw up. "Who would do this?" he whispered.

The man's eyes flickered at the noise. He was alive.

"Help me," the man croaked.

Ricky stepped forward, but Jak stopped him with a gesture. There was something else there, Jak realized, something watching them.

He turned, scanning the snow-spattered trees and bushes, their outlines barely visible in the starlight. And there, prowling among the bushes, was a white-furred mutie wolf, its massive head low to the ground, snout twitching as it sniffed at the air. It, too, had scented the blood and been drawn to it.

The wolf looked up, twin tusks jutting sharply from its bottom jaw, its pale eyes fixing on Jak's. The albino watched as the wolf's nose twitched again and its black lips curled back to reveal a fearsome set of teeth. Then it charged them.

WITHIN THE COPSE, Krysty spoke gently with Nyarla in a quiet voice while Ryan conferred with the other members of his crew.

"Must have come from somewhere," Ryan said quietly. "She isn't dressed for this climate."

"What language is she speaking?" J.B. asked. "It didn't sound completely like English to me."

"She's using English words," Ryan said, "but there's an accent. Thick accent."

"Sounded Russian," Mildred suggested.

"That'd make sense," J.B. said. "According to the maps, Alaska is close to the border with the Russkies. Easy enough to sail that distance. Little extra ice and you could probably walk it."

"She has a family," Ryan said.

Doc cleared his throat. "Let me voice what is doubtless primary on all of our minds," he said. "That the girl there is a slave of some kind, mayhap transported from the west and kept for entertainment."

Mildred looked unconvinced. "You're making some big assumptions. Huge ones."

Doc inclined his head. "And yet we have seen such scenarios played out time and again, Mildred. The girl's demeanor, and her cries for help, infer that she was running from our two friends back there. Would you not agree?"

"Yeah." J.B. nodded. "That's a given. You reckon they're this *Pomoshch* fella she was shoutin' about, Doc?"

"I feel it may be more simple than that, John Barrymore," Doc said. "*Pomoshch* is likely Russian for help."

Sitting with Nyarla beside the thick trunk of a conifer, Krysty was trying to find out what she could.

"It's cold, isn't it?" Krysty said. When Nyarla didn't answer, she continued on. "How did you end up out here dressed like that?"

Nyarla looked introspective, her eyes focused in the middle distance. "Run," she said in her heavily accented English. "I run."

"From whom?" Krysty asked gently.

"They want me to dance for them," Nyarla replied. "To do dancing." She looked disgusted, and Krysty suspected that by "dancing" she actually meant something more intimate.

"Who?" Krysty asked. "Who wanted you to dance?"

"They live in ice," Nyarla replied, her head turning toward the north. "My father says it freeze their hearts, that is why they so *kholodnyi*...so cold." She pulled the blanket closer, snuggling into its warming embrace.

"Is your father there now?" Krysty asked.

Biting her bottom lip, Nyarla nodded uncertainly. "He run. With Elya."

"It's okay," Krysty said. "You're safe now."

"Nyet," Nyarla replied, her eyes suddenly fierce. "They come. They always come."

"Who do?" Ryan demanded, having overheard the last of Krysty's conversation with the troubled young woman.

"The frozen men," Nyarla said. "From *Yego Kraski Sada*—the fields where time stands still."

THE MUTIE WOLF unleashed a howl as it charged down the slope toward Jak and Ricky, where the naked man lay sprawled in the snow. Fast-thinking Ricky had his Webley Mk VI revolver out of its holster and in his hand in an instant. The weapon featured no safety and had been rechambered to fire .45 Automatic Colt Pistol bullets. But Jak warned him back, stepping directly into the path of the wolf as it thundered toward them.

"Just want meal," Jak said gently.

The huge wolf emerged from the bushes, and Ricky gasped. Even on all fours, the mutant creature was almost four feet tall, and its muscular body was closer in size to a pony's than a canine. Perfectly camouflaged for the snow, the beast had dappled gray-white fur and pale blue eyes that seemed full of intelligence. Jak held its stare, fixing it with his own.

The wolf stopped in place, eyeing Jak warily. "We all hungry," Jak reassured the creature. "Not enough food to go 'round. Not out here."

On the ground, the naked man was whimpering, wrestling against the staked ties that held him by wrists and ankles to the ground. His extremities had turned a lifeless shade of gray, with white stripes where the ropes chafed against him.

Ricky took a step toward the man and leaned down to examine the ropes. Tied to the man, each rope was a foot long and brutally nailed into the ground through a wooden stake. The stakes looked impossible to pull free, but Ricky was sure he could untie the knots given a minute or two. What good it would do the man gutted the way he was, he couldn't imagine.

A few feet away, the wolf stared at Jak as the albino stood his ground. It snarled again, lips pulling back from its vicious teeth. Each tooth was four inches long and looked as sharp as a knife.

"No dinner today," Jak stated. "Not here."

The wolf tilted its head as if listening. Ricky watched, amazed by the performance. It was almost as if Jak had an instinctive bond with the animal. Something about his manner seemed to calm the angry beast, cowing it despite its greater size.

Jak had prior experience of taming animals. One time, a few years ago, he had been partnered with a mutie mountain lion, their curious bond inexplicable to his human companions.

For a long moment, the two faced off, Jak's gaze never leaving that of the wolf, his hand held close to the .357 Magnum Colt Python he wore holstered at his hip. If it came to it, Jak would shoot the beast, but something that size might take more than one shot, and Jak didn't like his chances of outmaneuvering a hungry wolf.

The wolf snarled once again, and Jak replied, his own lips pulling back from his teeth, a noise of warning issuing from deep in his throat. Then, magically—or it seemed so to Ricky—the wolf backed away, hunkering down as if in supplication to Jak.

The albino turned back, a cunning smile on his lips as he walked toward Ricky and the staked-out victim. It was at that instant that they heard the gunshot cut the air.

The wolf went down in a hail of bullets and Jak and Ricky dived for cover as that same stream of bullets clipped the ground close to their feet. They were under attack.

Chapter Four

"What the nukeshit was that?" J.B. cursed as the distant sound of bullets cutting the air echoed across the landscape.

"It came from down there," Doc said, using his swordstick to point past the tree cover toward the distant, snowcapped hills.

Nyarla scrambled to her feet, unwrapping the blanket to free her arms. "Papa?" She was going to run, Krysty could see it in her eyes.

"It's okay," Krysty said, reaching for the young woman's wrist. "We're safe up here."

Nyarla shook her head, the fear clear in her wide eyes.

Mildred and Ryan had joined J.B. and Doc as they peered through the trees at the northern edge of the clearing. More gunshots were coming from that way in ones and twos, abrupt rattles echoing through the silent air.

"How far?" Mildred asked.

"Close," Ryan replied, drawing his SIG-Sauer. "And I'll bet scrip for ammo it's Jak and Ricky."

J.B. pulled out his mini-Uzi as Ryan led the way through the trees, with Doc and Mildred following.

Krysty remained behind with Nyarla, holding an arm over her shoulders to try to calm her and to keep her warm. "It's okay," she encouraged. "Shh. It'll be okay."

Downslope, Jak and Ricky were scrabbling for cover as a fifth shot cut the air close to their hiding place. With the first shot they had dived for the nearest clump of bushes, their shaken leaves sprinkling loose the snow that covered them like dandruff.

Ricky had his DeLisle carbine in his hands, its black barrel pointing ahead of him like an extension of his body. "Where are they, Jak? You see?"

Jak looked calm, but he was roiling inside. He was pushing his senses to their limits, reaching out with sound and smell and sight and touch to try to detect from which direction the ambush was coming. "Up there," he said as another bullet issued from the distant blaster with a muffled burp. "Ridge."

Ricky watched where Jak had indicated, his eyes tracing the snowy line that mounted an undulating curve of ground. The stretch of ground was dotted with occasional trees, maybe just one or two every twenty square feet, with a further line of trees capping its highest point—an ideal spot to hide with a scoped rifle and wait for prey, Ricky realized. Between here and there was open territory, the snow-covered ground looking pale blue beneath the night sky, twinkling ice crystals shimmering here and there like tea lights.

The eviscerated man still lay staked on the ground a little ways to the left, moaning. Jak realized what he was now—he had been staked out to attract bigger prey, like leaving a steak or string of sausages to distract a dog. The mutie wolf was someone's dinner, most likely several someones given the bastard size of the brute, Jak thought, and he and Ricky had just stumbled into the chill zone at the wrong instant. But now that they were in it, it was going to take some quick talking or quicker chilling to get them out alive.

Jak eyed the distant tree line again, watching for the muzzle-flash of the longblaster. The echoes were muffled, making it hard to triangulate just where their distant chiller was. Jak waited.

"I don't like it," Ricky whispered, looking up at the trees.

"Cover me" was all Jak said in response. Then he bolted from the cover of the bush, sprinting in a rapid zigzag pattern, scrambling past the twitching corpse of the wolf and up and around in a long arc that would end at the distant trees.

A flash came from the tree line followed a split second later by the loud report of a longblaster. An instant later, a bullet whipped past Ricky, kicking up a plume of powdery snow as it impacted with the ground close to the gutless victim's foot. Ricky hunkered down behind the snow-covered bush, rattling off a blast from the powerful DeLisle. A .45 bullet whizzed away from the weapon's silenced barrel with just a whisper of parting air.

Ricky was already moving, scrambling across the icy ground toward another cluster of bushes, not waiting to find out if he had hit their opponent. The answer to that question came a moment later when another thunderclap echoed through the air as a bullet flew down the slope. A 9 mm round hacked through the bush behind Ricky like an arrow, cutting through the space where he had been hiding not three seconds earlier.

In a swift, long-practiced movement that he had learned from his Uncle Benito, Ricky brought up the DeLisle and rattled off a second shot, sending the bullet hacking through the undergrowth and up into the line of trees. The bitter tang of cordite hung in the air, but Ricky was on the move again, his legs pumping as he scrambled to the next patch of cover, close to the fallen body of the mutie wolf.

After a moment, another bullet whizzed back in response, clipping the hindquarters of the wolf just a couple of feet from where Ricky hid.

Damn, he thought, this guy's using night lenses. There was no other way he would be able to track Ricky with such accuracy on the night like this.

Ricky moved again, scampering away from the body of the wolf as his foe sent another bullet downslope in his wake. All he could do now was keep moving, seeking new cover until Jak made his move.

Jak, meanwhile, was still running up the slope, taking a circuitous route. He had his Colt Python revolver in his hands, six rounds chambered once more after his battle with the ill-tempered caribou outside the redoubt doors. He was close to the trees now, and grimaced as another muzzle-flash illuminated the darkness with the snap-bang of a longblaster's discharge.

Then Jak was weaving into the group of low trees, his Colt Python stretched before him like an accusing finger.

He saw the chiller immediately—a man wrapped, like the others, in rags, his face and head covered in scarves. A pair of night-vision goggles lay beside him, a few spots of snow settling on their cool titanium frame. The man was lying in the dirt, snow melted around him from his expelled body heat, his battered Mosin-Nagant longblaster propped on a low outcropping. The weapon was a two-hundred-year-old design, featuring a rudimentary crosshairs arrangement, a raised circle of steel at one end, in which the target could be ringed and then shot. Jak was impressed that the man had managed to hit the wolf at that distance.

The shooter turned as Jak appeared amid the trees, alerted by the crunch of his boot heels on the snow. Jak brought his Colt around in line with the shooter's head, squeezed the trigger, watched emotionlessly as the man's head kicked back and to the side with the impact of the bullet. The man went down in a flail of limbs, his Mosin-Nagant slipping from the outcropping, a red blossom flowering across his head scarf.

But before Jak could acknowledge his victory, a second shooter appeared, dropping from the branches above his head and landing on Jak's shoulders. Jak crashed down to his knees, releasing his grip on the Colt Python as he slammed into the dirt.

"Tough break, meat bag," the man atop his body snarled as Jak's head reeled. "You should've looked more careful afore you jumped in."

Jak heard the familiar sound of a handblaster being cocked as he sprawled in the frost-speckled soil. He struggled to move aside, driving his body away even as the half-seen shadow brought the weapon around in a tight arc. Then Jak felt something hard strike his head—the butt of the blaster—and he felt the bile rise to his throat as his head went crashing to the ground once again.

RYAN, J.B., MILDRED and Doc fanned out as they emerged from the tree cover. They could hear the shooting from close by, and ran with heads low, searching for its source.

"Jak?" Ryan called quietly. "Ricky? Where are you?"

Ricky's voice replied on Ryan's second urging. "Over here," he responded. He recognized Ryan's imposing silhouette moving among the shrubbery from his latest hiding place behind a fat tree stump. "On your left."

Ryan took a half-dozen strides and met with Ricky a moment later where the lad was crouching beside the dead tree.

"You okay?" the one-eyed man asked. "We heard shots."

J.B. joined them a moment later, and Mildred and Doc followed, giving the area a once-over as they hurried to join with their companions.

"Nice bit of roadkill out there," Mildred said, indicating the mutie wolf.

"More over there," J.B. added, pointing to the naked figure lying in the snow.

"The man's still alive, J.B.," Ricky stated, keeping his voice low and his eyes on the distant line of trees. "We found him when the shooting started."

"Fireblast!" Ryan muttered. "Seems we can't go five minutes without someone or something trying to chill us."

"Listen," Mildred said, raising her empty hand for quiet. "Hear that? Shooting's stopped."

The friends listened, but all they could hear was the insensate moaning of the staked man.

"Means one of two things," Ryan said. "Either your shooter's been decommissioned, or Jak has."

"It's not Jak," Ricky said insistently. "Shooter knew I was here. We were exchanging fire up till a minute ago."

"Could be reloading," J.B. suggested.

"Or could be coming to chill your asses," an unfamiliar voice snarled from behind the group.

STILL HIDDEN in the shadowy copse of trees overlooking the redoubt, Krysty kept Nyarla close to her, trying to share her body temperature with the freezing young woman. Nyarla was slipping back into shock,

Krysty knew, could feel the way her body shook not from cold so much as sheer terror. *What is she so afraid of?* Krysty wondered.

The sounds of the nearby firefight seemed to have ceased. It had been almost two minutes since the last shot had echoed through the snow-daubed trees.

Another thought plucked at the edge of Krysty's mind, something Nyarla had said just before Ryan and the others had responded to the gunfire. *Could it be possible?* she wondered. *Could a place become so cold that time itself would become frozen?* It seemed incredible and yet Krysty had seen many inexplicable things in her journeys across the Deathlands. One more would be nothing less than par for the course.

As she pondered that, Krysty saw a shape moving through the trees toward her. "Ryan?" she asked, her hand automatically going to her hip holster.

The figure didn't answer, and Krysty subtly relaxed her grip on Nyarla, pushing her behind her protectively. Even as Nyarla changed position, the figure emerged from the wooded curtain. It was a man dressed in snow-dusted furs that made his body seem huge and round like a balloon. His face was masked with wrappings of dirty cloth and he held a slim, blowback blaster with a matte black finish in one gloved hand.

Krysty had unholstered her .38 Smith & Wesson by then, and she swung up its snubby barrel where it could be seen. "Freeze," she commanded, unaware of the irony of her statement as snowflakes swam through the air around her.

The man reacted instantly, snapping off a single shot from his Russian-made PSM blaster even as he ducked behind one of the trees. The bullet whizzed past Krysty's side, embedding in a tree behind her and her charge.

She moved, scampering toward the fur-wrapped figure as he darted behind the line of trees, her breath coming through clenched teeth and hanging in the air, where she had been in foggy little markers. The figure in the trees shouted something Krysty didn't quite understand, and then his blaster barked again, launching another shot past the side of his tree cover toward the open area. Krysty fired back as he broke cover, cursing as her shot clipped a branch in a shower of falling snow, missing her quarry by a foot.

Krysty pushed herself harder, running for the man in the trees as another bullet clipped the air close to her left ear. Then she heard a scream, and she turned just in time to see Nyarla struggling in the bear-hug grip of a second attacker, this one dressed in similar ragged furs to the first.

Krysty turned, swinging around her Smith & Wesson, trying to get a bead on the man as he pulled Nyarla off her feet. The woman shrieked, her hands bunched into fists, her feet kicking as she tried to pull herself free. She was moving too much, Krysty knew; there was no way she could make the shot. Mildred maybe, or Ryan, but not her. Not running like this.

Behind Krysty, another shot rang out. She flattened against the nearest tree trunk, her head turning left and right as she sought multiple targets.

"On your knees, *bitch*," the first man shouted in a gruff voice from somewhere behind Krysty's right shoulder. Nyarla and her captor had disappeared, sinking back into the darkness beyond the open area of the copse, leaving behind the woollen blanket that Mildred had loaned her as the only evidence of their passing.

Krysty scanned the trees, searching for their silhouettes in the ill-lit woods, looking for a moving shadow among shadows. She heard a scream, abruptly muffled by a man's hand, but the trees and the faint illumination from the stars were contributing to disguising the source, the falling snow adding an extra layer of confusion. She just couldn't narrow down their position.

As Krysty peeked out from her hiding place, her emerald eyes darting left and right, another shot rang out close to her head. She leaped back as the bullet clipped the tree she was using for cover, kicking up a shower of broken bark just six inches from her skull.

It was too dangerous. There were at least two of them out there, both of them armed—plus the trapped woman was a factor, too. Krysty had promised to protect Nyarla, not get her shot in the cross fire of some ill-judged scuffle over nothing.

"Okay, okay," Krysty called out. "I'm putting my blaster down. Just don't hurt the woman."

"Na koleni," the now-familiar man's voice called from his hiding place. "On your knees." He sounded close to Krysty—real close.

"Okay," Krysty said again, stepping out from behind the broad trunk of the conifer, her arms raised with her blaster still in her right hand, pointed into the branches.

"On your knees," the man repeated, peering out from tree cover just eight feet from where Krysty had been hiding. His colleague stepped forward into the clearing as well, still clutching the slender form of Nyarla; she was no longer moving.

Holding her revolver above her head, Krysty dropped to her knees, the cold of the ground radiating through her pants' legs in an instant. "What did you do to her?" Krysty asked. "Why is she—?"

She didn't finish the sentence. The armed man closer to her had stepped behind Krysty and brought the hard edge of the compact PSM down on the back of her skull. All she knew then was a blackness that seemed to overwhelm her vision of the snow with a creeping lethargy of purpose.

BEYOND THE CLEARING and just a little way down the slope at the edge of the wooded area, Ryan and his companions found themselves surrounded by a whole squad of the raggedly dressed strangers.

They had turned as one to face the newcomer who had issued the snarled warning that he would chill their asses, their weapons already targeting where the voice had come from. But twelve ragged figures emerged from their hiding places in the trees, several of them pulling themselves up from mounds of snow they had used as camouflage. Each man was dressed in the thick layers that the frozen climate demanded and each one held a weapon, including several semiautomatic pistols and a pair of Kalashnikov AK-47s with their stocks removed. At the back of the group, Ryan saw Jak, held tightly by a man dressed in rags with a pair of night-vision goggles visible above the scarf. Jak stood limply, as if dazed.

"You want to try it?" the man with the goggles snarled. "Be my guest. All the more food for us after we've chilled you."

As the man spoke, two more figures clambered down the slope from the copse of trees, carrying the slumped forms of Krysty and Nyarla in their arms.

Outnumbered and with his colleagues' lives in danger, Ryan ordered his companions to stand down.

Ricky looked agitated, shooting Ryan a furious look. "We can take them," he whispered.

Ryan shook his head. His people were compromised, so much so that he couldn't risk a firefight at such close quarters. For now, they would stand down and wait for a better opportunity to arise.

Reluctantly, the companions handed over their weapons to the ragged group of ambushers and were led away.

THE CARIBOU WAS DEAD on its feet now. It trudged wearily onward, kicking up powdery snow with each heavy step, but Symon could feel the death in the beast now, expanding through its freezing body in a black wave. Three steps later the animal sunk to its knees, its great head slumping to the snow. It let loose a withered snuffling noise as it lay there, its hind legs still standing, its chin buried in the snow, and closed its eyes.

The man turned to his daughter, doing his best to offer her a comforting smile. "We walk from here, Elya."

Tarelya, eleven years old and with the same blond hair as her late mother, nodded almost imperceptibly. "I'm cold, Papa," she said in Russian. "This is a place of death."

Symon Vrack found it hard to argue as he clambered down from the horned beast. The landscape was bleak and cold, ice crystals glinting on the soil, grass shoots poking through the white snow in sparse patches. Mist swirled over the land in bobbing waves like the swell of the ocean, obscuring and revealing the surrounds in a game of peekaboo. Snow was falling in a light but constant curtain, enough to blanket the ground and the lifeless trees that made up the landscape, the air cold enough to turn one's breath into misting clouds of vapor that hung above the mouth like speech balloons in a predark comic strip. Vrack hadn't wanted to come here, nor had the mutie caribou. When they reached the Tall Wall, the creature had bucked and complained, rearing back from the translucent barricade and stomping its feet. But the ville men were just behind them, and Vrack had urged the beast on.

That was hours ago. How many had it been? Vrack couldn't tell anymore. When he looked back he could see himself trudging through the snow with his daughter on the back of the mutie caribou, following the footsteps that it had already walked. Ahead, he saw himself and his daughter making their way down the snowbacked slope toward a cluster of trees, hunched over against the unrelenting wind and the falling snow. He watched for a moment as the figures continued, disappearing behind the curling mists that swept the place in frozen clouds.

"Come," Symon said, grabbing his daughter's arm. "We will not die."

Tarelya looked at her father hopefully as he half pulled her down the slope. Behind them, the disembodied mouths were biting at the air, teeth chattering as they ate the flashes of light that sparkled in the atmosphere with charged static. Symon suspected that those mouths could bite through a person's arm or leg if he or she remained still long enough to be reached. He had already lost his son Evan on the trip here; he would not lose his daughter, too.

Seeing where her father was looking, Tarelya peered back over her shoulder. "Are they still there?" she asked. "I don't see them."

"We march quickly," Symon told her, "like the guards. To keep ourselves warm."

Tarelya nodded, recalling the guards in the ville and the way they had looked at her. That had been the last straw for her father. He was a fisherman by trade, not an especially successful one but proficient enough to feed himself and his family. The winters were harsh here, but then so were the summers. Her father would joke sometimes about how many pairs of socks he wore in the summer—"Six or seven, at least until the sun sets."

But three months ago the Tall Wall had come to them, cutting closer to their cold little house than it had ever come before, like a terminator line during a solar eclipse. It had eaten into space, stealing land, consuming it, leaving it just beyond reach. The stories of His Ink Orchard had been clear enough—to enter it was death, to go beyond the Tall Wall was to invite death. And no one had ever returned.

Symon had upped stakes and moved his family, searching for new fishing grounds. Instead he had found the ville, with its despotic baron and his appetites, coupled with the near-infinite weaponry to enforce his will. Symon had tried to barter with the man, but they had taken his rifle and they had committed him to the mines while his two daughters had been taken away. It broke Symon's heart. When he saw the scars on Tarelya's back he had determined to make a break for it. His Ink Orchard was the only place to hide. No one would dare follow a person in there willingly; no one would be so foolish. There was no escape once the barrier was crossed; it was suicide. But even suicide was preferable to seeing one's daughters worn down by forced labor or used as a slut.

"Where will we go now, Papa?" Tarelya asked.

"There," Symon told her. "The trees. They offer almost no shelter, but almost none is better than none at all."

Around them, the air fizzed with ghost colors, sparking through the mist like fireflies, each spark another meal for the bodiless mouths that roamed His Ink Orchard.

Chapter Five

The companions found themselves force-marched to a settlement like no other. The hunters had disarmed them before tying them up, giving them enough movement that they could walk but ensuring that no one could run away. After Nyarla had escaped them earlier, they were taking no chances. After being disarmed, the companions were made to gather around a small wooden cart while they awaited the arrival of other captives, who were subsequently brought into the open by a second group of men.

The group was comprised of twenty hunters, though they had lost two of their number to the companions during the scuffle outside the redoubt, plus the third man who had been chilled by Jak in the tree line overlooking the wolf trap. The strangers hadn't taken those losses well, beating Jak while the others were tied.

The hunting party included four riders on the mutie caribou, two of which had been recovered from where they had been left wandering close to the hidden redoubt. The caribou appeared to be drowsy, ill-tempered animals, and they took a lot of prodding and urging to keep moving. They also stank with a musty, damp-fur smell. Out here in this frozen wasteland, they were probably the only animal large enough to carry a human, Ryan reasoned as he watched their riders heel and curse them to movement across the snow.

The strangers had collected their dead and their wounded—the man who had been trampled by the caribou was still alive, albeit delirious with pain and blood loss. He had been rolled onto the back of one of the hulking caribou, his broken limbs bent at angles that should not be possible for a human body.

The hunters had also hauled the wolf's carcass onto the back of a wag. It looked smaller in death than it had in life, its thick fur flattened now and clinging to its cooling corpse.

The wag had two wooden wheels and a yoke in front which Ryan, J.B. and Doc had been strapped to and told to pull. It was hard work, the wolf's carcass was so large it drooped from the back plate of the wag's bed, and movement was made more difficult thanks to the short ropes that had been used to tie the companions' ankles, forcing them to shuffle rather than take full strides.

"Only a fool would make a tied man drag this thing," J.B. grumbled as the three of them hauled the wag up a steady incline. But the hunters didn't hear, or if they did they deemed response unnecessary. Instead, they simply marched alongside, shouting orders in a combination of Russian and English that sounded like a man clearing his throat, their blasters poised to threaten anyone who stepped out of line.

Nyarla had lost her blanket and shivered profusely as she strode along with the others of the group. She had been unconscious when the party had left the chilling zone, but had soon revived after a few slaps across the face from one of the well-wrapped hunters. Warily, Mildred had stepped in and assured the man that such brutality was unnecessary. "She's awake," Mildred insisted. "But she won't regain her senses if you keep hitting her like that."

The man had drawn back his hand into a fist as if to hit Mildred, but he reconsidered the action when Nyarla muttered something coherent for the first time in a quarter hour. "You—carry her," he had growled at Mildred. "If she slows us down I shoot your face."

Mildred nodded, grimly accepting the cruel terms of the proposal.

From what Ryan and the companions could guess, there appeared to be three other prisoners with them as well as Nyarla. All three were men in their thirties or forties, underdressed for the climate. One looked as if he had been dragged out of bed, as he wore no shoes, wincing with every barefoot step on the frozen ground. The hunters cuffed him across the back of the head when he complained, and so he fell silent and merely sucked breath through his clenched teeth with each icy step as his toes turned blue.

As they trekked the two miles to the group's base camp, the snow eased, its flurries turning to just occasional white spots that spun through the air like dandelion seeds. Ricky was shivering as they marched. They were all cold, but he had never known weather like this in Puerto Rico, had no idea that such extremes of cold could exist.

"Why would anyone want to live here?" Ricky asked Krysty as they marched, keeping his voice low.

Krysty was walking with Jak at her side, an arm around his back below his ribs, helping the albino keep pace with the others following the vicious beating he had been subjected to. "People will live anywhere," Krysty told Ricky. "They can't help themselves. Humans have such a capacity for adaptation that they will keep pushing themselves well beyond what you might expect."

"You've seen places like this before?" Ricky asked, his eyebrows raised in surprise.

"We've traveled all over," Krysty replied in a whisper. "Been here in Alaska four or five times."

Ricky nodded, looking around at the icy landscape in the dim light cast from the stars. Everything out here looked blue, the snow retouched by the indigo sky. Landmarks were few out here, just the odd cluster of trees marking the points between characterless bushes, the odd rock poking up through the frozen soil. Now and then, the companions' trek took them past the tops of old buildings, buried now beneath the carpet of snow, preserved by the ice.

Their brief journey took them in parallel to a sheer drop that fell away from the roughly marked path they followed. Even from up here, they could hear the crashing waves, and when J.B. peered over the side he saw great chunks of ice floating in the water.

"Must be a forty-foot drop," he told Ryan in a low voice. "The impact would likely break a person's back, and anyone who survived would freeze to death in five minutes."

A lot had changed in Nome since it had served as a military town on the northwestern tip of Alaska a hundred years earlier. The nukes had ruptured the land, casting it adrift with great fissures. What remained of the once-proud town had become frozen in the ice, whole buildings lost beneath snowdrifts that had formed a hundred years before during that awful nuclear winter. Ryan and his companions were indifferent to the starlit remains of a destroyed society; they had seen worse and they doubtless would again, assuming they could survive this encounter with the ice hunters.

They trekked over an icy incline, Doc using his

swordstick, which his captors had overlooked, to help his aching body climb as he, Ryan and J.B. drew the wag behind them. There, over the incline, they saw their destination. It looked like a glacier sliced in two, one-half missing to expose a sheer wall of ice that towered eighty feet into the night sky. Even in the dim light, they could make out the shadowed rounds running up its face at regular intervals, a honeycomb of caves burrowed into the ice behind which ancient buildings waited. There were fires flickering in those caves, the pulse of flames shimmering like specters. The glacier stretched back in the darkness farther than the companions could make out, weak flames like trapped stars burning in the ice.

To one side of the ice wall sat another sheer drop, a great rent in the frozen earth that stretched across twenty feet or more. As they drew closer, Ryan spotted simple bridges had been constructed across the chasm, two made of wood struts and a third no more than a rope stretched taut with two guide ropes running along above it. There were vehicles crouched at the base of the glacier, several wags like the one the companions had been enlisted to pull, and a couple of dilapidated trucks, their scarred paintwork showing rusted metal. There were also around a dozen caribou penned in a corral, a wooden roof and free-standing wall to one side where they might shelter from the elements when the weather got too wild.

"It looks beautiful," Ricky whispered as he stared at the twinkling facade of the glacier. "Like a tower block made by Mama Nature."

"Gaia works with a soft touch," Krysty agreed, "painting pictures across the landscape in ways we can only wonder at."

Voices and cooking smells wafted from the strange settlement as the companions drew closer, shouts like a party coupled with the grunting of animals, shrieks of joy or terror. At the base of the eighty-foot-tall structure several men patrolled in bored resignation, dressed in the thick ragged outfits that the hunting party had worn, their faces wrapped with scarves. They carried long-blasters in their mitten-covered hands, the mittens featuring a furry trim across the tops to keep out the cold.

"Nothing like a warm welcome," J.B. muttered as they approached the frozen ville. "And this here *is* nothing like a warm welcome."

This close to the strange ville, the companions could see ladders running up the sheer ice wall, placed helter-skelter along the glistening facade.

A voice called from behind Ryan, J.B. and Doc, ordering them to halt. They did as they were told, bringing the cart to a stop and resting their weary arms against the crossbar of the yoke with a sense of relief. Ryan turned to his side, eyeing Doc and the sec man, who waited just a few feet behind him.

"How you holding up, Doc?" Ryan asked, keeping his voice very low.

"This is tiring work," Doc admitted, flashing his oddly perfect teeth to his one-eyed colleague. "But we press on, do we not?" He sounded out of breath.

Ryan stared past Doc, taking stock of his captors and their weapons. They were a well-armed bunch, dressed for the freezing weather and clearly used to working as a team. They spoke among themselves, employing a mix of Russian and English just as Nyarla had. Ryan tried to piece together what had happened. He guessed that Nyarla had been their captive, probably working in some menial capacity—by her dress he would guess she could be a gaudy slut. But she had been brought along with the hunting party when they had gone questing for food, probably as live bait just like the naked bastard who had been nailed to the ground where Ryan had located Ricky just prior to the ambush. Using live humans for bait in a dead environment like this meant one less mouth to feed when they butchered whatever it was they caught, Ryan realized.

But Nyarla had said something else as well. She had called the hunters "frozen men" and had said that they had come from *Yego Kraski Sada,* the fields where time stands still.

Ryan puzzled over that as he, J.B. and Doc were unlatched from the yoke under the wary surveillance of armed guards. His other companions, along with Nyarla and the three ill-dressed prisoners, were led off toward the glacier. He watched as Krysty, Mildred and Nyarla were led up one ladder, encouraged by the jeers and whistles of two of the patrolling guards who had come to watch. They were splitting off the women, he realized, which inevitably meant trouble.

"Hey, eyes front," one of the fur-wrapped men growled as Ryan watched Krysty disappear into one of the high caves, her red hair receding from view in the darkness. "Hey," the sec man called again. "I'm talking to you, prick. What, are you deaf as well as half-blind?"

Ryan glared at the man, fixing him with his lone blue eye, his mouth a slash of barely restrained fury. "Where are you taking my friends?" he demanded.

"None of your business," the fur-wrapped man replied, leveling his Kalashnikov in unspoken warning. "You wait here."

Behind the man, fur-wrapped locals were hauling the carcass of the great wolf from the back of the primitive wag, dragging the creature across the hard-packed soil with the assistance of several of the more burly hunting party. Beside them, two women were dragging the body of one of the hunters' fallen colleagues across the icy terrain, pulling him by his splayed feet and leaving a bloody smear on the icy ground. Neither woman appeared to be particularly emotional and Ryan watched for a moment, wondering what they would do with the body. Were they going to bury him or was there some other ritual that these brutal ice dwellers would perform on their dead? Ryan wasn't surprised to see them begin stripping the corpse's clothes away. Nothing was wasted in the Deathlands, and warm clothes in any environment, especially one as cold as this, would be recycled over and over.

"Not exactly the meek sort, are they?" J.B. observed as he stood beside Ryan, watching the women remove the corpse's clothing and personal effects.

"We'd best be careful," Ryan said quietly. "Scavies like this are liable to take our boots soon as we take our eyes off them."

J.B. nodded his agreement. "You keep close to Doc. Left on his own, he can get a mite too trusting, if you ask me. Remember what happened the last time he was in the frozen north."

Ryan silently agreed. Doc was a valuable asset to their group and his marksmanship and ruthlessness in battle were faultless, but he had grown up in another era, over two hundred years before, where trust of one's fellow man came easily. Even now, after the years he had spent trekking the Deathlands, Doc could let his guard down too quickly, longing to find a glimmer of humanity in this cruel new world. Old habits died hard, it seemed.

While Ryan and J.B. watched, the two women were joined by a man wrapped in furs and carrying a long shaft of wood. Ryan guessed that the shaft had begun life as a tree trunk—it was roughly six feet long and three inches in diameter, with its bark stripped away and one end sharpened to a vicious point. The man dropped the pole, leaving it on the snow with the women as they stripped the last of their dead colleague's clothes from his pale body, which was already turning blue, the flesh puffy with cold. In a hotter climate, it didn't take long for a corpse to decompose, Ryan knew. But out here, decomposition could take months or more to set in; corpses could remain almost unsullied for a whole season until the frost started to thaw.

Ryan watched in grim silence as the women placed the dead man on the spit, emotionlessly driving it through his anus and up into the cavity of his bowels. The shaft was shoved with some force, a grim explosion of blood leaking down the dead man's bare legs as one woman worked the wooden pole into his sprawled body, tapping its blunt end with a wooden hammer while the other guided it into the cavity of the corpse's back passage.

Satisfied, the man strode away, clomping past Ryan in his heavy fur boots. The man noticed the one-eyed stranger watching, and he snarled something in his guttural tongue in Ryan's face before laughing. Ryan didn't understand the words but he recognized the language— Russian, like his old enemy Major Zimyanin.

The man passed then, grasping the hand of one of the sec men and laughing once more. Ryan watched them, his eye narrowed. The sec man saw Ryan watching and he laughed. "Curious, are you?" he asked in heavily accented English. "Be thankful it ain't you, my friend. But that day will come, too, you can bet your good eye on that."

JAK, RICKY AND THE three nameless prisoners were marched to another ladder that led to a clutch of caves across from where their female companions had been taken. Made of splintering wood, the ladder reached all the way to the top of the glacier, halting at the upper-most cave entrance where a sec man stood swinging an iron chain around and around.

One of the hunters, dressed in rags with a pair of night-vision goggles pushed up onto the top of his hood, shoved Jak toward the ladder. "You climb, white man," he said in a thick accent before turning to the next man, one of the disheveled-looking captives. "Once he's up to your head, you follow. And you," he said, jabbing at the remaining men with a gloved finger, "do the same once the man in front of you is at that height. Keep the line moving, no stragglers." The man held a blaster in one hand and had a knife strapped in a leather holster close to his left buttock. He used the former to make it clear that he would shoot anyone who didn't follow his commands.

At the rear of the group, Ricky glared at their guard, his teeth chattering in the wind.

"You have a problem, youngster?" the man growled, bringing his face up close to Ricky's.

"Only your breath," Ricky replied. "It smells of goat dick."

The man's face turned red with anger, and he balled his empty hand into a fist, knocking Ricky hard in the stomach and causing the handsome, dark-haired teen to double over with a gasp of expelled breath. Ricky staggered forward for a moment, slumping against the man with a groan of pain, holding his gut.

In response the sec man simply laughed, shoving Ricky away. Still doubled over, Ricky smiled to himself as he pocketed the hunting blade he had lifted from the sheath at the man's side. He had a weapon now; he only needed to find the right opportunity to use it.

Down below, Ryan, Doc and J.B. had been freed from the wag's yoke and they were commanded forward at a slow march under the watchful eyes of two guards. Doc used his swordstick to steady himself—an added consideration since both his wrists and ankles were still tied, causing him to waddle a little like a penguin.

The three companions trudged to one of the ladders that scaled the ice wall, followed a few steps behind by two armed sec men. Close up, the ladder looked rotted, its wood peeling paint and showing dark patches where the damp had seeped inside.

"Like winter in Vermont," Doc said as he took a wary step on the frozen ground and secured his grip on a lower rung of the ladder. "When my mother would make me clear the leaves from the roof gutters."

Doc's reminiscing again, J.B. thought. The man's mind was sometimes in two places at once, thoughts of his home two hundred years ago often intruding in his present life. It was hard on Doc, trying to carve a life as a nomad like the others when he was so far from the world he knew. He was a learned man with numerous qualifications from his own time. Yet here in the Deathlands, there were things he still had trouble processing, such as man's inhumanity to his fellow man.

Once Doc was a few feet up the ladder, the twin uprights shaking dangerously in place, J.B. was ordered to follow him, and then Ryan. The two men moved without complaint, but both remained alert to possibilities, searching for an escape.

The ladder towered sixty feet in the air, and as they climbed the companions got a closer look at the open mouths of the caves. People were huddled within, some peering out to see what the fuss was about. But the icy caverns seemed to stretch farther back than the faint starlight allowed them to see, and Ryan got the sense that there could very well be a whole community living within this block of ice; a ville in an ice tower block.

As they climbed, the companions saw, too, that there were shelflike ridges running horizontally along the front of the ice wall, just a couple of feet wide, connecting the cave mouths. Presumably, Ryan thought, there are more connections inside, like a rabbit's warren.

In the lead, Doc reached the crest of the ladder first. A man and a woman waited there, watching the ill-matched line of men clamber up toward them. The man held a knife, the kind used for skinning small animals, and he thrust it in Doc's face as the gray-haired man came within reach.

"You, keep moving," the man growled. He wore warm, heavy clothes with a scarf over his neck that left his features bare, exposing the round face and ruddy features of an Inuit. "Hurry it up."

Beside the man, the woman was working a longer knife with a wicked, serrated blade in her hand, using its point to work the dirt from under her nails in her other hand, which was clutched around the sleeping body of a newborn. She, too, had the black hair and features of an Inuit, and she spit something at Doc as he disengaged himself from the ladder, taking care not to drop his swordstick.

But what Doc saw at the top was enough to make him stop dead in his tracks.

"I said hurry it up," the dark-faced man beside him growled as Doc stared.

Human bodies were hanging from the ceiling. Doc counted seven in all and each one was naked, the flesh turned a pale gray-pink from the cold, and each had a great hook thrust through their chest. Three women were there, their plump breasts sagging between either side of those vicious, two-inch-wide metal hooks.

Chapter Six

Reluctantly, Doc took another step forward, and J.B. and Ryan followed behind him. The old man took another step into the icy food locker—for it was clear that that is what it was—past the bodies in the darkness. He tried not to look at them as he walked through the room, feeling the acrid taste of bile biting at the back of his mouth.

"Keep walking," the flat-faced man snarled from behind him, "all the way through."

Reluctantly, Doc walked onward, his right shoulder brushing against one of the bodies where it jutted in the ill-lit storeroom. The body swayed back and forth at his touch, the hook creaking on its thick chain. There, up ahead, Doc saw another doorway, its arch low, carved directly into the ice wall.

"That's it, old-timer," the man behind him chided. "Keep going."

With a palpable sense of relief, Doc stepped through the far door and out into the space beyond. He stood in what appeared to be a small lobby from which a half-dozen low doorways spoked in various directions, including the one that led to meat locker behind him. A man was seated there, thankfully alive and wrapped in a fur coat with a blanket of fur over his legs. The man held a snub-nosed .38 in his lap, pointing it vaguely at Doc as he stepped through the doorway.

"Welcome to the rest of your life, meat," the man growled, before using the barrel of the blaster to indicate one of the open doorways. "Go through. Two of you." He peered into the meat locker, where Ryan and J.B. were just striding in Doc's wake. "Third one, you with the hat—you wait, I'll show you where."

With his wrists still bound, J.B. took a moment to adjust the brim of his fedora and smiled bitterly at Ryan.

"Sounds like you're getting special treatment," Ryan told him, keeping his voice low.

"Pays to wear a hat," J.B. replied, sotto voce. "Makes a good first impression."

A moment later, the two men had joined the gunman in the ice-walled lobby, and Ryan strode on, following Doc into a frozen chamber just four feet square. Behind Ryan, the gunman was busy sealing the doorway with a wooden sheet that swung in on some kind of track-and-pulley system.

The chamber's walls were carved from ice, and a single glassless window was stuck in the far wall of the room, like a ship's portal. Doc stood at the open window, taking deep breaths of the chill air that blew through it. But he stepped aside to let Ryan take a peek. It was dark out there, too dark to see.

"Any idea where we are?" Ryan asked.

The old man looked queasily at Ryan, still sucking in deep breaths. "Hard to say. You saw what was back there as well as I. Do you think that mayhap they plan to eat us?"

Ryan's expression was staunch as he eyed the old man in the darkness of the cell. "Don't know, Doc," he admitted. But he suspected that the old man was right. Judging by the locker of hanging corpses, they were in the hands of cannies—the nukeshitting dregs of the Deathlands.

MILDRED, KRYSTY AND Nyarla had been incarcerated in a warm room deep in the bowels of the ice fortress, where five other women were already sleeping. Twelve feet by ten, the room was roughly hewn from the hard-packed ice, and featured a small brass heater in its center in which coals and incense glowed. The incense filled the room with its cloying pungency, a scent so thick that it caused Mildred to cough when she was initially thrust into the room and drew her first breath within. From their journey through the icy corridors of the ville, Mildred surmised that the incense was used to hide the stench created by the gas heaters, masking the smell of burning animal fat.

The walls of the room were hung with silks and carpets, both to provide decoration and to help trap the heat. The carpets looked old and worn, their colors muted over time. Behind them, a wide wooden door was rolled back into place, sealing the room like a jar. A single window was set in the outside wall. It looked out into the darkened ice and snow beyond and featured a pane of glass so thick that it had ripples across it. It was hard to make out anything, Mildred found as she parted the curtain to look through the window. All she could see was the towering structure of the glacier ville a little distance away, surrounding a courtyard on all sides.

"We're a story up from ground level," Mildred told Krysty, keeping her voice low so as not to wake the sleepers in the room. "Maybe we could jump or climb down?"

"If we could get this open," Krysty said, pressing her hands against the cold glass and working them along the edges of the windowpane. It was locked solid with no catches that could be worked. "Big if," she added grimly.

Nyarla had hurried over to the brass burner, and Krysty and Mildred could see she had been here—or somewhere very similar—before. The other women were huddled close to the heater, too, sleeping where the warmth was strongest. Two of them stirred for a moment, surveying the newcomers before rolling over and going back to sleep. They were clearly used to a lot of comings and goings in this room, and a steady turnover of new faces, Mildred guessed.

Mildred and Krysty looked at the room with distaste, knowing pretty well what it was. "Gaudy house or harem," Mildred said, voicing what the other thought.

"Looks like there's just the one door," Krysty said, searching the room and moving several woven tapestries aside.

Mildred's dark eyes scanned the door itself, her hand unconsciously moving to where a holster should have been strapped to her hip. Holster and blaster had been removed when the companions had surrendered to the hunters, while Mildred's bag of medicines had been thoroughly searched and potential weapons removed before she'd been allowed to keep it. The door looked sturdy, made of a solid wood such as oak and rolled on a chiseled track outside the room like a train wheel, sealing the chamber like a stopper. The door was entirely blank, just the unaltered grain of the wood showing on this side, with no handle or turning device. That left them with no facility to open it from the inside and also meant there was no way of telling whether they were being watched, or when someone might be listening outside.

Mildred's fingers clenched as she brushed the side of her leg where her blaster should be, and she shook her head with irritation. Their captors had also given her and the rest of them a pat down, checking for any additional weapons. They had discovered Jak's stash of knives that way, but they had missed the surgical scalpel that Mildred habitually carried in a sheath in her pants pocket next to a pencil; it was so small that it might easily have been mistaken for another pencil by cold-numbed fingers.

For now, there was no way out of the room, not until someone on the other side of the door decided to open it. The noise of the door opening would be enough to alert them, so Mildred joined Krysty beside the heater, where several of the women were moaning in fitful sleep. Nyarla hugged herself, trying to get the warmth back into her frozen body. Krysty kneeled while Mildred adopted a position behind her and briefly examined her head where she had been pistol-whipped by the man in the woods. There was a lump there, a little swelling that bulged in her hairline.

"You feel anything? Light-headed, any trouble focusing your eyes, things like that?" Mildred asked as she pressed two fingers lightly to the swelling.

Krysty drew a sharp breath at Mildred's touch, then assured her she felt okay. "Felt a bit sick at first," she said, "but it's passed now."

Mildred ran her hand through Krysty's hair again, checking for any other signs of damage. There was no blood, and just the one swollen lump at the back of her skull, like a robin's egg trying to break through the skin. Krysty winced when Mildred ran her fingers over it, but it didn't seem to be anything too worrisome. There was, of course, always the chance of internal bleeding with a skull injury like that, but Krysty was strong. And besides, there was nothing that Mildred could do while they were stuck there.

Mildred then moved across to check on Nyarla, keeping her voice low as she asked some simple questions about how the young woman was feeling. Like Krysty she seemed fine. It transpired that she had been rendered unconscious using a drug of some kind, sounding to Mildred like chloroform or similar from the way she described it.

After that, Nyarla returned to her spot next to the heater, and Mildred and Krysty could feel the heat radiating from it as they crouched to join her. Mildred was pleased to note that some color was coming back to Nyarla's cheeks, but she still looked exhausted and scared.

"It's okay," Mildred soothed. "We're safe for now."

"No." Nyarla shook her head. "They'll come for us. The men. They always do."

Krysty fixed Nyarla with her emerald eyes. "We'll look after you," she promised. "No one will come tonight."

Slowly, the young woman nodded, but her fear remained palpable. Krysty thought it best to change the subject, to take Nyarla's mind off of the threat of being raped here in this awful hive of ice. She recalled the thing that she had said earlier, about the place where time had frozen.

"When we spoke earlier," Krysty began, "back in the woods, you said something about a frozen area where time itself had stopped. You gave it a name—*Yegok Rask...?*"

"Yego Kraski Sada." Nyarla nodded.

"Yego Kraski Sada," Mildred repeated.

From the floor beside her, one of the women spoke up, her eyes still closed and a thin woolen blanket pulled up tightly to her chin. "We call it His Ink Orchard in English," the woman said.

"Yes," Nyarla agreed, "it is dark place where God sows time like crop. My father, he tell us to stay away from place. People, they go there and we don't see them again. They get...held."

Mildred looked from Nyarla to the sleeping woman. The woman had short hair dyed a vibrant shade of rusty red by some food coloring. She looked about twenty, maybe twenty-five, and her face was flat and tanned in the familiar manner of an Inuit. As if aware that she was being stared at, the woman's eyes flashed open.

"Do you know about this place?" Mildred said. "His Ink Orchard?"

The woman nodded, her eyes narrowed in the flickering light of the burner. "Everyone knows about it," she said quietly. "Whole herd of babas got lost out there once, couldn't get them back. After that no one would go there."

Mildred didn't know what babas were but she guessed it was local dialect for sheep or cows or goats, most likely something that could be farmed and eaten in the unforgiving climate. "How far away is this place?"

The red-tressed woman closed her eyes and gave her head a visible shake of irritation. "Closer every day," she said with a resigned sigh. After that she rolled over, pulling the blanket over her head intending to go back to sleep.

"So, what do we do now?" Krysty asked, pitching

her voice low so as not to wake the other women in the room.

Nyarla had fallen asleep already, her tired body curling into a fetal position, light snoring emanating from her open mouth. Mildred looked at her and smiled. "We sleep in shifts," she said, "and try to avoid getting surprised again."

Krysty nodded in wordless agreement, and she made her way back to the door to assume the first watch, crouching there with boot heels touching her rear.

Mildred was grateful that her friend had volunteered without asking. She needed sleep. The cold seemed to have drained the last of her energy.

J.B., MEANWHILE, had been locked in a similar cell to the one that Ryan and Doc had been forced to share. His also had a small window that was open to the elements, and it looked out onto an open area to where he could just barely make out the twinkling lights of the stars.

The sour-faced Inuit sneered at J.B. as he shoved him in the back, forcing him to stumble into the room due to his bindings. Off balance, J.B. crashed to his knees with a whoosh of expelled air, causing the bored-looking Inuit to guffaw. He got up again slowly, reaching for his battered fedora where it had tumbled from his crown.

"Don't get too comfortable in here," his captor taunted. "Not enough meat on your bones to get you anything but a short stay."

With those ominous words still ringing in J.B.'s ears, the man stepped back through the doorway and sealed the cell shut with a great plug of carved wood. The wood had been tooled to show figures, barely visible in the faint light. J.B. studied them for a moment as he brought himself up off the floor. They showed men and women with naked bodies and devils' faces, the work of some deranged mind.

Wary of the restraints he wore, J.B. sidled to the window. He felt the ice breeze of the north wind pound against his face as he peered out into the night. The area appeared to have been burrowed out of the center of the glacier, which suggested that the ville had a donut shape.

Freezing cold, the open area was large enough to generate its own sound, a low hush where the wind played through it from outside. J.B. gazed at the night sky, locating Orion's Belt and, from there, Taurus and Canis Minor, all the while wondering just what the hell they had walked into this time.

Eventually, the sky still dark, J.B. fell into a restless sleep, his body shivering and quaking to remain warm.

"FUCKING CANNIES," Ryan muttered, shaking his head as he stared out the window of the tiny cell.

The ice chamber was so tight that they would have to sleep sitting up. Ryan, a tall man by any reckoning, leaned his back against the wall, thankful for the blanket effect of his fur coat, while Doc lay as best he could, his legs bent against the wall with the window, his frock coat covering him like a bedsheet.

"Did I ever tell you about my dear Emily?" Doc asked, his hushed words breaking into Ryan's thoughts of escape.

In the darkness, Ryan nodded. He had, many times. But the old man didn't seem to remember. It was like this sometimes with Doc—he would drift away from them, into a fugue of memory, where the past became more real than the now. He was getting better as time went on, but occasionally his mind still slipped away.

"She looks so beautiful," Doc continued, "as she bakes cakes in the kitchen for Rachel and Jolyon. And the smells, my goodness, the smells! That woman could tempt the angels down from Heaven to sample her wondrous pastries and iced delights."

The old man's voice wended on in memory, his words slurring as sleep gradually overcame him. Ryan's mood lightened as Doc's words tapered off. It had to be nice having memories of better times to slip away into, Ryan thought. All he had was death and loss, his own son snatched from him, only to return to his father to suffer heartache and bitterness.

The old man snored while Ryan sat still, his lone eye fixed on the stars glimmering through the open hole of the window. He could hear the restless noises of the mutie caribou from somewhere nearby, their lowing echoing with the ominous fury of a distant earthquake.

Ryan was weaponless, but he wasn't helpless. If it came to it, he would revert to his fists, his muscular body trained by the hard school of the Deathlands. And Doc still had his swordstick, disguised as the walking cane. The old man had played up his infirmness when he had climbed the ladder, drawing attention to his need to use the cane to steady himself. None of these ice scavengers had given it a second thought, which left Ryan and Doc with one weapon between them.

Ryan's mind worked furiously, plucking at the problem of their incarceration high up in this glacial roost. To escape from up here would require not simply getting access out of the cell, but also making their way through the caverns that had been drilled into the ice, past that grisly meat locker where men's bodies swung in icy silence. There would be guards, Ryan knew, sec men, made strong by the cold weather. From his initial observation they appeared well-armed—almost everyone they had passed at this eerie ice ville bore a blaster or a knife of some kind.

Ryan replayed the location in his mind, mapping each turn they had taken, trying to work out which path to take should the opportunity to escape present itself. A few feet away, Doc snuffled, rolling over on his side and pulling the collar of his coat tighter over his shoulder to keep warm.

As he sat there, Ryan's thoughts turned to Krysty, his lover. Perhaps one day they would settle somewhere, give up this hand-to-mouth existence, the constant cycle of running and chilling. Mebbe raise a family of their own just like the one Doc Tanner had left behind in the 1800s. "Memories are waiting to be made," Ryan told himself quietly as the cold breeze blew against his tired face. "Just waiting to be made."

JAK AND RICKY had been thrown into a larger cell in the warrenlike ville along with the three men who had been brought under armed guard to join the party. Jak had slumped to the floor, and he lay unmoving. This cell was much closer to the ground than the ones that their companions had been placed in, its walls made from compacted ice with seams of earth running through it in dark, dirty smudges. The room had no windows and no furniture. The only light came through the ice walls, the blurry flickering of a gas heater seen through layers of frozen water. The effect was like a painting or a child's night-light, but it was enough to let them see their own misting breath hanging in the air.

There were two other figures hidden amid the darkness, Ricky realized as soon as the great wooden door was rolled over the exit like a screw-top lid. One lay sprawled against the wall farthest from the light, his skinny body bent in on itself to keep warm. The other pulled himself very slowly to his feet and greeted his new cellmates.

The other men were complaining, albeit timidly, one of them moaning about his missing wife. "She's eight months gone," he pleaded to the cool air. "If they harm the baby I'll chill every last one of the bastards, I swear."

Ricky looked at the man with disdain. He wasn't the sort who would chill anyone. He looked more like the kind who hid at home while people like his uncle had done the real fighting.

Ricky turned back to Jak, whose pale flesh was painted an orange tint by the shimmering light of the nearby fire. "Jak?" Ricky asked quietly. "Jak, are you okay?"

For a long moment Jak didn't respond. He lay still, sprawled half-on and half-off a threadbare rug that had been placed on the floor of the cell. He had taken an awful beating at the hands of the cannies, Ricky knew.

"Head hurts," Jak said finally. "Feel like it went up against wag, headfirst."

Ricky smiled at that.

While the other prisoners sorted out their sleeping arrangements, Ricky showed Jak the knife he had lifted from the sec man. "I bet he's missing it by now," Ricky said with a smug grin.

Jak agreed. "Be careful with that. Our time come."

Ricky nodded, his smile disappearing and his face turning serious. Jak had far more experience in these situations than he did; while he wanted to mount an escape he figured that his friend would know when the right time to strike was, just like a mountain cobra waiting for the climber to pass.

Jak leaned back down, pulling up his jacket so that it bunched under his shoulders to give him a little padding to lie against.

"You hurting, Jak?" Ricky asked. "Is there anything I can do?"

Jak shook his head, wincing as a burning pain raced across the back of his skull. "Sleep," Jak told him.

"Please stay alive," Ricky whispered as he laid his slender body beside Jak. For a moment, his hand reached to the blade he had lifted, where it was hidden in his waistband. He pushed it around to the crease at the small of his back, making sure he wouldn't roll onto it in his sleep.

Around them, the men continued to mutter and complain. At some point, one of them realized that the figure lying against the wall farthest from the illumination hadn't responded to any of their questions and he went over to check on him. The man's eyes were open and there was a thin film of ice over each one. He had been dead for a week, his body perfectly preserved by the subzero environment. His corpse made for an uncomfortable cellmate.

WHEN THEY FOUND THEM they were close to death, sheltering among the dead trees whose branches scraped at the air like arthritic claws. Cupped in her father's arms, the girl had a film of ice over her clothes and the exposed skin of her face, and the snow had begun to settle where she had closed her eyes. Her father clung to her like a precious treasure he had pulled from the frozen ground, his arms wrapped around her, his coat open, better to press her against his body. There was ice in his hair where his hood had slipped, and his scarf had frozen to his face, an icy line across his mouth and nose.

"Wake up," the man who found them said. He was a broad-shouldered man with skin like tanned leather and the perpetual stoop of one who had been walking against the wind for too long. He had climbing equipment, including a thick rope, strapped to his furs. Beside him, a second man and a woman surveyed the area with weapons poised. "Are you alive?"

The man in the snow grumbled, the layer of ice on the scarf splitting in the folds as he moved his jaw. "Alive, yes," he mumbled, his words accented thickly with Russian. "Alive."

"I'm Piotr," the man who had roused him said. "We need to get out of here now. It's not safe here."

Lying in the snow, Symon Vrack moved his aching limbs, so cold he could no longer feel them, checking that his daughter was still there. "Tarelya," he whispered, "wake up. Quickly now."

In his arms, Tarelya roused with a groan. "So cold," she said.

"Yes, it's cold," Piotr agreed. "Come on, before the crows get here."

Symon looked askance at Piotr as he stood. "Crows? You think birds can fly in this?" The snow was falling in thick clumps now, billowing in the strong wind that rushed against the slope with the determination of a prizefighter's punches.

"The crows walk and leap," Piotr explained as he helped Tarelya up. "They're not birds."

Standing at the edge of the tree line, the woman dipped her head at the newcomers in greeting. She wore goggles over her eyes and her head was wrapped in woollen scarves that covered her mouth and her hair, leaving just the bridge of her nose exposed. "You've seen the mouths?" she asked, and Symon and his daughter nodded. "Crows is what we call them," she explained. "Short for chronovores. They eat time."

"How can something eat time?" Symon asked, woodenly brushing the snow from his clothes.

"We don't know," Piotr admitted, shaking his head. "End Day keeps on going, getting more compressed with every moment it continues. We are living in Hell."

Symon nodded. He had heard his place called by many names, one of which was the land that God had abandoned for darkness. Hell fitted the place as well as any other.

Chapter Seven

They were awakened when two burly sec men drew back the pluglike door and began beating them with sticks. It was still dark outside the cell, and Ryan was catnapping, alert to the movement of the door. Doc mumbled complaints as he came to, swiping the sticks away from his torso again and again, the men laughing and jeering. The men ignored his complaints, jabbing and poking him, issuing unintelligible taunts in their native tongue.

Ryan watched all this through one slit eye, his back crushed against the wall of the room beneath the open window, his legs stretched out before him across the cell. There was a third sec man standing at the door, Ryan noticed, this one armed with what appeared to be a rapid-fire longblaster, possibly an AK-47, Ryan wasn't sure from that angle. He readied himself as one of the men stomped across the tiny cell toward him, a cruel sneer on his face. The man held a paddle-like stick, as wide as a hand and fifteen inches long. Ryan guessed that it was salvaged from somewhere and had served another purpose years before.

"Heh, One-Eye," the man growled as he drew the paddle back, preparing to strike Ryan to awaken him.

As the paddle swung, Ryan's left hand snapped up and grabbed it above its wide end, yanking it upward away from him. The move surprised the paddle's wielder and he stumbled into the wall, striking his head just to the side of the open window. Still in his sitting position, Ryan's other hand snapped up and grabbed the man by his throat.

"Try that again and I'll chill you," Ryan snarled in the man's face, "right here in front of your girlfriend."

The man's face showed genuine surprise, his eyebrows rising comically on his forehead.

"Yeah, you droolies understand English, don't you?" Ryan continued, shoving his hand deeper into the man's throat and pushing him away.

With a wounded expression, the sec man pulled the paddle back, his sadistic game over before it had begun. Ryan pulled himself from the floor as the man backed away toward his partner. The other sec man had stopped jabbing at Doc and simply stood there, his own paddle hanging forgotten in his hand.

When Ryan stood he found he was almost a foot taller than either of the guards. "Now," he commanded, taking charge of the situation, "you have some reason for waking us or what?"

The men spoke to each other for a moment, then one of them—the one who hadn't tried to rouse Ryan—pointed his wooden stick at the one-eyed man. "You come with us. You follow, yeah?" His accent was so thick it made the words grate against Ryan's ears as he tried to make sense of them.

"Yeah, okay," Ryan said, and he checked on Doc, helping up the old man.

Outside the cell, they found themselves back in the ice-walled corridor, the strong smell of gas emanating from the dim, flickering lamps that were dotted along the floor.

J.B. was already standing out there, his hands bound

and his hat crooked on his head. When he saw Ryan emerge from the other cell he smiled grimly. "Good to know the gang's all here," he said. "My cell was bastard cold. Is Doc all right?"

Before Ryan could reply, Doc emerged from the cell, ducking his head under the lintel and smoothing his frockcoat. "That's quite all right, Ryan, I can answer for myself. My night's slumber was as restive as one would expect," he explained as one of the sec men bound his hands loosely, "but this old body of mine is not ready to give up quite yet."

Once they had been bound, the three men were led down a series of icy corridors to the exterior of the glacierlike ville, using slopes and occasional ladders to descend to ground level. Once there, they joined other gathered prisoners, including Jak and Ricky, who waited in a pen overseen by three armed guards dressed in furs. Jak looked exhausted to Ryan's eye, and his face displayed a line of nasty purple bruises running from brow to jaw where their captors had beaten him the night before.

Catching Ryan's eye, Jak shrugged indifferently. "Looks worse than is," he assured the one-eyed man.

Before long the group was marched away from the ville. There were thirty prisoners—all male—in the party and they were guarded by five men, three of whom rode on the backs of mutated caribou, their curling antlers daubed with bright paint in tribal design.

The sky was still a dark shade that Ryan took to be dawn, though later he would come to realize that the sun never really rose in these parts at this time of the year, leaving the days a sort of grim twilight even at the height of noon. The sec men didn't bother to explain where they were being taken, but one of Ricky's and

Jak's cellmates, a pasty-faced, drawn-looking man who had been incarcerated in the ville for several weeks, enlightened them.

"There's an old bomb site just to the east of here," the prisoner began, "close to where one of those earth-shaker missiles came down, I heard. Place was an army base once, before the nukecaust turned it into shit. Right now the site looks pretty much what you'd expect, but there's still some good stuff to be found there, blasters and so on. These ice demons been pushing us deeper and deeper into the ruins, seeing what shit we can scavenge up."

Doc tsked with surprise. "A mining operation," he said in a low voice. "We're miners, indentured laboring miners."

Ryan shot him a warning look. "At least we're alive, Doc," he said. "Till we can get to Krysty and Mildred, that's the best we can hope for."

Doc nodded apologetically. "Of course, I quite forgot myself."

As he spoke, one of the guards leaned over from his caribou steed and lightly rapped Doc across the back of his head with his rifle butt. "You, be quiet."

Chastised, Doc fell to silence and continued to trek out eastward with the other prisoners under the instruction of the dour-faced sec men. Snow littered the ground in sickly little patches like a rash amid the frozen soil, great untouched swathes of white running in a long line where a frozen tributary of the Nome River lay sleeping.

Ricky sidled up to join Ryan and J.B., his head turned against the chill wind. He checked for a moment, making sure none of the sec team was watching before turning to Ryan with a cunning smile on his face. "It's okay, Ryan," he whispered. "I have a plan to get us out of here. Just follow my lead."

Before Ryan could reply, a sec man shouted something at the group and they were forced to thin out again. Ryan didn't like it. Ricky had only recently joined the group, and was inexperienced. The kid had the arrogance of youth, too, which was fine in its place. But when you had a team to worry about, going off half-cocked could sure as shooting end up with someone chilled. Ryan made certain to find time during their forty-minute march in the bitter temperatures to instruct J.B. and Doc to keep an eye on Ricky. J.B. had been with Ryan right from the start, and Ricky seemed to idolize the man. Putting the two together made a certain amount of sense, at least until they reached their destination.

HAD ANY MAN in the group of prisoners had the frame of reference to think it, they might have wondered if they were looking at a Salvador Dali painting brought to startling life. A great basin had been carved into the land, runnels of snow streaking across its surface as it stretched three miles across into the distance. The giant pit had sunk into the earth by at least half a mile, trees and the remains of buildings clinging to its sloped sides like pus on the head of a popped boil.

Beyond the vast indentation in the earth, the air in the distance seemed to shimmer like a mirage, occasional flecks of color running across the dark sky. Ryan wondered if these were the fabled Northern Lights or if they might be something else. So much of Earth's environment had become scragged by the nuclear exchange that it was often impossible to judge what was going on in the atmosphere anymore.

The thick tail of a missile poked out from the center of the basin, a metal tube painted yellow and black with four fins studded equidistant around its sides. The fins tapered down toward the buried front of the missile, disappearing in a mound of snow and churned-up soil. A radial pattern of cracked earth spread from this epicenter, thick lines of broken soil running outward like cracks on a windshield. And around this, a mining colony had been set up—a great structure of underground tunnels held in place by metal scaffolding and thick wedges of wood, some of them still discernible as the tree trunks they had started life as.

Three sec men waited at the main entrance where it burrowed underground, wrapped in furs with blasters resting on their laps or beside them. They looked up as the group appeared, and one of them shuffled over on wide-soled snowshoes.

"About time you got here," he said. "We're freezing our balls off out here."

"What's the shift haul?" one of the mounted guards of Ryan's group asked, leaping down from his mutated steed.

"Not great," the man in the snowshoes said regretfully. "New seam over here—" he pointed "—but we're still trying to shore up the walls."

The dismounted rider jabbed back at the group of prisoners with his thumb. "We've got some new muscle. We'll get to it, see what's inside," he boasted.

The man with the snowshoes looked up at that, eyeing the prisoners more carefully for the first time. "Some of these slaves are new?" he asked with a broad smile. "Hearing that almost warms my frozen balls. Maybe we will get a decent haul out of this dump before sundown."

Overhearing that, J.B. eyed the dark sky with disapproval and leaned over to whisper to Ryan. "You reckon sundown will be any time this week?"

Ryan smiled at the comment despite himself.

The prisoners were walked into the gaping mine shaft and led, under armed guard, through the underground complex. The place was shored up with creaking wooden poles and metal struts, a series of dim gas lamps poised along the low ceiling at steady intervals. The burning lamps made the air stink, but they were too widely spaced to provide good illumination. As such, the line of prisoners-turned-miners had to pick their way slowly along the uneven floor of the mine shaft while the sec men berated them and hurried them along.

Spreading from a single entry point, a number of mine shafts had been dug deep into the earth beneath the sunken basin. As Ryan and his colleagues moved through them, they saw the walls had been shored up with metal plating scavenged from old military vehicles and packaging, the familiar olive-green paint scuffed almost to oblivion, but still visible to the trained eye. J.B. noted a fragment of stencilled lettering similar to that he had spotted on their arrival at the redoubt the night before. He had to tilt his head to read it, but when he did so he laughed. Upside down, the stencil read This Way Up.

After a couple of minutes walk through the underground passageway, they reached a fork and the prisoners were split into two groups. Ryan and Doc found themselves among the group following a wide pathway leading to the right of the underground development while J.B. was tossed in with a group of twelve prisoners that included Ricky and Jak. He hurried to join them, but one of the guards pulled him back.

"What's the rush, speedy monkey?" the man taunted. "You'll get where you're going, just have some patience."

It rapidly became evident to J.B. that the mines had been burrowed into an existing military complex, and he suspected that it had already been underground before the subsidence resulting from the missile attack. Some of the original corridors still existed among them shored-up mine shafts like ghosts of another era.

The group was split again shortly thereafter, leaving two groups of six captives, each group guarded by a lone sec man. Their guard was armed with a compact pistol that he displayed proudly in his belt, trusting he needed nothing else to keep them in line. He was probably right—most of the captives were worn down from days or weeks in the frozen cells of the ice fortress, and all of them had their wrists loosely bound with cord or metal links that granted enough freedom of movement for them to work but would still hinder them from overpowering their captors.

J.B. eyed the sec man's blaster, recognizing the weapon from his vast catalog of knowledge as a Colt Anaconda, a vicious six-shot pistol with plenty of punch. If he could get his hands on that then mebbe…

The mismatched party moved on, passing caved-in storerooms that had been stripped bare, the last of their broken contents strewed across the floor or heaped in piles along the walls. The only reason to come down here was to find weaponry, J.B. knew, and it looked like these ice pirates had been scavenging this site for years. No wonder that just about everyone in the ice ville had been armed to the teeth. They had the twenty-first-century equivalent of a munitions factory here, a fully stocked museum of death that they could raid at any time.

Little wonder then that they were top dog in the local territory—who would stand a chance against a heavily armed ville?

RYAN AND DOC meanwhile had been placed with a larger group of prisoners. Within a few minutes, however, the prisoners had been split into smaller groups and, accompanied by one sec man per group, were led into different sections of the underground complex. Ryan made sure to stay near Doc. It wouldn't do for them to become any more split up than they already were.

A five-minute walk brought them to a hollowed-out chamber whose low, curved ceiling echoed their footsteps. Six people were in the group now, including Ryan and Doc, along with a sec man dressed in thick furs and armed with a Kalashnikov longblaster and a Smith & Wesson he had rammed into his waistband beneath the furs.

"Now you work," the sec man spit. "Find ammunition, yes?"

One of the other prisoners spoke up and Ryan recognized him as part of the group that had been picked up along with his team outside the redoubt the night before. Despite the cold, the man was sweating profusely, his eyes wide with distress. "H-how much?" he stuttered. "How much do you expect us to find?"

Ryan looked around the vast chamber, assessing their surroundings. The man had a point. Even in the dim light of the wide-spaced lamps, it was clear that this storage area had been plumbed almost dry. The overall effect was more like a dump now than a military warehouse. There were stacks of crates and all of them had been broken open and emptied, many so carelessly that they were now little more than firewood. The floor was uneven with debris strewed everywhere, including ragged clothes and a mound of electronics—circuit boards and wiring whose copper lines glinted as they caught the illumination of the nearest gas lamp.

"You bring me your weight," the sec man said, "head to toe. You carry as much as you can, the rest we come back for. You bring less than this, you don't eat tonight. Clear?"

Grimly, the prisoner nodded.

The sec man eyed Ryan's broad shoulders. "You, tough guy, huh?"

Ryan didn't answer.

"Over here," the man instructed. "And you," he added, indicating Doc.

The storage area was large enough to house half a football field, but a great chunk of the ceiling had caved in over time. Some sections were propped up using thick metal posts, and Ryan guessed it had been backbreaking work shoring the roof up like that.

While the other prisoners got to work exploring the piles of junk in the vast room, Ryan and Doc were brought over to a stack of the metal poles waiting to be added at the edges of the ruins. The sec man pointed to them, indicating the tools that had been left there. There were two shovels along with a hammer, thick rivets for the scaffold poles and metal clasps that would lock them in place.

"You dig the shit back," the guard explained. "Once you have enough space, you prop ceiling up so we can search here. You unnerstand?"

Ryan nodded. Backbreaking work was right, and it

would be made all the more wearying by the fact that he and Doc were still shackled at the wrists.

Grimly, Ryan and Doc each picked up a shovel and started sifting away the clustered junk.

While the six prisoners worked, the guard sat back on what appeared to be a scarred plastic lawn chair that he had propped near the doorway. Ryan slyly looked around, assuring himself that it was the only way in and out of the room.

"This is an impossible task," Doc grumbled as he raked away a wedge of debris. The debris appeared to be a congealed amalgamation of concrete and metal plate, melded together in the white heat of the explosion that had ripped through the complex.

"Impossible or not," Ryan told him, "we're all out of options right now. For now our hands are tied. Literally in this case."

Doc nodded grimly, glancing to the lounging sec man in the lawn chair. The man had the Kalashnikov braced across his knees as he leaned back in the seat, pushing the chair back so that it balanced on the back legs, the front legs no longer touching the ground.

"I can feel something here," Doc whispered when he was sure the sec man wasn't watching them.

Ryan shot him a look. "A blaster?"

"No." Doc shook his head. "Not here—but here," he said, indicating his skull. "I have the strangest sensation that Emily has cooked me dinner tonight."

Emily Tanner, Doc's wife, had been dead for two hundred years.

"Snap out of it, Doc," Ryan ordered. "I can't have you going to la-la land on me right now." He had seen the old man drift in and out of lucidness before now. The man was plagued by his fractured memories, his brutal journey through time leaving his mind sometimes out of sync with reality. Their situation had to have triggered this latest bout. Ryan could only hope that Doc could keep it together long enough for them all to get out of this hellhole alive.

Doc nodded, shoveling another payload of detritus out of the way, feeling the muscles working in his shoulders. But in his mind, something seemed almost to be calling from the shadows, not a voice perhaps but another sense, a familiar smell or a sound he had not heard in two hundred years.

THE DAY PASSED in grim exertion. J.B., Jak and Ricky had been set to work sorting small caches of ammunition, single bullets that had been removed from their clips or strips in some forgotten past. There were three other prisoners working with them in a dimly lit cavern, its walls still scarred with ancient, peeling paint that hadn't been altered in a century. Together, the group perched on a line of crates and formed a little production line while their captor oversaw from outside the doorway.

The sec man couldn't imagine a threat from these prisoners. They were in a room with ammunition but no blasters—how much threat could they pose?

It was hard work, boring in its repetition and made uncomfortable because of the claustrophobic conditions of the cramped, warrenlike cave. Around the three-hour mark, another sec man came down the tunnellike corridor to relieve his companion. They spoke in a guttural combination of Russian and English, clear enough that J.B. could make sense of it if he listened. Their conversation was of no import, he decided, just the usual young man bragging about sexual feats that likely neither of them had actually achieved.

While the sec men were engaged in their conversation, J.B. leaned across to Ricky and Jak, speaking in hushed tones. "You said you had a plan, Ricky?"

The kid nodded. Then, glancing around to ensure they weren't being watched, he pulled out something that had been hidden inside his jacket lining. It was the sheathed hunting blade, the one he had lifted from the guard he had argued with outside of the glacier-like ville.

J.B. made a face. "That isn't going to do us a shit-load of good against these bastards," he said, shaking his head. "You never heard the expression 'bringing a knife to a blaster-fight'?"

Ricky smiled. "We'll wait until the other guy disappears," he said, using a tilt his head to indicate the two sec men. "I figure if we move fast enough we can take out one guard. Me and Jak will disarm him while you get the others moving."

J.B. looked over at the other prisoners with whom they shared the production line. They looked dead inside, all their spirit gone. It would be a challenge getting these half-starved wretches motivated. They had to be cajoled not to simply soil themselves where they sat.

J.B. turned back to Ricky and Jak, sitting opposite him on the production line. "You have an exit figured?"

"Same way we came," Ricky said. "At least we know it gets us back to the surface."

"There's going to be guards that way," J.B. warned. "Likely a lot of them, too, I reckon."

"I reckon so, too," Ricky agreed. "But we'll have the blaster by then."

J.B. glanced at the two men outside the room, surreptitiously eyeing their blasters. They were still engaged in their conversation about the sluts of the ville. "Best you're going to get there is a six shot," J.B. averred. "Not exactly ideal."

Outside the cavern, the two sec men had finished their conversation and one of them came striding back into the room. "No talking," he snapped, running a paw over a line of bullets that had been sorted and tossing them to the floor. "You! Start over. And stay quiet."

J.B. looked at the man and said nothing. He'd heard out Ricky. Now he was busy worrying about all the flaws in the kid's plan.

THE OPPORTUNITY CAME later, when J.B., Ricky and Jak were well into their seventh hour of bullet sorting. Their original guard had returned about an hour before, and he sat outside the small cavern half-asleep. Even so, J.B. was sure they wouldn't be able to sneak up on the guy—he never quite drifted into sleep proper, no matter how long they waited.

Unseen, Ricky had been working the knife at his wrist ties while the others sorted. The cord was frayed now, and he felt certain that it would snap with just the slightest of pulls.

Jak had his own ideas, his scarlet eyes flicking to the guard with regular suspicion.

The man snuffled, then shoved the fur-trimmed hat back on his head until it sat low to his skull. "You still working in there?" he snarled, poking his head and shoulders inside.

Ricky looked at him. "The stench in here is making my head spin," he complained.

The sec man smiled sadistically, showing a line of tiny steel tombstones where his rotted teeth had been repaired by someone with little skill. "Yeah, what you want me to do about it, shitface? This ain't no vacation."

J.B. placed another 9 mm bullet into the appropri-
ate storage box before speaking up. "Not mean ruffle
feathers, but kid's young. He's right—place stinks," he
added, glancing significantly at one of the other work-
ers whose pants showed a damp patch among the urine
stains. "Should let kid grab fresh air, clear head. Might
croak."

The sec man looked at J.B. with a scowl before re-
lenting. "Yeah, whatever. You," he said, pointing at
Ricky, "and you, whiteface. Come with me. No tricks.
As for the rest of you, there's a man posted at the end of
this tunnel. None of you are going anywhere. Get me?"

Ricky rose, stepping out of the cavern and into the
tunnellike corridor with Jak following two paces behind
him. Warily, the sec man watched them both pass, his
hand close to the Colt Anaconda holstered at his hip.

The kid kept his hands low and, in the darkness of
the corridor, snapped the frayed cord that held them.
J.B. would have argued that he acted too soon, but Ricky
saw his best chance as being before they reached the
man at the end of the tunnel. He shifted his sleeve ever
so slightly, uncrooking his arm and letting the hidden
blade drop into his hand, subtly hidden from the guard's
view.

"Come on," the sec man snarled, "keep moving." He
shoved Ricky in the back.

Seizing his opportunity, Ricky moved like a blur.
The hunting knife appeared from its hiding place in
his hand, and he lashed out with it at the guard, whipping the blade across the man's face in a rush of bloody
movement. The air around the man's face streaked with
scarlet as Ricky's blade hacked at his flesh, and he
stumbled toward Ricky with a curse.

"Fuck you," Ricky snarled in response, driving the

vicious little blade behind the man's left eye socket and wrenching it across his face, both hands gripped on the leather-strapped handle.

With a screech, the guard stumbled against a wall, his shoulder slamming into it with a clang of metal. Blood poured from his face and he brought his left arm up to try to staunch the flow, holding what was left of his face in place. With his other hand, he reached for the blaster strapped at his waist, drawing the weapon from its holster.

Jak moved faster, pivoting on one heel as he raised his other foot to kick the blaster out of the sec man's hand. The heel of his boot connected, sending the blaster flying across the tunnel with a loud pop of discharging ammo. A single bullet ricocheted from one of the metal-plate walls before drumming against the tunnel ceiling in a shower of sparks.

J.B. was moving, too, charging from the cavern straight at the sec man as his colleagues assessed other threats. The gunshot had echoed through the underground complex and already the sounds of running feet and voices raised in confusion were coming from the nearest tunnels.

"You two go," J.B. ordered. "I'll follow you."

Ricky didn't like leaving J.B. but Jak knew better than to argue. He had partnered with the Armorer for a long time, trusted J.B. to have his own plan of escape. Jak slipped his right hand from his bonds in an instant, compacting the bones and pulling it through the now-oversize loop. Then, snatching up the sec man's blaster, Jak gave Ricky a friendly shove on the back, urging him back the way they had come. Together, the two friends charged along the corridor that they had just come from, a blaster and a knife between them.

Up ahead in the ill-lit tunnels, Jak's remarkable eyes spotted the guards moving in their direction, their blasters ready. "Back," he instructed Ricky, shoving the youth against the wall.

"What is it, Jak?" Ricky asked, keeping his voice low.

Jak's eyes flashed to the blaster, checked its ammunition. Just five shots, not enough to hold off all the sec men and get Ryan and the others to safety. "Out of here," Jak whispered. "Find 'nother way."

Ricky nodded, turning back the way they had come. Sec men were appearing there, too. They were trapped like rats in a maze.

Chapter Eight

J.B. knew the jig was up the second he spotted the three guards silhouetted against the walls of the mine shaft. The other prisoners had proved as meek as sheep after shearing, much to his irritation, which left everything up to him. He wanted Jak and Ricky to escape. At least with them out in the field, the group stood a chance of getting out of this hellhole they had managed to walk themselves into when they had left the redoubt with Nyarla.

The bloody-faced sec man had both hands to his head now, screaming himself hoarse as he tried to hold his ruined face in place. There was no question that Ricky could act quickly when he needed to, even if it might not have been the best moment to try to escape, even though J.B. hadn't told him not to.

"Best give the kid a chance," J.B. muttered, striding purposefully toward the sec man with the ruined face.

The man couldn't see a thing. Blood was pouring into his eyes, and his left eyeball looked to have ruptured with Ricky's savage attack. Grimly, J.B. pulled the rope around his wrists taut and stepped quietly behind the sec man, hooking the rope over the man's throat. Then he yanked, pulling the man back and cutting off his screams in an instant.

RICKY SAW THE TUNNEL up ahead where J.B. was struggling with the bloodied guard. The Armorer had lost

his hat, and he was using his wrist bonds as a make-
shift garrote, dragging the man's neck back as he stran-
gled him.

Jak whispered something from behind Ricky, grabbing the kid's wrist and drawing him in a new direction.
There was a gap between the metal-sheet walls. It was
barely visible and doubtless Ricky would have missed
it had he been alone. Jak's night vision, however, was
legendary, a compense for the problems his albino eyes
sometimes suffered during daylight hours.

Ricky followed Jak into the new tunnel. Its walls
were scrappy and unfinished, and great hunks of debris littered the floor in increasingly messy arrays. It
had to be an old mine shaft, Ricky realized, abandoned
after its contents were dug up. Behind them, Ricky and
Jak could hear the commands of guards as they reached
J.B. and the others. Annoyed shouts echoed down their
shaft, followed by a single crash like a hammer blow.
Ricky winced at that, hoping against hope that it wasn't
J.B. getting a rather brutal comeuppance.

He and Jak continued up the shaft, ignoring the increasingly irritated cries echoing behind them.

J.B. HAD BEEN STRANGLING the sec man when the others
appeared at the bend in the tunnel. There was no room
to maneuver in these corridors; it was like trying to
head off a rabbit in its warren. The wily Armorer figured that gave him the upper hand for about ten seconds.

Drawing his strong arms back, J.B. pulled the strangling sec man toward him and turned him around, forcing him to arch his back and using him as a shield as
the other sec men targeted him with their weapons.

"Put him down," one of the men commanded.

J.B. eyed the blaster in the man's hand—a .44 caliber

that looked like a mutated Magnum, the kind of weapon Jak would have been comfortable with. If J.B. had the firepower figured right, that blaster could punch a hole right through his human shield. He held his breath, his eyes narrowed as if daring the man to shoot.

There was a moment's hesitation, and the sec man seemed to acknowledge for the first time the awful state that his partner had been left in, following Ricky's attack. Then he lowered his weapon a little, his face blanching in revulsion.

The man with the bloodied face spoke up then, his voice croaking where J.B. still had his throat held tightly. "Chill me," he gritted. That was the one thing J.B. hadn't wanted to hear.

To his credit, the other sec man didn't hesitate. He raised his blaster and fired, sending a single titanium-sheathed bullet into his partner's chest. The man's chest exploded in a geyser of blood, and J.B. stumbled back with the impact, feeling the force of the bullet strike against his own body even through his human shield. He struck his head against the wall and blacked out in an instant.

At the lip of the tunnel, the three sec men were rushing toward the prisoners even as another two appeared.

"Two prisoners are missing," one of the sec men said. "Find them. Quickly."

THE MINE SHAFT LED upward in near total darkness. At first the rise was gradual, but after a while Jak and Ricky started to find it more of a climb, with little flights of makeshift steps set up at intervals closer to the surface. Jak led the way, his incredible night vision priceless in such confines. Jak guessed that this had once been a corridor within the military building itself, but the earthshakers had destroyed the foundations and left it lurching at this impossible angle.

Debris was all over where the roof was unstable and some of it had almost entirely blocked the shaft, leaving the two companions with little room to maneuver. Somehow, Jak found a way through even the worst of it, his movements almost instinctive.

After what he'd guess was three or four minutes of frantic passage through the dark confines, Ricky spotted light ahead. It was dim, but he checked it by the simple process of looking behind him once before looking back at where he had seen it. Behind it was dark, like a black sheet had been hitched in front of his face; but ahead there was the square of illumination, faint but discernible and getting bigger even as they moved forward.

"Look, Jak, light!" Ricky whispered.

In the darkness, Jak's nod went unseen by his colleague. He had noticed it already, had it figured for an exit and was heading toward it with grim determination. "Man could be there," he reminded Ricky. "Chillers."

Ricky clutched his stolen blade tighter, wishing he had his Webley or some other blaster instead. Jak could handle a knife better than he could, he knew, and he wondered if they ought to trade, blaster for knife. But before he could suggest it, Jak halted right before him, pulling up so sharply that Ricky slammed into him with a fierce expulsion of breath.

"What is it?" Ricky whispered as he recovered himself.

Jak's head twitched left and right as he tried to locate the out-of-place sound he had heard. It was coming from behind them. Footsteps. "Go," he told Ricky. "Company coming."

Ricky picked his way ahead, wishing on his sainted

mother's life that he had Jak's knack for seeing through the darkness.

Behind him, Jak remained silent. He was moving much slower now, the blaster held low to his side as he listened to the sounds of the approaching footsteps. Then a flickering gas flashlight appeared without warning, popping into existence as their pursuers rounded a heap of debris. They saw Jak at the same moment he targeted them.

"There they are," the lead man bellowed. "Stop them!"

Jak unleashed a shot from the blaster, deafeningly loud in the enclosed space, hoping to take out the flashlight. The blaster pulled to the left, he discovered, throwing his aim quite considerably. In the light of the muzzle-flash, Jak saw the startled expressions of his pursuers—three of them in all, barely twenty feet behind him down the tunnellike shaft. Then came a crash of metal and plaster as the slug embedded itself in the wall, spewing dust.

The cloud of dust hung in the air, dotting across the beam of the flashlight as the men continued their pursuit. They were wary now, but they didn't shoot back. They either wanted their prisoners alive or they wanted to conserve bullets. Either way, it gave Jak an extra few seconds to get moving.

He found Ricky up ahead, close to the exit to the mine. The teen looked young to Jak, fear gripping his handsome features in the dim light that emanated from the doorway. A frigid breeze was coming from the open doorway, blasting several feet in with an accompanying howl like a wolf in distress.

"Come," Jak said, glancing back over his shoulder and gauging the distance to their pursuers. The sec men had fallen back a little. They were twenty-five feet or so away from them now, working their way past a low hunk of ruined ceiling that bulged down like the belly of a pregnant dog.

Jak saw the opportunity and took it, whipping up his blaster again and firing off two quick shots into the cracking ceiling. The off aim on the blaster would make it next to useless in a firefight anyhow, he figured, so he might as well spend what little ammo he had on a sure thing. The bullets streaked away with a double boom of sound, and Jak was already running to the exit as they struck the ceiling behind him. The ceiling creaked for a moment, then it tumbled down like a vomiting drunk, blocking the sec men's path and filling the whole shaft with dust and debris.

Then they were through the doorway and out into the open air, Jak still with two bullets left in the stolen blaster and Ricky with nothing more than a blood-stained hunting knife. Beside them, a man coughed and spit a curse in Russian. A sec man in a thick fur coat and hat sat smoking a hand-rolled cigarette. Surprised, he dropped the cigarette and reached for the Heckler & Koch longblaster he had stashed at his side. Jak shot him in the forehead before he could get the rifle off the ground, and the man sank back against the mine wall, blood and brains mingling with the frosting of ice crystals there.

Without a word, Jak and Ricky hurried forward, checking for more guards. It looked like they were alone for now. The man Jak had just chilled had to have sneaked off for a cigarette while his colleagues worked. Still, Jak figured they wouldn't have long before more sec men arrived from one direction or another, alerted to their presence by the blaster's loud report.

They took a moment to take stock of where they were. They stood on a steep incline where two trees bowed toward them like hunchbacks, the broken remains of a wire fence visible beyond. Though dark, the sky showed flashes of color, as if some great cosmic artist was washing his brushes in it. Jak figured they were on the far side to the main entrance where they had entered the mines. It was easy to get turned around in the darkness like that, moving underground the way they had been forced to.

"Where now, Jak?" Ricky asked, snatching up the H & K. "We can't just leave J.B., Ryan and Doc." His brown eyes seemed to plead with Jak, deferring to his friend's greater experience.

Getting away from the mine was the only intelligent course of action. They could always come back for Ryan and the others, mount a sneak attack either here or at the ville that looked like an icicle. Jak was a fine tracker—he was certain the albino could find it without trouble.

Jak led Ricky up the slope, fidgeting with the blaster in his hand in irritation. He had one shot left, so he had better make it count.

At the top of the rise they ran into more trouble. Two sec men were tending to their mutated steeds, the fearsome caribou gorging themselves on the remains of what looked to be a mutie fish, twice the size of anything Ricky had seen in the waters around Monster Island. The men had the caribou—four in all—tethered to a short post that was stuck into the dirt to the side of the haphazard remains of the wire fence.

Silently, Jak pointed to the right, and Ricky saw a narrow gap in the fence there, just out of sight of the sec men. He nodded and began scurrying toward it, and Jak followed a moment later. The men seemed unaware of their presence, most likely the gunshot had been muffled by the lightly falling snow and the snorting of their mounts.

But as Ricky approached the breech, one of the caribou yowled out a hideous roar and the sec men turned. The beast had scented the blood on Ricky's knife, and it wanted a taste of whatever meat it had come from.

Jak turned, scampering backward as he watched the sec men react. Thirty feet away, they were reaching for their longblasters, which had been holstered in the saddles of two of the mounts.

Ricky was through the gap and running, clambering higher up the slope, his body held low to keep his center of gravity down. It was a good strategy, Jak acknowledged—not only did it help his ascent, but it also made for a much smaller target for the distant sec men.

A shot rang through the air, swiftly followed by another. Chillers like these had been mining this army base for who knew how long, Jak realized—they weren't likely bothered about wasting a few bullets if it meant keeping their prisoners in line. And if they died, well, they could always use them as bait for the mutie wolves just like the man he and Ricky had found spread-eagled in the dirt back at the redoubt.

His head down, Jak ran through the gap in the fence. Behind him, the wire grating of the fence sparked where a bullet struck against it, shaving metal from the structure.

Ricky was at the top of the incline now, out of the vast crater where the missile had struck. Jak didn't like where he was headed; all of a sudden he had a feeling that something real bad was lurking out there where the lights smeared the sky.

Another bullet cut the air behind him, driving Jak

on as it clipped against the snow just a few feet away. He weaved, dodging purely by instinct as another bullet whizzed through the air. The sec men were tenacious, and their shots weren't wide enough to give Jak confidence in evading them for very long.

Ahead of him, Ricky was still running, puffs of snow kicking up in his wake. Jak dived to the ground as another bullet spiraled by overhead, wincing as it struck a tree trunk at head height. Swiftly, the albino brought his blaster around, wondering if he might be able to knock one of the sec men out of the fight with a single well-placed bullet. That was all he had, he reminded himself—just one bullet.

By the tether post, the two sec men had coordinated themselves, Jak saw. One was using a longblaster to track the escapees while the other one had just mounted one of the steeds and was urging it to chase them. Take out the mounted one, Jak figured—they could hide from his ally, and maybe the sudden death of the rider would send the steed into a frenzy.

But as Jak steadied his aim, he heard Ricky call to him. He sounded frightened.

"Jak, help!"

He turned and saw Ricky just a dozen feet ahead of him. The kid seemed to be stretched, his whole body elongating as he moved forward, like a picture that had been poorly copied.

"I can't stop!" Ricky screamed as parts of him blurred away, a series of images flashing across Jak's vision faster than he could comprehend.

Behind him, the rifleman took another shot, sending a bullet into the snow just inches from Jak's knee with a resounding boom. Jak made a decision then, the kind of life-or-death decision that could change a person's destiny. He sprang from the ground and ran, his arms pumping at his sides, the blaster still hanging from his right hand. He raced forward, chasing after Ricky as his young ally disappeared in a blur.

Snow kicked up at Jak's passing as he bolted toward the space where Ricky had vanished. And then, without warning, Jak began to blur out of existence, too.

LOCKED INSIDE HIS radiation suit, Don Nectar took a moment away from his work to listen. He had been reworking the quantum infuser of the scoop reverberator—Section 93-B according to the hundred-year-old designs he had found and begun to amend—trying to minimize the frequency of distortion to a level that might prove endurable for a human body. But as he worked, he had heard the voice calling to him from close by, like a ghost on the wind.

He stopped work, inclined his great helmet head this way and that, trying to locate the source through the thick weave of material. The radiation suit muffled outside sound, but that didn't seem to matter. It wasn't as if the caller was in the room with him, down here in the great subbasement where the generators whirred and clunked as they powered the time portal he knew he would need to get home. No, the call was coming from farther away than this room, and somehow closer still, just a skipped heartbeat away from him. He knew it, recognized it. The voice was like a missing part of himself, a chunk of his soul screaming out for release.

"Lost souls," he muttered with a shake of his head. "Shall we ever know peace in our lifetime, you and I?"

Nectar turned back to Section 93-B and brought the

ratchet wheel around until the teeth bit home. The voice was closer now, almost with him. That much he knew for certain.

Chapter Nine

The two sec men were hurrying toward the line of demarcation as Jak followed Ricky into the blur, their blasters raised to attack. They watched in annoyance as first the dark-haired adolescent, then his white-skinned partner, blurred through the unmarked line.

The rider on the mutant caribou pulled back on the reins to halt his mighty steed, and the beast growled in complaint, rearing back just a few feet from the invisible line that indicated the danger. "Dammit," he gritted as he watched the snowlike blur that he suspected had once been Jak. "Lost them." Baron Kenojuak wasn't going to be happy about that, but there was no way he was chasing them into His Ink Orchard. No way at all.

JAK FELT WIND in his hair and his stomach lurched as if he was falling. Around him, the ground seemed to be shifting, rolling under him in a blur. He looked down, watching his own feet as they tramped through the snow. There was a disconnect, somehow the two facets didn't join—his feet were moving normally and yet his surroundings blurred as if he was moving at incredibly high speed, faster even than a cross-country wag.

And then he tripped, stumbling over a rock jutting from the snow, falling to the ground in a tangle of limbs.

Automatically, Jak bunched up, rolling in a ball even as he struck the snow-speckled earth, the blaster clutched protectively to his gut. He came to a halt a moment later, his senses reeling from both the fall and the invigorating sense of speed that had threatened to overtake him just moments before.

"Shit," Jak spit as he pushed himself up off the ground, checking that the blaster was still okay. It was. He turned his head, searching for Ricky. The kid had been just a few yards ahead of him when this whatever it was had overtaken him, turning him into a human blur.

Almost as an afterthought, Jak looked at his own hands, his arms, his body. No, he was in one piece.

Behind him, the mining area was lost in a sea of fog, cold mist brushing across the ground in rapidly moving lines. The wind was picking up here, had picked up already. The sky was as dark as twilight, but there was something shimmering across it, brushes of light like bruises on the clouds.

And there was no sign of Ricky.

Jak hadn't been able to view his passage through whatever invisible barrier he had traversed. He had sensed the passing, felt his body being drawn as if by powerful forces, like his bones and organs were being momentarily yanked through his flesh.

He sat there, blaster gripped in his hands, gazing around him at the sprawl of snow and ice and mist that went on as far as the eye could see. "Shit," he muttered again, shaking his head.

FOR RICKY, hitting the hidden barrier had felt like being thrown from a fast-moving wag, that sudden sense of unexpected movement as the door was opened and one was shoved through the gap. He had continued to run, the guard's shots echoing behind him, determined to stay out of their reach.

One of the bullets had cut through the…barrier, wall, field? Whatever it was, one of the bullets had cut through it as Ricky entered, clipping past him. Ricky had watched it sail over his shoulder, lunging onward across the snow-smeared ground until it was lost in the clouds of low-lying mist hugging the soil.

Ricky stopped—or he tried to. Bringing himself to a halt had proved far more difficult than he had expected. It was as if he was on a merry-go-round, going faster and faster, each revolution adding to his momentum. When he finally did stop, he did so with all the grace of a tranquilized rhino, crashing into a clutch of dark-limbed trees whose skeletal branches showed no signs of life. Somehow, somewhere, he had dropped the Heckler & Koch longblaster, but that was the least of his concerns.

Ricky sank to the ground amid the eerie copse, looking up into the sky. Either his head was spinning or the sky was; right now he simply couldn't tell which. But as he lay there, something else crossed his vision, poised just inches above his face. It was a bullet, cutting the air and aimed right at his forehead.

J.B. WAS BEING held under armed guard, his hands and ankles shackled and he was sporting a vicious cut across his forehead. He had been brought up to the surface with brutal rapidity, had awakened to find himself being dragged by the arms through a mine shaft, his back and legs trailing along the ground. When they reached the surface, J.B. had still been woozy, so one of the sec men had kicked him hard in the shin until he jumped.

"Wakey wakey," the sec man snarled. "You are in a lot of trouble, little man."

J.B. looked around. They were back at the surface,

himself and four sec men. The Armorer had been placed in a chair—a dilapidated swivel seat that had been recovered from the mess belowground—and two sec men watched him with their blasters pointed at his face. He said nothing, figuring words couldn't help him right now. Instead, he assessed the blasters that the sec crew had armed themselves with.

One of the leathery-skinned men was wearing J.B.'s battered brown fedora, and he paraded in front of his colleagues doing a mincing kind of strut. It was the same man who had shot the sec man in the tunnel. "Look at me," the guy mocked, "the big, bad chiller of no one." They all guffawed at that.

"You're wearing my hat," J.B. said, a note of warning in his tone.

"And just what are you going to do about that, little goblin?" the sec man taunted. "Strangle me, too?"

J.B. held the man's glare, saying nothing.

"I knew Pamploma—the man you chilled—well," the sec man said.

"I didn't chill him," J.B. pointed out reasonably. "You did. Shot him one right in the belly. Nasty way to chill a man, if you want my opinion. Slow way to die."

The chiller grimaced angrily.

"My hat?" J.B. said without emotion.

With clear irritation, the sec man removed the fedora from his head, spit in it, then shoved it onto J.B.'s head before stomping away.

J.B. watched him go then slyly peered around the little camp. There was no sign of Jak or Ricky, which could mean they got away. J.B. hoped so—his own chances were looking pretty slim right now.

EVENTUALLY, RYAN and Doc were relieved of their task and accompanied back to the surface along with their fellow prisoners. They had worked the mine for more than twelve hours straight, shoring up the walls and digging through the rubble, and Doc was almost doubled over from exertion by the end of their unforgiving shift.

"These bones cannot take much more of this punishment, my dear Ryan," he said as they pushed a cart to the surface. Doc leaned against its handles, Ryan noticed, using it to prop himself up.

The cart featured a bent wire frame and had been half-filled with ammunition and rubble along with a handful of recovered blasters. There were four blasters in total, but two of them were in pieces and the barrel of the third looked as if it had been crushed. The ammunition was in similar condition, and Ryan reflected that the haul was hardly worth the exertion involved; had the ice dwellers not used slaves, the mine would have been abandoned long ago.

When they got to the surface, Ryan instantly spotted the state that J.B. was in. The cut on the Armorer's forehead had dried, but it left a mean red streak that had run right down his face. Ryan checked himself, tamping down the urge to go to his friend.

"It appears John Barrymore has been busy," Doc observed quietly, stretching the painful kinks out of his back muscles as he leaned against his swordstick.

Ryan looked all around, his lone eye roving across the heads of the exhausted prisoners-turned-miners. There was no sign of Jak. Or Ricky. Where were they?

JAK PULLED HIMSELF back to his feet and forced himself to take a step. Mist was billowing all around, and he had no idea which direction he had come from. He was a tracker, with senses like a wolf—he shouldn't get confused by a little mist like this. Yet, Jak had to admit he was lost.

He looked around. The ground showed a patchy quilt of snow, clumped here and there in high drifts, while other parts of the ground remained free from its white pattern, showing instead the glittering lines of icy blades of grass.

Trees were dotted here and there, their branches bare, a whole line of them poised on the horizon like jurors waiting to pass sentence.

Above, the sky showed slate gray with only the barest hint of the sun's illumination, like those few minutes before dawn when the sun was still crouching just below the horizon. Within that muted sky, Jak perceived flashes—and they were just flashes—of color, popping in and out of existence like fireworks. He had seen radioactive glow before, and it reminded him a little of that and also the deranged patterns he had witnessed during travel via mat-trans. Whatever it was, it spoke of energies unrestrained, darting in and out of existence in the blink of an eye.

"Ricky?" Jak called, risking attracting the sec men.

There was no reply.

"Ricky?" he called again, louder this time.

Once again, no response.

Jak eyed the ground, searching for evidence of his friend's passage. It should be easy enough to spot, tracks in the snow.

Jak was right—finding Ricky's footprints wasn't hard. Turning himself to face them, though, that was a whole other experience. It felt almost as if he was underwater, in those murky swamps around where he had grown up in Louisiana. Water with so much crap in it

weighed on the body as one tried to swim through it.
But here, it was the air.

There was something going on here, something Jak
was only subliminally aware of. It was like everything
was taking longer, even the most simple movement of
his body to follow Ricky's footsteps.

Following the prints, Jak trudged up toward a cluster of half-dead trees. Their branches hung limply at
their sides. Jak pushed on, shoving one of the scrappy-
looking branches aside and spotting Ricky lying faceup
in the snow, gazing at the air above him. For a moment, Jak took him to be looking at the sky, and then
he stopped, realizing what it was Ricky was staring at.

A single bullet hung in the air above Ricky's head,
just six inches from his nose and pointed in the direction of his face.

RYAN, DOC AND J.B. joined the other prisoners on the
long trek home, their muscles aching from a hard day's
work. J.B. was made to walk behind the other prisoners, his wrists and ankles still bound, leaving him just
enough rope to walk but not to run.

From what Ryan could gather from what little the
sec men let slip, Jak and Ricky had fallen off the edge
of the world. The more he listened to their conversation, conducted as it was in fractured Russo-English,
the more he realized that "the edge of the world" was
an actual place to these people, and he figured it for
the area beyond the mines where he had seen the lights
playing across the sky.

"It makes a perverted kind of sense," Doc agreed
when Ryan ventured his opinion in a low voice. "You
may recall that John Barrymore described our arrival
point as farther than any map reached."

Ryan nodded. That didn't exactly answer the question about where his missing companions were now, however, but perhaps it gave an idea of where they had headed to escape the clutches of their brutal jailers.

One thing came across loud and clear from the sec men's guttural conversation. None of them had any desire to follow the missing prisoners beyond the edge of the world. They seemed to view it as an area of supernatural activity, something that one of the men described as *Temno Bozh'ego Sada*. Ryan had come across those kind of superstitions before. The Deathlands was a breeding ground for ignorance and idiocy. Having a bunch of inbred Inuits figure a place for the world's end didn't surprise him any more than that Jak would see such a place as a viable escape route.

The question was whether they were coming back—if that were even possible. Ryan might not buy into the superstitious mumbo jumbo these meatheads were spewing, but he still figured a place like this *Temno Bozh'ego Sada* likely got its rep because no one came back from it. For now, at least, it was down to him, Doc and J.B. to figure a way to free Krysty, Mildred and Nyarla, then get out of this mess alive. Unless, of course, the women had already gotten their own plan in place.

WHILE THEIR MALE companions toiled in the mines, Krysty and Mildred had spent their whole day locked in the twelve-by-ten cell with its draped walls. They, along with the other women who shared the cell, remained largely undisturbed; the only time the mighty wooden door was rolled back was to allow an elderly woman entry to bring food. The food was simple fare, tough day-old bread, unrecognizable vegetables and cured meats that had been cut in tiny slivers that were barely large enough to taste. Between them, the eight women who shared the cell had perhaps enough food to adequately feed three.

"One thing's for sure," Mildred said grimly as she chewed on the bread, "at least neither of us is getting fat while we're here." Neither Mildred nor Krysty would touch the meat, fearing it was human flesh.

With little else to occupy them, Mildred had taken up her scant medical supplies and looked over the other occupants of the room. Along with Nyarla, three more of the women were under twenty, one dark-haired girl just barely fifteen. The girl had a little puppy fat to her face, and sported a vicious scar down below her chin where someone had tried and failed to hang her. Why this had occurred the girl wouldn't reveal, and she shied away from Mildred's ministrations. Mildred suspected that she had been treated savagely all her life, such was the level of fear showing from her demeanor.

While Mildred checked over the women, all of whom were suffering the initial results of hypothermia, Krysty examined the door in the daylight. It sealed the doorway entirely, acting like the stopper on a jar of jelly, which meant that it couldn't be forced from within, at least not by a normal human. Krysty wondered whether her other strength, her Gaia power, could move the door. There was only one way to find out, and only one chance to do so. Now was not that time.

The eldest of the other women in the room was a twenty-five-year-old named Kirima. She had the dark hair and wide features of an Inuit, with slim body, long legs and remarkably slender hands. Though distrustful of the newcomers at first, she soon opened up to them after Mildred had cleaned a wound she revealed on her neck hidden by her long hair.

"The men come," Kirima explained, "and they make us do things, whether we want to or not. Some of the girls haven't minded so much, some of the men are quite nice really. But a few are just bastards, brutes that want nothing more than to hit and fuck." She pressed her hand against the little patch of material that Mildred had affixed to her neck with some scavenged medical gauze from her bag of supplies. "That's how I ended up with this. Bascha couldn't get it up so he cut me open with his knife. Blood turns him on."

Mildred thought about the wound that she had just dressed. It was a slight wound, long and designed to bleed for a long time without healing over. Even when she had dressed it, the wound had still been weeping. "How long ago was this?"

"With Bascha?" Kirima asked. "Two days, I think."

Mildred said nothing, but she knew the woman was lucky that the wound hadn't gone septic. The freezing environment had probably helped keep the wound from becoming infected.

The other women related similar stories, of how they would be made to perform sexual acts for the ville's baron, an easily bored man called Kenojuak. Even the young teen, whose name was Narja, related terrible stories of her experiences here. Mildred had heard it all before, one way or another. Whatever the Death- lands had brought, it had managed to shove women to the very bottom of what little society remained, used as baby carriers and sluts.

Once Kirima had finished her tale of woe and her wound was patched up to Mildred's satisfaction, the doctor strode across the room and spoke quietly with Krysty. "You hear that?" she asked.

Krysty nodded. "Some of it. Enough."

Mildred raised her eyebrows. "Figure we might have some male company sometime soon. I plan to be ready for it."

Somberly, Krysty nodded again. "Men with their pants down tend to be easy targets. Figure it for our chance to get out of here."

"Yeah," Mildred agreed. "Let's hope so."

"You see it, don't you, Jak?" Ricky whispered, as if afraid that his voice would disturb the bullet where it hung just inches before his face.

"Sure do," Jak agreed. He still had the blaster in his hand, and his grip tightened on it as he eyed the bullet.

"It's moving," Ricky said, keeping his voice low.

"Not think it…" Jak began, then stopped. He did see it, the movement was incredibly slow but the bullet was very gradually continuing toward Ricky. "Yeah, okay."

"How can it do that?" Ricky wanted to know, his voice rising a little with fear and frustration.

"Not know," Jak decided. He arguably had a simpler outlook than Ricky or his other companions, living much more in the present than even his fellow survivalists. For Jak it wasn't simply necessity that drove him to be that way; there was something instinctive, almost feral about him.

"Where it come from?" Jak asked, taking another step closer to the hovering bullet.

"Don't know," Ricky said. "I fell and when I looked up it was just there, hanging over my heart. I've watched it for what feels like an hour as it ran up the length of my chest, real slowlike."

"Real slow," Jak agreed absently. He was close enough to the bullet to see its markings now, close enough in fact to pluck it from the air if he had the inclination to. He wondered what that might do to the slow-moving projectile. Would it speed up, drop, or burn against his skin the way a fast-moving bullet would? Maybe it wouldn't react at all.

"I'm going to try rolling out from under," Ricky said. "I think there's room."

Jak was still looking at the bullet. He recognized the type, it was a 7.62 mm. Jak had loaded bullets like that before now. It was the kind of bullet a person would use for a longblaster. He had the strange feeling it had come from the sec man who had begun blasting at them outside the mine, had followed them through the invisible barrier that separated that place from here.

On the ground, Ricky shimmied to one side, compacting the snow as he moved out from under the hanging bullet. The bullet continued to float there, following its sluggish path toward the nearby tree.

Once he was out from under it, Ricky breathed a heavy sigh of relief. He knelt on the snow, staring at the bullet that hung impossibly in the air. "You have any clue what's going on?" he asked.

"Sec-man bullet," Jak proposed, indicating the bullet. "It follow here."

Ricky looked at the trees, the snow and the ground-hugging mist beyond, his head reeling a little. "Where are we? It doesn't look like anywhere special."

"Mebbe not," Jak agreed, "but feels it. Figure we stepped in whole load shit."

Ricky nodded. "Yeah. My fault."

The two companions leaped back suddenly as the bullet picked up speed, whistling through the air for less than a second before embedding itself in the nearest tree trunk, its passage finally complete.

"Wha—?" Ricky spit, kicking himself away from the impact site.

Jak glared at the open air where the bullet had been, eyed its passage and destination point. To stop, to slow like that, then to suddenly speed up. Jak had never seen anything like it. The whole occurrence made no sense.

He turned back to Ricky, pushing a hand through his alabaster mane of hair. They both took a deep breath. The bullet had embedded in the tree. They were safe.

It was then that the mouth came, emerging through the dead undergrowth.

Chapter Ten

With evening came unwelcome visitors. Krysty had been leaning against the sill, gazing through the thick glass through which the central courtyard of the ville could be seen. She was in tune with Gaia, the Earth Goddess, and being locked away from her like this hurt Krysty, driving a wedge of discomfort through her soul.

Unimpressive to begin with, the Alaskan sun had dwindled to nothing outside, and the room itself had been left lit only by the gas lamps that were dotted between the tapestries. At the far end of the cell, the door began to draw back. Immediately, Krysty was on her feet, her hand automatically brushing to the place where her blaster should be...would have been had she not been disarmed. Beside her, Mildred had stood up, too, the strap of her satchel yanked swiftly over her shoulder.

The two women looked at each other, silently wondering if this was it, if this was to be their chance at escape. Around them, the other women had tensed, watching the opening door with wary eyes.

As soon as the door was pulled aside, two men strode into the room. Each held a blaster, the one on the left's looking so scratched and beaten that Mildred wondered if it could even fire.

"Back up, ladies," the man to the right said, his yellow teeth showing through his thick beard. "Party time has arrived."

One of the women whimpered at that, but the two men ignored her. They were looking at Krysty, her bright red hair and statuesque figure diversion enough for any man.

"Baron's looking for some company tonight," one of the men said, picking something from his teeth. His eyes fixed on Krysty. "You, strip."

Krysty stood staring at him, her emerald-colored eyes showing a barely restrained fury.

"What, bitch, are you deaf?" The man laughed, taking a step toward Krysty.

She made a show of wrinkling her nose while brushing at the air with her hand as though the man's breath stank, which it did.

The man reached out, his smile becoming more fixed, eyes narrowing. "I told you to strip, bitch," he snarled.

As his fingers touched Krysty's arms, she stepped forward, hooking her right foot behind his. In less than a second the man had toppled over, slamming into the floor. Struggling to catch his breath, the sec man looked up at Krysty angrily from where he lay.

The red-haired beauty glared at him, baring her teeth. "Next time I'll snap your neck, little man," she hissed.

The sec man's colleague was on her by then, jabbing his blaster at Krysty and Mildred, warning them away. "Back up, back up," he shouted. "I got enough bullets here for all of you."

But did he have enough time, Krysty wondered, *to shoot all of them? Not likely.*

Mildred's hand grasped Krysty's arm and steadied her. She knew just what Krysty was thinking. "Not yet," she said in a low voice. It wouldn't do to get the other captives chilled because of a rash decision now, and even if they did manage to overpower the sec men Mildred figured there would be hell to pay for anyone left behind.

Reluctantly, Krysty stepped back.

The sec man on the floor recovered, but he kept clear of Krysty and Mildred, gravitating instead toward two of the other occupants of the room. Mildred winced as Kirima and Narja were made to strip before being marched away at blaster-point to the waiting bed of the baron. At least they had survived—for now.

"I TELL YOU I FELT HER, Ryan," Doc explained, "as clear as I see you there. My Emily was with us in the mine. Not standing with us, but near enough that I could feel her presence."

The two men had been accompanied back to the ice ville, where they were split from the other prisoners and locked in a new cell. The cell was on a lower level than their first, granting a superior view of the open area that the ville had been built to encompass. The cell was still small, however, with only a narrow slit of open window, far too narrow for a man to fit through. As well, the floor had a gentle slope to it, pitching from right to left in such a way that it made one nauseous to stand up for too long.

With little sense of order, the sec men had endeavored to keep the two men apart, but Ryan had muscled another prisoner out of the way during the walk through the icy tunnels, ensuring that he and Doc arrived together for the lock-up ritual. They were joined this time by another prisoner, a man called Hurst, who slumped down in one corner of the tiny cell and began chewing his fingernails with some ferocity.

J.B., meanwhile, had been returned to his own cell, but that was a deliberate ploy on the part of the sec men. They held him responsible for Jak and Ricky's breakout and, while they showed no intention of chasing after them into the area they referred to as *Temno Bozh'ego Sada,* they very definitely intended to punish the Armorer for his part in the escape and the death of their colleague. J.B. took the treatment solemnly, his eyes alert, searching for an opportunity to somehow turn the tables on his captors.

"You were out of it, Doc," Ryan told the old man as he gazed through the narrow window into the circular courtyard. "All the work down there, and it was hot in those tunnels. Would get to anyone after a while."

"No," Doc enthused, shaking his head, "this was different. My Emily was close, calling to me. And the whitecoats, too."

Ryan perked up at that. "The ones who sent you here?" he asked. This was a new avenue for the old man to pursue. Usually his ramblings went back to the better life he had led in the 1880s, not to the terrible experiments that the scientists had performed on him in the twentieth century.

"I cannot explain it properly," Doc said, irritated at his own failing. "It is like…like the smell of bacon on the griddle will remind you how hungry you are. This was a sense, my dear Ryan, the sort of thing a man knows without needing to question it."

Turning from the courtyard, Ryan looked Doc over. Even in this icy cell the man looked every bit the gentleman in his Victorian-era clothing. Doc was an anachronism, a refugee from another time. Ryan had seen the man almost lose his sanity coming to terms with that, had watched, powerless, as the old man had been haunted by his own memories.

"You really think it was something out there?" Ryan asked.

"I can assure you," Doc insisted, "there was something about that mine."

"The mine or the surrounding area?" Ryan asked perceptively. He was thinking about the way that Jak and Ricky had apparently disappeared, the place the locals referred to as the edge of the world.

"The...feeling," Doc said, choosing his words carefully, "and that is all I can really describe it as, began when we emerged from the redoubt." He dipped his voice low when he said this last, glancing warily at their fellow prisoner. The man didn't appear to be listening.

RICKY ROLLED OUT of the way as sharp teeth snapped at the air above him, barely six inches from his right leg.

Beside him, Jak was already back on his feet, scrambling across the snow-dusted ground and bolting out of the natural enclosure of trees. "Move," he called back to Ricky. "Out there."

Ricky didn't need telling twice. He leaped to his feet, hurrying from the copse like a sprinter in the starting blocks, his feet kicking up powdery snow in his wake. "What was that, Jak?" he cried as he chased after the albino.

"Not know," Jak admitted as he slowed and turned, bringing the blaster to bear. He was very conscious that he only had one bullet left.

Behind them, the mouth was turning in the air. At first glance it had looked just like that, a disembodied mouth hurtling through the air two feet above the

ground, spiny teeth arrayed in four rows across its men-
acing grin, two sets of two like some undersea creature.

If Jak could figure out what to shoot he would, but
all he could see was that mouth, nuzzling around the
tree trunks, searching for its prey. Jak watched it, the
hackles rising on the back of his neck. He had never
seen anything like this, a creature without a body, just
a hole in the air.

"What are we going to do?" Ricky asked breathlessly as he reached Jak's side. "What the hell is that?"

Jak watched the thing silently, ignoring Ricky's
squawking. He wanted to get the thing's measure, try
to figure out how it moved, whether it followed a pattern. He suspected it might be artificial, some kind of
remote-controlled thing that was employed to terrify
and hunt down unsuspecting intruders to this place.
After all, Jak reasoned, the barricade that they had
passed through had been erected by someone; maybe
the same someone who wanted them to stay away from
this place, wherever it was that they were.

Amid the trees, the mouth nudged left and right,
searching for something. The jaws snapped closed with
a nasty clip-clopping sound, again and again, biting at
the empty air. There was something more of its presence, Jak realized as he watched it. At first he had taken
it to be just a mouth hanging in the air, but there was
definitely more to it than that. It had a body, narrow
and tubular like a worm, extending behind it in a writhing coil. The body was hard to see; it flicked left and
right, more discernible by the way it knocked against
the brittle shafts of the dead tree trunks than by any
visual presence.

Beside him, Ricky saw the thing, too. "You think it's

some kind of stealth tech?" he asked quietly, fearful of attracting the mouth thing.

Jak had seen stealth tech before, and he could see how Ricky might think that was what they were witnessing. The body was like a shimmer in the air, as if a lens had been placed over his eye, subtly changing Jak's view of the environment. But if it was stealth tech, why would anyone leave the mouth showing? Unless maybe it was broken, a faulty circuit in the thing's makeup.

With a blurt of warning, Ricky knocked Jak aside. Above them, a second mouth had shimmered into existence, cutting through the air on a rocketlike path toward the two companions.

Jak spun on his heel, bringing the Colt Anaconda around and aiming at the mouth where it writhed across the snowy ground, widening as it neared him for a second time. But before he could shoot, the impossible mouth launched itself from the ground, butting against Jak just above his left hip and knocking him from his feet.

The albino went crashing to the ground and the blaster sailed from his grip. Before he knew it, the mouth was hurrying across his body, bearing down on his face. Though he couldn't see it, Jak could feel this one's body as a weight against his torso. The mouth snapped at his face, and Jak reached up without thinking, clutching the thing behind its jaws where he estimated its throat had to be. The jaws snapped closed an inch from his nose, four sets of teeth clacking together with a hollow finality.

IN THE ICE VILLE, J.B. was thrown back into a similar cell to the one he had occupied the night before. The sec men had worked him over for his part in getting their partner Pamploma chilled. They had used their fists and feet and short clubs to pound him, but J.B. had taken the beating in grim silence. If anything, the feel of the men's short attack had brought a little sense back to his frozen limbs.

He had lain in a daze when another figure had emerged from the icy tunnels wearing a towering fur hat, with dark hair that stank of oil. The man had spoken quietly in a voice that had a hissing quality like a snake's. "He has spirit, this one," he whispered. "I hear his friends stepped beyond the edge of the world." He laughed, sending a brutal kick into J.B.'s aching ribs. "This one lives until tomorrow," he informed the others.

The man with the oil in his hair said something more as he left, but J.B. couldn't make sense of it, the words half-lost as he strode down the ice tunnel away from the cell. Behind him, two sec men worked the stopperlike door, wheeling it back into place and sealing J.B. inside. He hadn't eaten, had hardly slept and he had been worked and beaten close to the limits of his endurance. J.B. lay on the cold floor and smiled grimly. He had until dawn to figure out a way out of here.

PIOTR HAD LED Symon and his daughter to a small group of buildings located at the foot of a gradual slope. "You have to be careful around here," he warned the newcomers. "Watchers come out sometimes, hunt in packs."

"Watchers?" Symon asked.

"Clockwatchers," Piotr told him with clear distaste. "Just be glad we found you first."

"Ha," the woman—whose name was Marla—laughed. "If the watchers had found you, you'd be slap-bang in the middle of getting fed to Old Father Time by now."

Symon could make no sense of the woman's words, and reasoned it was best not to pry. Though tight-knit, this group seemed friendly enough. For now, maybe they could provide shelter from the elements and any sec men who might try to follow. They'd be mighty pissed about the stolen caribou; Symon figured that much for certain. Maybe even enough to follow him and Tarelya past the Tall Wall after all.

When they reached the base of the slope, amid swirling snow flurries that danced on the air, Symon and Tarelya saw the buildings lined up as dark humps blanketed by snow. The buildings were the tired remains of a twentieth-century ville and many had been repatched, great sheets of metal slapped in place, bolted there with great braces and rivets. A frozen river stood static to the side of the farthest building, a bombed-out artillery tank lurching in the ice, stuck fast with its turret poking down toward the riverbed.

Overhead, sparks flitted across the sky, bringing with them a sound like crackling electricity, making the air charged. It was like standing by an electricity pylon, a palpable sense of motion that churned from the air.

"Look," Marla said, pointing to a patch of sparking sky.

Symon and his daughter peered up. The sky was fluttering with colors, and amid them a dark cloud of solid forms swarmed toward the ground. "What is it?" Tarelya asked.

"Crow feast," Marla explained. "They've found a weak spot in the discharge. They'll keep working at it until it breaks away."

"They're drawn to them," Piotr added by way of explanation. He was working the door of one of the ramshackle little buildings; it wasn't locked, but the door had begun to frost over and it took a moment to clear the ice away.

Symon and Tarelya followed him inside, their two companions bringing up the rear. Inside, the building had been partitioned over and over to create a series of smaller rooms, presumably easier to heat than the larger building it had started life as, an old supermarket with shelves now draped in material.

"What is this place?" Symon asked.

"Here? This was a house once," Piotr told him. "Still is, I guess. There was a military base near here, and this community served it. Nothing fancy, just a few stores and a bar."

"How did you end up here?" Tarelya asked with all the abruptness of a child.

"When whatever it was that happened, happened," Piotr told her, "me and Graz there were caught up in it. We'd been fishing a little to the north and we got trapped. Marla came later."

"Riding accident," she explained, lifting the goggles to reveal two hazel eyes. "Horse slipped on the ice while I was crossing paths to the east, I fell and when I woke up I was on the wrong side of the barrier with no way back."

"You mean the Tall Wall," Symon said, explaining it to his daughter. "What is it, do you know?"

"Nah," Graz said. He seemed younger than Piotr, with a ginger beard streaked with white and pale eyes that displayed a definite squint as if he was peering into the sun. "Can't get close enough to find out. No one can. What we know we pieced together since we got here."

"And in answer to your question, miss," Piotr continued, "we don't rightly know how long we've been here. Feels like one day. One bastard long-long day. A hundred years of a day."

"You called it…End Day," Symon recalled, "when you found us."

"Yeah, End Day," Piotr agreed. "A day without end, which I figure means when it does end we won't get another."

"Like purgat'ry," Graz said. "Big ol' limbo. You heard of those places, Symon?"

He nodded. "The waiting rooms for Heaven and Hell. Before my wife died she said about them—"

"Maybe she's here," Marla said flippantly. A moment afterward, she apologised, admitting that the comment was uncalled for.

Piotr and Graz stood at the window, pulling back a heavy curtain. Outside, the snow was still falling. Amid it, the swarm of black shapes could be seen, mouths rushing out of nowhere like a stream, pouring toward an unseen marker across the snow less than a mile from the building. In the air above the epicenter of the swarm, the sparkles seemed to have grown more intense. Creatures flitted through the air right above the building they were in, disembodied mouths with twin sets of needlelike teeth that shone in the twilit air.

"We'll have to move soon," Graz said, "if they keep coming like this."

"Where can we go?" Piotr asked him. "There's nowhere left. They keep eating at the rents, making it impossible to cross the pockets of broken time."

Symon had stopped behind them, and he peered over their shoulders at the feasting creatures. They looked like nothing more than mouths, and only occasionally did he get the suggestion of something behind those wicked grins, a substance, a shape, a form drawn in darkness. Just what new Hell had they escaped into?

Chapter Eleven

In His Ink Orchard, Jak reared away from the strangely disembodied jaw as the needle-sharp teeth clacked together again, snapping for his throat. He could feel the creature that was connected to those teeth, had grasped it around the throat—or maybe belly—as it squirmed in his grip. Its unseen body felt cold against his hands, a fierce, penetrating chill that ached into his skin and down to his bones in a matter of seconds.

This close, Jak could smell the thing's breath, too. It smelt musty, like dust burning in the sunlight, and of things unborn. The jaws snapped again, driving Jak back against the ground. The back of his head slammed against the snow as he pulled himself away.

Ricky brought up the knife, staring at the strange disembodied mouth that was lunging at Jak's throat. The Deathlands was full of muties created from the radioactive fallout of the nukecaust, and growing up in a place called Monster Island Ricky had seen his fair share of abominations. But this thing, with no discernible body nor eyes to see with, well, it creeped him out. As for the stolen hunting knife in his hand, Ricky was suddenly reminded of the words of wisdom J.B. had imparted just a few hours before—about bringing a knife to a blaster-fight.

In the fraction of a second it took to acknowledge them, Ricky had already dismissed his fears, leaping at

the eerie mouth and thrusting the tip of his blade at it.
He plunged the blade into the only part of the creature
that he could see, driving it between the front teeth and
pushing with all his strength.

Still clasped in Jak's hands, the mouth creature
pulled away from him, the jaws snapping together as
they tried to dislodge Ricky's blade. Jak used the thing's
own momentum to toss it to one side and it went flying over Ricky's shoulder as he let go of the knife. The
friends watched as the disembodied mouth went spinning through the air before slamming against the soil
with a great *whumph,* spitting the knife free.

Ricky moved swiftly, galloping across the ground
and snatching up his knife as the strange creature
writhed in pain. They could both see it now, the full figure of the thing. It slithered against the snow, kicking up
an S shape in the frosty white carpet as it twisted back
and forth. Its body was snakelike but fatter, more like an
overgrown grub. Four tiny eyes came into view above
the vicious teeth, as black as a widow's cape, watery
like the eyes of a spider. The lower set of eyes touched
the top lip of the creature where those hideous jaws
snapped, and the lips themselves were colored a deathly
gray, like a dead thing. Between the wide-set eyes, two
thick nostrils lay flat to the curving face, and behind
that the body protruded in its ghastly, wriggling total-
ity. The body was segmented like an insect's, with thick
rings of fat protruding between each armored plate. It
had been those armored plates that Jak had grasped
when he had tried to hold back the creature, their cold
alienness sending goose bumps up and down his arms.

"What the hell is that?" Ricky asked, staring at the
creature but not daring to step any closer.

Carefully, Jak reached for his blaster, not taking his

eyes from the writhing wormlike thing. "Not know," he admitted. "Hungry grub."

"Yeah," Ricky agreed, horrified, "but if that's the grub what do you think the adult looks like?"

Holding the Colt Anaconda before him, Jak held the creature in the blaster's sights for a moment before easing pressure off the trigger. "Got your blade?" he asked.

"Yeah."

"Let's move. Not want find out what mamma grub does when pissed."

With his eyes fixed on the writhing creature, Ricky walked backward, slowly backing away from the hideous, hungry thing. "Where are we going, Jak?" he asked. "We should turn back, right? Help J.B. and the others."

Jak looked behind them, the way that they had come. Cold mist clung to the ground like a blanket, masking the path he and Ricky had taken. Finding their way back wouldn't be easy.

"FUCK, BUT THE BARON is a lucky bastard," Bascha muttered as he watched the two women plod up to the door he was guarding. Stripped naked, both women shivered as they walked before the armed sec men who had dragged them from the cell. Stripped and washed, they were being delivered to the baron's quarters deep in the heart of the ice ville.

"Sure is," Bascha's partner, the occasionally loudmouthed Serb, agreed. "Mercy, Bascha. What I wouldn't do to get fresh flesh like that delivered to my dorm."

"Yeah, but only the baron of the ville gets to do that," Bascha said. And man was the baron a lucky bastard. He watched as the doors to the baron's quarters pulled back, admitting entry to the two gaudy sluts. Neither of

them could have been much over twenty, Bascha reckoned—in fact he knew one of them from just a few days
before, when he had jabbed the tip of his knife into the
back of her neck while they had been engaged in fore-
play. Kirima? Was that her name?

Baron Kenojuak's quarters were located in a tower
at the highest area of the ville, part of the old structures
that had once been a tiny town before the nukecaust.
Now all that remained were the ice-coated interior
walls, their outsides blasted away by earthshakers,
leaving them little more than ruins that the locals had
adapted for their use. The aged internal doors and serving hatches of the tower had been given a second life
as windows, staring down to the courtyard that served
as the "theater of spectacle" on those days it was used.

Bascha was a sec man, and this day he and Serb had
pulled shift guarding the baron. Serb had a big mouth
on him, but Bascha kind of liked him—even if he did
get them into trouble sometimes because he didn't know
when to shut up.

Bascha watched as the two women were marched
naked into the baron's quarters. The one on the left
had enjoyed his company a few days ago. He had got
off on that, seeing the helpless woman squirm while he
pushed his short blade against the tendons of her neck,
her lithe body covered in a sheen of sweat. The other
one was a petite blonde called Narja, pretty and wide-
eyed, and Bascha figured he would have her maybe
once the baron was done.

The doors to the baron's quarters peeled back, and
both women trembled with cold as they strode inside,
two more sec men following behind them with blasters poised should either of them try anything. Bascha's
eyes roved over the svelte forms of both women, think-

ing about how much better they would look if they wore something different. That was an obsession with him, women's clothes.

The doors closed behind the women, leaving Bascha with his thoughts of what the women should wear.

Inside, the baron's quarters were warm, flickering gas and oil lamps hanging at regular intervals around the vast entry room where he met his nightly brides. Baron Kenojuak was thirty years old and a handsome man, ruggedly so with a square jaw and dark hair slicked back from his forehead with oil. He wore a simple robe that left his chest bare and his dark eyes played delightedly over the forms of his visitors. They stood before him, Narja more timid that Kirima, this being her first time in the baron's company. He was working an apple in his hands, stripping the peel off using a short-bladed knife, working the juicy flesh around in his mouth.

Baron Kenojuak's eyes never left the women as he addressed the two sec men who had escorted them. "You may leave," he commanded.

The sec men turned and left without a word, leaving their baron with his women.

They had been brought here naked for two reasons—to ensure they were not armed and to hasten the process should the baron desire them immediately. He looked them over in delight, instructed the younger one to come to his side. Narja looked at Kirima for reassurance.

"It's okay," the older woman whispered. She had seen the baron hurt girls before, and angering him was a sure way of making that occur.

"Come, sit," Kenojuak instructed again.

Narja joined him, watching as he continued to peel the apple with the blade.

"Are you hungry?" Kenojuak asked.

Narja nodded. She was afraid to speak.

"Do my people not feed you?" Kenojuak asked, his eyes flicking to the fruit in his hands, then up to the girl. From the corner of the room, Kirima watched fearfully, hoping that the new girl would remember to say the right thing and not anger the baron.

"They f-feed us," Narja stammered. "But it's not nice food. Sometimes I don't—"

"Don't what?" Kenojuak snapped, bringing his face close to the girl's. She shied away, terrified, but he tossed the apple aside and grabbed her by the wrist. "Don't what?" he repeated.

Narja looked at him fearfully while Kirima took a step forward.

"My baron, please..." Kirima begged, but the baron silenced her with a look.

"Fruit," he said, his grip tight around Narja's wrist, "can be peeled to reveal its flesh."

Narja watched as he brought the little paring knife closer to her, raising it close to her face.

"Other things have flesh, too," Kenojuak growled. "Even nasty, ungrateful little brides who believe they should be treated like princesses."

"Pl-please, my lord," Narja stuttered, her eyes fixed on the shining blade.

"With an apple," Kenojuak continued, ignoring the girl's pleas, "one sometimes finds a flaw, just beneath the skin." He brought the knife down, tapping it against her nipples. Narja felt the blade touch her navel, playing across her skin. At the edge of the room, Kirima was trying to look away, but something inside her demanded she watch.

"The only thing one can do," Baron Kenojuak said,

"other than to throw the whole fruit away, of course, is to cut around that flaw that offends and consume all that remains."

Narja shrieked as she felt the blade pierce her side, crying out in pain.

Outside the baron's door, Bascha heard the shriek and he smiled. The baron was getting the best out of these two girls. He always did.

MORNING CAME with all the charm of a smoker's cough. J.B. estimated he had had maybe three hours' sleep in total, and that had been interspersed with bouts of wakefulness as the cold of his ice cell got to him, turning his bones to frigid sticks inside his flesh and driving wedges into the cuts and bruises he had suffered at the hands of the vicious mining guards.

He was awakened by a sec man wearing gray furs in a sort of layered series of leaves, like a topcoat and cape, his face uncovered and displaying an impressive gridwork of scars as well as an indigo tattoo down past his left eye. The Armorer had been awake the very moment that the wide door had begun moving, his catlike senses alert to the sounds of the movement. There was another noise, too, the sound of a mob, its echoes coming up from the open window overlooking the circular courtyard. J.B. sat up, bringing himself into a ready crouch as the door was drawn back.

"You're awake then, eh?" the sec man began, a cruel smile appearing on his face around the stub of his cigar. The smile revealed a missing canine tooth in his upper set, two more gaps in his lower front teeth.

"Early bird chills the worm," J.B. acknowledged and the sec man smiled wider at that before jabbing J.B. in the gut with a swift-as-hell rabbit punch. The lack of space in the cell forced J.B. to carom against the nearest wall, clutching at his gut and struggling for a few seconds to catch his breath.

"You better hope that's the case, prick," the sec man told J.B. with a puff of smoke from his cigar, "'cause, brother, you got a rat's-piss-short life ahead of you." And then the sec man laughed, a great booming sound like a blaster. Idly, J.B. matched the timbre of the man's laugh to the boom of a Winchester 1300 Defender in his mind's eye.

The sec man reached forward and pulled J.B. roughly by the arm, slinging him toward the open doorway. "You can walk?" he asked, but it seemed more like a statement of fact.

"Yeah," J.B. murmured, pushing at the brim of his hat where it had become crooked on his head. With his other hand, he shoved the cigarette lighter he had palmed into his shirt, pushing his fingers between the open shirt buttons and feeling the hard, cool metal press against him.

J.B. was led at blaster-point through another set of ice tunnels. "What happened to my friends?" J.B. asked as he shuffled down an incline, his hand grasping a safety rail made of a knotted rope wedged into the ice wall.

"They'll have a good view, don't you worry," the sour-faced sec man told him, slapping him across the back of his head with his open palm. J.B. reeled forward at the blow, stumbling down the icy slope.

The Armorer didn't exactly know what the sec man meant, but he could guess it was nothing good. He continued to follow where the sec man guided, trudging through ill-lit tunnels that stank of gas heaters and climbing down a series of short internal ladders until he guessed he was near the bottom level of the strange ville. After a while J.B. became conscious of the sounds of a great many voices coming from up ahead, the cheering and baying of an excited crowd.

They turned a corner and the sec man indicated a short staircase that ran five steps down to a narrow walkway, metal glinting in the roof above it. The walkway was just three strides long and at its end J.B. could see sunlight and falling snow. People crowded either side of the walkway, raised above it behind high walls that twinkled where sunlight caught the ice crystals. The people wore heavy clothes, with dark winter tans, and most of them had the black hair of the Inuit.

The loud cheering was emanating from beyond the open mouth of the tunnel, and J.B.'s heart sank as he heard the all-too-familiar sounds of violence, of metal striking metal, blade cutting flesh. Suddenly something came flying past the opening, hurtling at some velocity. For a moment, J.B. took that object for a ball, and he watched as it thumped against the side of the tunnel entrance with a wet splat before sinking to the floor. The rumble of the crowd's cheers grew louder, and J.B. saw what the round thing was—it was a man's head.

Adjusting his glasses, J.B. walked forward, his eyes fixed on the mouth of the tunnel. One of the people sitting above the abbreviated staircase noticed J.B. walk past, reached out and knocked his hat from his head.

"New meat!" the man shouted with a triumphant shrill.

J.B. reached down to pick up his fedora, and when he glanced up he saw that all eyes had turned to him, watching from the high walls that overlooked the walkway. There were over a dozen people watching J.B., cursing and making obscene gestures. One man was pissing over the wall, directing the yellow stream of urine at J.B.'s head. Behind him, something clanged and J.B. turned to see what it was. A grilled metal gate had been pulled down over the far end of the tunnel, just above the top step.

"Well," J.B. muttered, eyeing the opening to the tunnel, "guess it's a mighty fine day for a stroll."

Chapter Twelve

The tunnel opened out into a small circle, roughly twenty feet across, set amid the towering walls of the glacier. J.B. stepped out from the tunnel entrance, shielding his eyes from the glare of the sun reflecting from the icy walls and ground as snow drifted from the clouds in languid flurries. Above, the sun sat low on the horizon, a gray-white orb that resembled a cataract. It had risen as much as it was ever likely to up here in the northern climes, and it gave off little heat.

J.B. shivered, taking another step into the round, past the decapitated head of his unfortunate predecessor. Blood had pooled on the ground, but it was already freezing, a sheen of frost running across it like a custard skin.

The Armorer stood at the edge of the circle, ignoring the jeers of the people behind and about him, snow settling on his shoulders. There was a figure standing at the other side of the circle, an imposing man, over six feet tall with the broad shoulders and impressive reach of a prizefighter. The man wore animal skin breeches, and a fur jerkin over his mighty chest that left his arms bare and his rippling muscles on display. His body was impressively tooled, the kind of body it took a lifetime's dedication to truly achieve. The fighter's feet were wrapped in strips of animal hide that came up past the level of the breeches; and he wore something else, too—a helmet that wrapped around his head, cinching his face into a narrow gap between protective strips. The helmet had two mighty stag horns protruding from its top like the branches of a tree, each one adding another foot and a half to the man's already impressive height. The man held a chain saw in both hands, wielding it like a sword. Its blade was pointing toward J.B., eighteen inches of whirring death. The man smiled grimly between the cinching lines of the helmet as J.B.'s eyes met his, wrinkling the flattened, broken nose at the center of his scarred face.

J.B. tipped a hand to his fedora, giving the man a nod, impressed that the man had access to precious fuel to run the chain saw.

All around, people had crowded in seats at the lowest level of the round, watching the early-morning spectacle. There were seats or standing room—J.B. couldn't be sure which—arranged behind sheer walls that stretched twelve feet high. The walls were constructed of metal and further protected by a line of metal barrels, their sloping sides glistening with frost, which guaranteed they would be near impossible to climb. To J.B.'s keen eye they looked like old oil canisters, laid down on their sides, Deathlands recycle-and-make-do once again in operation.

Higher, above the rows of spectators, the ville itself reached upward, towering eighty feet into the air. Windows, ladders and walkways were visible along its walls, and J.B. could see more people watching from up there, transfixed by the death games below, women holding babies to their breasts as they watched. This was where both of his cells had been, he realized, looking out onto this courtyard that served as a theater of blood. This ring was the center of ville life, a stage where death was dished out on a regular basis.

The courtyard was sealed now, its ground dotted with snow and ice that clung there in little patches like wedding confetti. Beneath the settling snow, the floor was painted with blood, dried streaks of it running the whole length of the circle, a great mass pooled at one wall. A lot of people had been killed here, J.B. realized, and a whole lot of them had wound up dying right there at one specific spot by the wall, close to where his chain-saw-wielding opponent waited.

Behind J.B., the crowd of Russo-Inuit was baying like rabid dogs, hurling abuse at him over the chugging sound of the chain saw. J.B. tuned them out, scanning the distant section of wall where the blood had most noticeably amassed. Like the rest of this savage arena, the sheer wall behind reached twelve feet in height, its occupants sitting above it so that they could look down on the vicious action. A man sat there, with a wind-tanned face and wearing a Pschent hat atop his head, his dark hair greased back with oil. J.B. guessed the man was in his twenties or early thirties. The towering hat added another eight or nine inches to the man's height with decorative streaks of silver and copper running through it. Got to be the baron, J.B. thought as he eyed the man. He sat on a chair with a raised back, several subservient types busying themselves about him, a woman with long dark hair kneeling on the ground before him. She clutched her sides, shivering in the cold air, her breath hanging in a bloom before her mouth.

J.B. took all of this in in just two seconds as his eyes roved about the circular enclosure. There were several more tunnels set back like the one he had entered through, one of them with a heavy barred gate drawn across it, behind which J.B. could see three or four dogs snuffling and bearing their teeth. The be-headed body of a man was on the ground close to the baron's throne, blood pumping like a geyser from the open neck, the seminaked body twitching where it lay. But there were no weapons, nothing that J.B. could envisage using against an opponent.

Ahead of him, the man with the stag-horn helmet issued a howling battle cry, his chain saw moving almost of its own volition in his hands as he began to charge at the newcomer. Time seemed to slow for J.B. as he watched the hulking figure come charging at him, the chain saw cutting through the air with its angry snarl.

Timing things to the last possible second, J.B. ducked aside, his feet skipping across the ice-strewed ground as he weaved out of the path of that lethal whirring blade. The chain saw cut empty air in a diagonal sweep, but already its horned wielder had shifted his own position, stomping a foot down to pivot to come at J.B. again. The crowd hissed and booed as J.B. scampered backward, the soles of his boots whipping rapidly across the frosty ground.

DOC CAME OUT of his sleep speaking, as if he had never been asleep at all. "Of course, I could not bake to save my life," he explained randomly, as if in midconversation. "I had on one occasion been asked to bake a cake for some visitors while Emily ran some other errands before they arrived. Of course the whole thing had burned black, smelled terrible and no one dared taste the ghastly concoction."

Ryan shot the old man a look, ordering him to silence. He was poised along with cellmate Hurst at the open window of the cell he shared with Doc, Hurst standing on tiptoe to better see what was happening in the circular atrium below.

"Something's happening down there," Ryan said as the icy wind brushed against his numb cheeks.

"What, pray tell?" Doc asked, rubbing his face with the heel of his hand as he tried to rouse himself from sleep. He could feel the cold aching in his bones already, like a dull throb running through every muscle, evidence of the hard work he and Ryan had been forced to do the day before.

"'Nother beheading maybe," Hurst suggested. "Can't be sure from up here."

"Another...?" Doc muttered, still playing catch-up.

"I can hear the crowd getting excited," Hurst said, "which means a new opponent, but it's hard to see. Looks like some little guy in a dumb-ass hat."

Ryan shoved the man aside and cranked his head out the window. "Shit! That's J.B. down there."

"By the Three Kennedys!" Doc exclaimed as he joined Ryan at the one-eyed man's side, peering down into the courtyard. "Ryan, we have seen the like of this before. It looks for all the world to me like a gladiatorial contest, a popular pastime of both the Roman Empire and many a baron."

Ryan nodded. "Yes, and J.B.'s up as the next challenger," he said, "whether he likes it or not."

"In Roman times," Doc mused, "a victorious gladiator was granted his freedom once he had served in a sufficient number of contests."

Ryan turned to the old man with a fearsome expression on his scarred face. "I suspect that won't be happening here. I can't quite see but I'm sure J.B.'s opponent is armed with something."

Beside them, Hurst nodded, a broad grin on his dirty

face. "Champ's in session." He chuckled. "Someone's going to taste the wrong end of his chain saw."

"Well, now, that could pose a problem," Doc admitted as he reached for his swordstick. He eyed Ryan with grave seriousness. "Are you thinking mayhap we should go down and assist our colleague?"

"You read my mind," Ryan told Doc with a firm nod.

The courtyard was two stories down from their cell, but the window was too narrow to pass through. Ryan turned to the cell door and drew a deep breath. "Get behind me, Doc," he said as he booted it with a powerful kick. Under the force Ryan struck it with, the door shuddered, but it still held.

From the rear of the cell, Hurst was back at the window, trying to see what was happening in the courtyard. But he didn't know where to look—the contest outside was just starting to heat up, but what his cellmate was doing was just as entertaining. "So long as I i'nt on the receiving end," he muttered, chuckling softly to himself.

Like an out-of-control engine, Ryan struck the door again, using both hands to lever it away. Outside, beyond the door itself, he could hear someone calling excitedly, ordering him to stop in a language he didn't know. Ryan ignored the order, cinching his shoulder up against the door and pushing again. His booted feet scraped against the icy floor, struggling to find purchase.

"Come on, damn you," Ryan cursed between gritted teeth. "Move."

The door shuddered an inch on its treads, revealing just the tiniest of gaps between the lintel and the heavy wood of the door itself.

"SOMETHING'S COMING," Krysty said. She was sitting cross-legged on the silk-draped floor of the cell, her body so still that she had slipped into a meditative trance.

Mildred turned from the window at the sound of Krysty's voice. She had been watching the proceedings in the courtyard, but the view was so obscured that she hadn't yet seen who the chain-saw-wielding madman's opponent was. As she turned, she caught her first glimpse of J.B. and did a double take. "What's coming, Krysty?" she asked, distracted by the sliver of battle that flickered across the narrow slit of window.

"Men," Krysty said. "Angry men. They wear their rage like a shirt."

"That's J.B. out there," Mildred cried, indicating the window. "Looks like he's about to get massacred."

Krysty opened her eyes and met Mildred's worried gaze. "The time's now," she said. "Get ready."

Ignoring the other women who crowded in the gas-heated cell, Krysty and Mildred took up positions on either side of the heavy, rollback door. Mildred reached into her bag of meager medical supplies.

Nyarla watched them. "What are you planning on doing?" she asked.

"What I always do," Mildred told her, pulling a scalpel from the hidden pocket of her pants. "Treat the sick."

As she spoke, the door began to pull back.

BARON KENOJUAK looked at the little man in the battered brown hat who stood in the arena and he sighed. Compared to the champion, the man looked positively dwarfish, and his little dance-step maneuvers were already becoming tiresome. Surely his men had only chosen this bespectacled idiot because there wasn't enough meat on him to eat. It was ridiculous. Chewing on a tough hunk of meat, Kenojuak spit it in the woman's face where she kneeled before him. He ejected the flavorless hunk with such violence that she jumped back before wiping the detritus from her cheek. The baron snapped his fingers and pointed her down. She was blocking his view. Kirima settled back down and began eating the half-chewed morsel, her flesh raw with the cold.

IN THE ARENA, J.B. dodged another attack from his opponent. The chain saw was heavy and it slowed the man. Maybe that could give J.B. some advantage here, he realized. As the blade came whirring past six inches from his outstretched left arm, J.B. wondered if he would have time to press any advantage before he ended his life carved up worse than a turkey at a drunken eat-off.

AS THE CROWD cheered, Baron Kenojuak turned away from the action, tearing another hunk of charcoaled meat from the spit roast. The meat on the spit was the sharpshooter who had tried to shoot Jak and Ricky two days before. Food was precious out here in the frozen wastes—nothing was wasted, not even colleagues. With the increasing loss of land to the north thanks to the energy fluctuations there at the spot known variously as the edge of the world and His Ink Orchard, now more than ever it was time to conserve and recycle what limited resources they did have.

The little man in the arena skipped backward, a grim smile plucking at the corners of his mouth. He didn't realize—as a stranger to the ville, how could he?—that the champion was shepherding him toward this spot, the imaginary altar where sacrifices were made to the baron and the gods of the ice. It was so obvious that it was becoming boring; the champion was simply too proficient.

Languidly, the baron raised one hand and snapped his fingers. "Cut his head off," he drawled between a mouthful of hot flesh. "Let's make something of this."

THE TUNNEL WAS LIT by gas lanterns, and they stank to high heaven in the enclosed space, yet they cast little illumination, too widely spaced to adequately light the area. As such, it took a moment for the two sec men to realize what was happening, that one of the prisoners had actually managed to shove their cell door back an inch and a half on its solid treads.

"Back away from the door, prisoner," one of the sec men hollered, pulling the Smith & Wesson Model 60 from his armpit holster and waving it at the gap.

Inside the cell, Ryan turned to Doc and gave him a nod. Doc had already snapped open his swordstick to reveal the blade within. In a flash of tempered steel, he whipped the thin blade through the narrow gap that Ryan had created, rapping it across the knuckles of the sec man. With a cry of surprise as much as pain, the sec man dropped his blaster to the ground and watched in horror as the weapon skidded toward the open cell. Ryan's hand snapped out in an instant, snatching the blaster and pulling it back through the tight gap.

The sec man's partner stared at the gap, then at him with increasing annoyance. "Buffoon! What did you just do?"

Before the first man could reply, Ryan sent a single bullet through his forehead from his position flat against the large wooden door. Behind Ryan, Doc was working his sharp sword across the slight gap that had been created between the door and outside. He ran the blade along the top edge, left and right, until he snagged the rope that operated the cantilever that, in turn, worked the door.

As the first sec man dropped to the ground, a perfect red circle in the center of his forehead, the cell door swung back and Ryan and Doc emerged. The remaining sec man turned, drawing his holstered blaster. Ryan took a pace forward and shot the man in the head, an explosion of blood and brains bursting across the back wall in a terrible instant.

Ryan leaned down and snatched up the second man's blaster—a 9-shot Stechkin pistol—from his dead hand, passing it back to Doc. "Keep close," Ryan instructed. Already, they could hear the shouts of other sec men and locals responding to the sounds of blasterfire.

Automatically Doc checked the new weapon, slipping off the safety. The blaster was finished in matte black and fitted with a suppressor that stuck out from it like a snout, adding considerably to the eight-and-three-quarter-inch barrel. Blaster in one hand and swordstick in the other, Doc followed Ryan through the narrow, icy tunnels as more figures began to emerge into the light.

KRYSTY'S GUESS WAS RIGHT on the button. The door rolled back to reveal two men with long dark hair and squashed, ugly features on their weather-beaten faces. Even this early in the day, the two men stank of rotgut and had the leer of the oversexed. They were men used to taking whatever they wanted, and the captive women had suffered their depredations before.

"Bascha," one of the women gasped.

Bascha—a dim-witted slob with more interest in women's shoes than in their intellect—laughed, rubbing at his crotch with one meat-stained hand. "Get me some livin' bird," he growled around the charred drumstick of a gull, "to go with the dead one."

Beside him, Bascha's partner, a similarly repellent piece of human detritus called Serb, laughed with all the comprehension of a rotten tree. "Bird," he said with a throaty chuckle.

They had been celebrating during the gladiatorial tournament, their shift over, and right now all they wanted was easy sex, the kind that confirmed their imagined superiority. In their ardor, neither man had noticed Krysty and Mildred standing as they were flush to the wall. And neither man realized what was happening when Krysty and Mildred launched their attack.

Mildred ducked low and swept one leg out to trip Serb, the shorter of the two, hooking his feet out from under him. He slapped against the floor like a discarded rag. He was fast, though…the alcohol burning in him and fuelling that bubbling rage he always had buzzing through his head. He turned, flipping Mildred off his back as she struggled to hold him down.

Beside her, Krysty booted Bascha in the groin with such force that he felt something rupture. He sagged to the floor on his knees, the whites of his eyes turning pink. Krysty kicked him again, driving the heel of her cowboy boot into his jaw. Bascha crumpled backward, lolling out the open door of the cell, his flabby arms sprawled out at his sides. Krysty stood over him, a steely look in her eye.

"Anything to say for yourself, rapist?" she demanded.

Bascha tried to focus his eyes on the voluptuous redhead, such was the agony he was feeling from her attack. All he could think was how nice her boots looked with their silver falcon design on each side.

Krysty drove her heel into the man's throat in a sav-

age strike, held it there and pushed as he hacked against
the pain.

Behind her, Mildred had outmatched her dim-witted
opponent, who was under the mistaken belief that every
woman in the Deathlands was inferior. As he swooped
his hairy arms around her and hugged her close to him,
Mildred proved him wrong, driving the blade of her
scalpel through his neck and into his windpipe, slashing the flesh there in a bloody stripe of red.

Mildred stepped away as the ville man's grip weak-
ened, his hands reaching up for his ruined throat. He
looked at her, distraught, his eyes pleading as he tried
to speak through the blood pooling in his windpipe.
Mildred fixed him with a no-nonsense stare. "Don't
know, don't care," she told him. She had long ago accepted that despite being a healer, she would have to
take life in order to survive.

His voice quieted forever, Serb sank to the floor in
a bloody ruin of red. Ignoring the choking sounds he
made, Mildred checked over the dying man's body,
searching for weapons. She came up empty and, over
by the doorway, Krysty found the same with her own
opponent. Evidently, neither man had come to the cell
armed; probably a standard precaution to prevent the
women getting their hands on a weapon.

Mildred hurried over to join Krysty where she
crouched over the fallen body of the other man at the
door. Kneeling, Krysty was warily checking the corridor beyond, scouring for possible sources of trouble.
It was almost empty now, just a single figure visible in
the distance, but she knew that couldn't last long.

"Come on," Krysty whispered. "While it's quiet.
Help J.B., find Ryan."

Mildred looked up the empty tunnel, its ice walls

glittering in the flicker of the gas lanterns poised down low to the floor. "It's too dangerous out there," she said. "We need to get our weapons back. And fast."

Behind the two women, Nyarla had prowled across the room to join them. "I know where men keep blasters," she said in her thickly accented voice. "I show you, you keep me safe. Yes?"

Mildred eyed the young woman. "Find us our weapons," she said, "and we'll do whatever we can."

IN THE ARENA, J.B. weaved out of the path of the roaring chain saw, his eyes fixed on its rotating blade. He wasn't the fastest of Ryan's group of companions, certainly not the most agile, but he could hold his own in hand-to-hand combat.

He held his attention firmly on his opponent, watching the way he was wielding the chain saw. The man used it like a sword, although judging by its heft the thing was heavy and didn't lend itself easily to that use. The device smelled of alcohol where a valve at the side of the handle coughed out clouds of dark smoke. Gasoline driven, J.B. knew.

And gasoline was flammable.

He leaped away as the chain saw cut the air by his left flank again, booted feet skimming across the icy ground. That was the third time that his opponent had come at him from the left, J.B. realized. That meant something—that he was trying to get him to a certain spot. The bloody spot in front of the baron, most likely, J.B. surmised, even as his heel touched down on that scarlet stain.

▼ If offer card is missing write to: Harlequin Reader Service, P.O. Box 1867, Buffalo, NY 14240-1867 or visit www.ReaderService.com ▼

BUSINESS REPLY MAIL
FIRST-CLASS MAIL   PERMIT NO. 717   BUFFALO, NY

POSTAGE WILL BE PAID BY ADDRESSEE

HARLEQUIN READER SERVICE
PO BOX 1867
BUFFALO NY 14240-9952

NO POSTAGE
NECESSARY
IF MAILED
IN THE
UNITED STATES

Send For
2 FREE BOOKS
Today!

I accept your offer!

Please send me two free
novels and a mystery gift (gift
worth about $5). I understand
that these books are completely
free—even the shipping and
handling will be paid—and
I am under no obligation
to purchase anything, ever, as
explained on the back of this card.

366 ADL FVYT   **166 ADL FVYT**

Please Print

FIRST NAME

LAST NAME

ADDRESS

APT.#   CITY

STATE/PROV.   ZIP/POSTAL CODE

Visit us online at
www.ReaderService.com

Offer limited to one per household and not applicable to series that subscriber is currently receiving.

Your Privacy—The Harlequin® Reader Service is committed to protecting your privacy. Our Privacy Policy is available online at www.ReaderService.com or upon request from the Harlequin Reader Service. We make a portion of our mailing list available to reputable third parties that offer products we believe may interest you. If you prefer that we not exchange your name with third parties, or if you wish to clarify or modify your communication preferences, please visit us at www.ReaderService.com/consumerchoice or write to us at Harlequin Reader Service Preference Service, P.O. Box 9062, Buffalo, NY 14269. Include your complete name and address.

GE-GF-13 ◄ Detach card and mail today. No stamp needed ◄ © 2012 WORLDWIDE LIBRARY ® and ™ are trademarks owned and used by the trademark owner and/or its licensee. Printed in the U.S.A.

Chapter Thirteen

Somewhere within that rat-run of ice tunnels that made up the ville, Ryan was making a swift check around him while Doc covered them. Hurst was watching them both from the now-open doorway to his cell, his mouth gaping open. He had lived as a prisoner here for a long time, and while he had witnessed a few attempted escapes, he had never seen such a bold prison break. These two newcomers were either extremely brave or really stupid—and if it turned out to be the latter, Hurst decided, then he would rather be found waiting obediently in his cell than running loose like a gaudy slut on jolt. That was a sure way to a chilling.

Ryan and Doc moved on, leaving the indoctrinated prisoner to his fate. They had met too many like Hurst over the course of their travels, people who had given up all hope. It was as if they wanted to be treated like dirt, to be abused by power-hungry barons who understood nothing of compassion.

The narrow tunnel they traveled had solid ice walls. Several windows were carved indelicately along one wall. Ryan peered through one and saw the pen that held the mutie caribou out front of the ville itself. Identifying this as the exterior wall, Ryan told Doc that they would follow it for it gave the best odds of finding egress from the claustrophobic tunnels.

The tunnel gently sloped, too, just like the cell he

and Doc had been locked within. Ryan figured going downslope was his better option. There was just one problem—figures were hovering there in the shadows, and a heated discussion could be heard echoing down the tunnel.

"I heard a blaster, something's happened."

"Tinck ain't at his post, must be something going on."

"We should go check."

"Yeah, maybe it's one of the cells. Damn these bastards, where did they find them anyway?"

Ryan listened silently, discerning at least three voices. Getting Doc's attention, he indicated ahead and showed three fingers. Doc understood.

An instant later, two people emerged into the soft glow of the floor lamp. They were armed, one with a club, the other a scarred blaster as long as his forearm, and both men had impressive beards that brushed against their dried-skin clothing. Ryan didn't hesitate. Already he had the Smith & Wesson raised, and he snapped off a shot at the blaster bearer.

The man slumped back as half his head exploded in a bloody splash. Ryan was already moving, bringing his blaster around as the second man spotted him. There were more of them behind, Ryan saw now, hemmed in by the narrow confines of the tunnel, unable to attack in force. That might help, if he and Doc could avoid getting shot anyway.

Ryan brought the heavy weight of his blaster around to pistol-whip the second man—no use wasting bullets where he didn't need to. As Ryan waded into the next sec man, he trusted Doc had his back.

Doc had spotted the men scurrying along the corridor that Ryan had seen, and he targeted them with the long barrel of the Stechkin. As he did so, another figure emerged from behind him, hurrying downslope and bringing his own blaster to bear in a burst of fire.

Doc ducked as a bullet whizzed past his shoulder, spun and fired, whipping off a hip shot from the Stechkin. Unsurprisingly, the shot went wild, missing its target entirely and instead burying itself in an icy wall. But it made the rear attacker halt in his tracks, sending him scurrying for cover.

Doc blasted again, this time targeting the individual with more care and drilling a slug into the man's back. The man went down like a house of cards, collapsing to the floor with a cry. As he writhed there, Doc fired again, sending a second shot straight into the man's spine, chilling him instantly.

Then Doc turned to face the remaining attackers as they amassed in the narrow confines of the ice tunnel.

Beside him, Ryan had just delivered the deathblow to the other sec man, snapping his neck before dropping him to the icy floor. Doc smiled grimly. "We are rather outnumbered," he observed.

"We've never let that stop us before, Doc," Ryan said, bringing up the Smith & Wesson revolver and sending a bullet through the head of their next attacker before he could get close.

The two men hurried on, making their way through the ice tunnels.

KRYSTY, MILDRED and Nyarla hurried along a frozen corridor, hunting for a stairwell that the young woman remembered from when she had first been brought to the ville.

"The men brought my sister, Papa and me here two weeks ago," she said. "We had come over the ice strait searching for food. My brother was with us then, too, but he…didn't survive the crossing."

"You came a long way for a meal," Krysty said. Her mind, though, was on the claustrophobic tunnels ahead of them, searching for possible ambush. They were higher in the ville than they had been, and the walls here, though coated with ice, were actually what appeared to be old housing from the predark. The ville had been constructed around an old housing or office project, and parts of that foundation remained quite clearly in place amid the icy warren of tunnels that made up the interior.

"*Yego Kraski Sada* got in the way," Nyarla explained. "At first it had been interesting, almost beautiful to watch the patterns it cast across the sky. But after a while it started to grow, consuming our old fishing grounds and leaving my father with nowhere left to hunt."

"This *Yego Kraski Sada,*" Mildred asked, "what is it exactly?"

"It is place where world ends," Nyarla said in a voice filled with gravity. "Dangerous place, no one goes there anymore."

She stopped then, indicating a sharp turn in the tunnel. "They took my father's gun here when they brought us," she explained. "They showed him how they would strip it down because they called it a piece of shit."

"An armory like that will be guarded," Mildred said, her voice low. Beside her, Krysty nodded.

Up ahead amid the soft gaslight illumination, Krysty could see shadows moving against the walls. They were man-shaped shadows and they held something in their hands. Silently, she ushered Mildred and Nyarla back, ordering them to wait.

Mildred still held a scalpel in her hand, and her thumb pressed against its rounded handle nervously. It was a poor weapon, cruel when it struck, but requiring such close quarters that it put its user in enormous danger. But it was all they had.

Ahead of Mildred, Krysty was prowling up the tunnel, her emerald eyes narrowed as she watched the shadows playing across the bend in the tunnel wall. There were two men there, she counted, holding either clubs or blasters. They didn't seem to be aware of how close she was, standing just around a corner from them.

Krysty stepped around the corner in a semicrouch, appearing before the men without warning and leaping at the closest with a balled fist. She struck the man in the jaw, driving his teeth together in a snap that cut through the knuckle-like nub of cigarette he had been inhaling on. The man danced back, cursing, while his ally turned toward Krysty with surprise, bringing up the machete-style knife—so that's what it was, Krysty thought—to strike her.

Krysty sidestepped the swishing blade, stepping inside the arc of the man's swing and driving the heel of her hand into his face. The man's nose erupted in a bloom of red, hot blood steaming in the air as it rushed down his face. He stumbled back, clutching at his broken nose, but Krysty didn't let up. She came at the man again, kicking him hard in the gut with the silver-tipped toe of her cowboy boot, striking with such force that he doubled over as he slumped to the floor.

Swiftly, Krysty stamped on the hand holding the machete, driving the hard heel of her boot into the man's fingers with an audible crunch.

His friend was just recovering from the surprise blow he had taken to the jaw. His eyes fixed on Krysty, still trying to process what had happened in the last five seconds. "Gaudies have escaped," he shouted with obvious surprise.

Krysty gave the man credit for realizing what had happened so swiftly, not that it would do him any good. Her left fist was already swinging out and up in a vicious rabbit punch, striking her foe just below the ribs. He stumbled back, slamming his head against the low wall where it met the ceiling in a curve.

Krysty spun, working her momentum into a roundhouse kick that knocked the sec man against the wall with a loud crack. He sagged down to the floor, his eyes closed, blood dribbling between his teeth.

"Come on," Krysty whispered, turning back to Mildred and their teenage charge.

The three women continued up the corridor and into the place that Nyarla had identified as the armory.

Mildred whistled as they entered the enclosed space that was used to store weapons. It was a chop shop with workbenches, vises and a small firing range—not long enough to improve one's skills, but with enough space to test a weapon. The walls were lined with various blasters and boxes upon boxes of ammunition. "J.B. sure would love this," she muttered.

A man was standing before one of the workbenches, filing down the muzzle of a chopped-together shotgun. He looked up at the entry of the newcomers. "What…? Who are you?" he sputtered, reaching for the shotgun.

"Is that loaded?" Krysty asked as the man trained the weapon warily on them.

The man fixed her gaze for a moment before lowering the weapon. Only an idiot would work on a loaded gun like that, and everyone in the room knew it.

"We're here to pick up our stuff," Mildred commanded, stepping closer to the man at the vise and showing him the glinting scalpel blade. "That's not going to be a problem now, is it?"

The man eyed the blade, processed Mildred and Krysty's no-nonsense looks and shook his head.

Three minutes later, Mildred, Krysty and Nyarla were making their way out of the ville, their weapons back in place and the weapons of their companions distributed between them. Mildred had also had the good sense to grab several extra boxes of ammunition, which she stuffed into her satchel where it sat incongruous among the medical supplies.

IN THE FROZEN ARENA, J.B. glanced back, eyeing the spot where the baron and his lackeys watched with studied disinterest. The ground was darkened with blood there, the decapitated body of the previous fighter still slumped where he had fallen.

So, he was being maneuvered. What good did that knowledge do him when he was facing a man who was using a chain saw like a broadsword? J.B. wondered.

As the chain saw cut the air again, J.B. turned to his right, dipping his body low so that the whirring blade clipped less than a foot over his head. J.B.'s hat went flying and he plucked it up before it could hit the floor. The falling hat gave him an idea—if he could just get enough space to try it.

Then suddenly J.B. realized where he was standing. His feet were placed in the dark wound on the ground, where the blood of dozens of victims had been shed. Behind him was the wall and the theater box-style area where the baron resided, watching the battle. This was it, this was where he got on the last train to the coast, single seat, headless commuter. Nothing like knowing you were about to die to get the blood pumping, J.B. realized as a wave of warmth seemed to ripple through his body.

The whirring blade of the chain saw swung toward the Armorer's head again, and the crowd booed as J.B. ducked. His battered fedora still in his hand, J.B. skipped it across the ground as he ducked, using it to scoop up a little dusting of the ice-flecked soil. Then, as the horned gladiator loomed over him, J.B. tossed the hat and its contents at the man's face, showering him with sharp flecks of ice.

The man in the helmet growled as ice and dust caught in his eyes, distracting his vision for just a single heartbeat. But it was enough. Still crouched low, J.B. powered his body at his towering opponent, head down, driving his shoulders and the back of his head into the man's gut.

J.B.'s attacker didn't fall with the blow, but he did skid back on the ground, his arms windmilling as he tried to keep his balance. In his right hand, the snarling chain saw swung wildly, cutting backward into one of the barrels that lined the arena, spitting a shower of sparks as it sliced through the metal drum.

An instant later the man had recovered. He held the chain saw steady in one powerful hand, the engine bucking in his grasp as he used his free hand to wipe grime from his face. J.B. saw the man's ugly grin appear amid the narrow lines of his helmet, saw that his front teeth were rotted stumps or missing entirely. But J.B. saw something else, too—where the chain saw had cut into the shell of the fuel drum, a dark liquid was spilling loose, forming an expanding puddle on the floor at his opponent's feet. J.B.'s nose wrinkled as he smelled the liquid's scent—a cloying greasy stench: cooking fat.

J.B. was a weaponsmith by training, but that didn't mean he was helpless without a blaster. Rather, he could see the ideal use of weapons in any situation, enough that he could employ whatever was around him to his advantage. It was something he resorted to when ammo was low. So when the situation called for it, when he had his back to the wall, metaphorically, John Barrymore Dix could make a weapon out of just about anything that came to hand. Right now, he had opted to use one of man's most ancient weapons—fire.

As the horned warrior recovered, J.B.'s busy hands had already reached into his jacket, pulling out the little lighter he had stolen from the sec man. His thumb worked the wheel once, twice, trying to get the spark to catch. Towering over him, J.B.'s opponent had recovered and swung the chain saw once again, thrusting downward in a vicious strike as the crowd cheered.

"Third time's the charm," J.B. muttered as the flame finally fluttered to life.

The Armorer dived out from the wall, rolling across the ground and reaching out with the lighter to touch the tip of the flame to the spilled contents of the barrel. An instant later, the liquid came to life in a whoosh of blue-gold flame as J.B. continued rolling over and over, generating as much distance as he could from those fearsome flames.

His horned opponent, however, wasn't so lucky—in a second, the first line of those flames had reached up his calves and was licking at the bottom of his fur jacket. He had been covered in the oil when his chain saw had cut through the barrel, and now all of that highly flammable liquid clung to his body like a second skin as the flames took hold.

The crowd was stunned, a ripple of shock running

through the spectators as their champion went up like a torch. J.B. watched in grim satisfaction as his hulking opponent stumbled backward in a column of rising flames. The flames were so bright it hurt J.B.'s eyes to watch. He shielded his eyes from the intensity as his opponent sank to his knees, the chain saw still spinning, his voice raised in agony. Then there came the sound of wrenching metal over the pop and hiss of the flames, and J.B. realized that the chain saw had cut into another of the barrels. His opponent screamed louder as a second barrel of oil splashed over his back and face, turning his horned helmet into a flaming star at the arena's edge while the gasoline in the chain saw caught light in a shock of explosion.

"Poor bastard," J.B. grumbled as he turned away.

Behind him, the fire was spreading, running up the arena wall behind his fallen opponent, burning toward the baron with his ridiculous headgear.

"Chill him!" Baron Kenojuak shrieked as his arena began to burn before his eyes. "Chill the outlander!"

"SHE IS CALLING TO ME," Doc said as they hurried along another icy tunnel.

"Who is?" Ryan asked with irritation. Now was not the time for the old man to start losing his grip on reality again, not when they were this close to freedom.

"Emily," Doc said, casually flipping his swordstick around to garrote another would-be attacker.

Ryan drove a solid punch into the next man who came at them, driving him backward into two of his fellow sec men. The cramped conditions of these tunnels worked to the two men's advantage—while they could be hemmed in, that required coordination. Furthermore, it was bastard hard, Ryan knew, for more than one man to round on them at any one time, turning the whole sequence of events into a series of one-on-one skirmishes. Short of running out of adrenaline, Ryan was confident he and Doc could hold their own—at least until someone had the bright idea of bringing a blaster to the fight.

"Emily's long dead, Doc," Ryan reminded the old man. "Where do you think she's calling you from?"

"I do not know," he admitted, shaking his head in confusion. "But I can…hear her. Sense her, if you will. Yes, that would be a more accurate reflection of my intuition here. 'Tis most vexing."

"Most vexing is right," Ryan agreed, blasting another attacker in the face with his stolen Smith & Wesson. "Emily got any idea how the fuck we get out of here?"

Doc laughed, missing Ryan's sarcasm entirely. "It is not that kind of a communiqué, my dear friend," he explained as he ran the blade of his sword through another attacker. "It is more like…knowing when you are almost home, recognizing the neighborhood even though you have been away for a very long time."

Ryan eyed the corridor with swift desperation. "Well, I don't know this neighborhood from squat," he snarled, "so let's just keep moving and worry about your ghosts later on, okay?"

And wasn't that just the shits, Ryan thought—right when he needed Doc most, the old man was losing focus.

The two men scurried down the sloped corridor and found themselves standing in a wide tunnel featuring a continuous curve. Nearby, they could hear the roar of the crowd as they watched J.B. getting pulverized by the ville champion. "We need to get to J.B.," Ryan growled, "before it's too late."

MILDRED AND NYARLA followed Krysty through the claustrophobic tunnels of the ice ville, working their way toward the courtyard where J.B. was battling with the deranged warrior. As they moved, Mildred quizzed Nyarla on what had happened to her father.

"After they…let it be known they wanted my sister, he ran," Nyarla explained. "He found a way to reach her and me and we all ran together. But we had to split up. He had one of their mounts by then, but it could only carry two of them. I was just slowing them down."

"Is that when we found you?" Mildred asked. Ahead of her, Krysty flicked her Smith & Wesson blaster through a doorway, shooting a surprised sec man through the chest before he had an inkling that he was under attack. Screaming and clutching at the wound, he sagged to the floor like so much deadweight.

Nyarla nodded. "They went east while I went west," she said. "He was heading toward *Yego Kraski Sada,* said we would rendezvous there. The ville men followed him, so I taunted them until they came for me instead."

Mildred looked at the young woman, figuring her for no more than her late teens, and tried to imagine how brave she had to feel to do that, how scary it had have been. "Is that when we found you?" she asked gently.

"I couldn't run any farther."

"What about your father and your sister?" Mildred queried. "Did you hear anything more? Do you know if…?"

"He would have gotten there," Nyarla said insistently. "I know he would. He's my father."

Krysty had led the way into a tunnel close to the lowest level of the ville. It ran in a continuous curve, following the walls of the vast courtyard, and the sounds of the baying crowd could be heard just beyond it. Together the three women followed the curve, searching for a way into the courtyard itself.

Up ahead, Krysty saw more figures moving, twin shadows among the flickering floor lanterns. She raised her revolver in a two-handed grip, waiting for them to step into the open. The figures moved warily, edging closer. They were thirty feet away now and Krysty saw the glint of metal in their hands where they both held blasters. She readied her aim, tracking the figures' movements, judging where they would be when they stepped into the light.

RYAN LOOKED UP and saw three people watching them, blasters raised and about to fire. He brought up his own .38, just two shots left in it now, and prepared to blast them to hell.

Chapter Fourteen

Baron Kenojuak was smiling in savage humor as everything before him was consumed behind the wall of flame. The champion, that chain-saw-wielding lunatic, lay close, sprawled among the metal barrels that had been placed against the walls to protect the crowds. Ironically, they hadn't protected them at all, not once the outlander had managed to get the contents alight. How the hell had he sneaked a lighter in there anyway? the baron wondered.

The champion's body was billowing with black smoke, his face and torso a pillar of flame. In his hands, the chain saw continued to whir as flames licked across its metal sheen, throwing flames in all directions as it spun.

The baron swept away the dark smoke that spewed across his sight, pulling himself from his throne to get a better view of the action, a cruel smile spread across his face. The little man in the hat was still alive, cowering behind the execution mound as flames nuzzled at its edges. Even if the champion was dead, at least this little upstart would be chilled soon, too, the baron assured himself with satisfaction. And the ville was constructed of ice—what harm could flames do to that?

"Chill him," the baron cried victoriously. "Chill the outlander!"

Around him, the crowd was becoming fearful as

those flames licked higher, sparks spitting out and showering some of the seats with their burning embers. The baron laughed as his people danced out of the way of those sparks, patting themselves down. "Chill him," he bellowed over the rising sounds of the flames. "Chill him for your baron!"

As he spoke, Kirima stood up behind him, her eyes fixed on the baron's back. She had been stripped naked and forced to serve the baron, suffered his depredations all night and had watched in horror as he ran the paring knife over her friend's skin until Narja was dead from blood loss. Resolutely, Kirima took a pace forward. Then, with grim determination, she shoved the baron with both hands, shunting him against the wall that ran around the edge of the arena.

Taken unawares, Baron Kenojuak stumbled just a pace forward before regaining his balance. He turned to the naked slut, cruel anger burning in his dark eyes. "How dare you lay your hands on the royal personage," he snarled.

Kirima backed away but she was surrounded on all sides by the baron's trusted aides. There was nowhere left to run.

"I'll see you turned into steak for that," Kenojuak continued. "Not even fit for humans but steak fed to the caribou!" But as he spoke the baron's towering Pschent hat caught a spark from where he was standing so close to the burning arena now, and in an instant it had begun to flame.

With a shriek, the baron swept the hat from his head. But the flame had caught the oil in his slicked-back hair and, in moments, his whole head went up like a candle. He screamed in agony, his hands reaching to pat down the flames—only to find the skin on his fingers catching light and burning.

All around, the followers of the baron backed away, surprised and horrified to see his head going up in flames. All, that was, except for Kirima. Leaping forward, she kicked the baron in his gut with an outstretched foot, driving him back toward where the corpse of the sharpshooter was being slowly spit-roasted. Still shrieking in agony, the baron tottered backward before tromping into the flames, and suddenly the rest of his body had joined his head in raging conflagration.

HER FINGER RESTING on the Smith & Wesson's trigger, Krysty watched as the two figures stepped out from the inconsistent shadows cast by the flickering lamps. Behind her, Mildred and Nyarla hugged the wall, each holding their own weapon as they sighted down the curve of the wide tunnel that backed onto the arena.

Mildred had reloaded her Czech-made ZKR 551 target pistol as the group worked their way down to this tunnel, but she cursed that she hadn't had an opportunity to check it over. Right now, all she could do was hope that they hadn't mangled its workings in that chop shop.

Two paces behind Mildred, Nyarla held out the stubby Colt revolver she had acquired from the armory. In spite of its short barrel, the revolver looked large in the young woman's hand and she held it with a mixture of determination and discomfort, clearly unused to wielding a blaster like this. Mildred had to trust that Nyarla wouldn't accidentally shoot her in the back.

Krysty saw the twin figures emerge from where they

had been obscured by the curve of the tunnel, readied to fire and then…

She stopped herself, bringing the revolver swiftly down to the ground, ordering Mildred and Nyarla to do the same.

For a moment, Mildred thought her friend had lost her mind, but then she saw why Krysty had backed down. Thirty feet ahead of them up the tunnel stood Ryan and Doc. Both men looked a little scarred and weary but otherwise they seemed okay. Ryan was bringing his own blaster down to a safe position as Krysty sprinted over to meet him. Ryan also began to run, hurrying to meet Krysty before sweeping her up in his arms.

The lovers embraced briefly, then returned to the matter at hand.

"J.B.'s in trouble out there," Ryan stated, "in some kind of arena. We were hoping to find a way in."

"Us, too," Krysty confirmed.

As she spoke, Krysty handed Ryan his weapons—the SIG-Sauer blaster and his Steyr Scout Tactical long-blaster, which she had strapped across her back. Ryan took the weapon and checked the scope, confirming it was still operative.

With the briefest of discussion, Ryan and Krysty continued around the icy tunnel, searching for a way into the combat arena. Keeping pace beside them, Mildred handed Doc his LeMat.

"Good to see you again, old girl," Doc said cheerily.

Mildred shot the gray-haired scarecrow a look. "Do you mean me or the gun?"

In reply, Doc gave her his most enigmatic smile, while Nyarla hurried to keep up with the group.

As they ran, they heard an explosion shake the whole

ville and up ahead a burning gap appeared in the curving side wall, glowing and sparking. A moment later, people began pouring through the gap, running for their lives.

"Come on," Ryan commanded. "Looks like J.B.'s fighting back."

CROUCHING BY THE chilling mound, J.B. turned as something exploded across the far side of the courtyard. Through the flames he saw the wall come crashing down as the seating area there gave way, scattering the baying mob as some were consumed in the fire. Behind this, the whole wall had crumbled to nothing amid the fierce flames. The people who survived the wall's collapse began to stream out of the newly created gap. After a moment's hesitation, J.B. followed, bullets kicking at his heels as he bolted out from cover and across the circle of courtyard.

The crowd was panicked now as the flames became more intense and lunged at the walls with their fiery tongues. J.B. saw one woman close to the gap in the wall slip and drop her blaster—a retooled Tokarev pistol with go-faster stripes painted across its black finish. The Armorer considered picking up the blaster, but already the flames were on it, making it literally too hot to handle. A second later, the Tokarev began to spit bullets as the heat engaged its firing mechanism, sending slugs spewing out across the arena at ground level. The problem with a blaster with no safety, J.B. thought grimly as he leaped over its lethal discharge.

Then he was at the gap in the wall, bullets pounding the ground all about him. It was a ragged hole, fifteen feet across. Flames played across the walls and a fiery plume of a barrel stood at one side, pouring black smoke into the immediate area. J.B. coughed, holding one hand before his face, his eyes tearing. He slipped through the flaming gap and out into the area beyond.

Standing there, waiting at the gap, were four familiar figures along with a fifth—Ryan, Krysty, Doc and Mildred, with the girl Nyarla, who, in a roundabout way, had got them all into this jam. Ryan and Krysty were in the lead, pushing a path through the surging crowd to get into the arena.

"Ryan!" the Armorer called. "It's me."

"We were just coming to find you," Ryan told the Armorer as he hurried over to greet him.

J.B.'s clothing was covered in dust where he had rolled around the icy arena and there was dried blood on his face. But otherwise he looked intact. He grabbed Ryan just above his hand in a tight grip, wrist-to-wrist. "Save me some other time," he suggested. "Right now, we should get going. This whole place is going up in flames."

Another ville person came running through the fiery hole, shouting angrily and wielding a Russian-made KS-23 shotgun in both hands. "Die, outlanders!" His shotgun blurted a single cacophonous burst of buckshot. But the fool hadn't bothered to aim, too caught up in the moment and distracted by the thick smoke swirling all about him. Utterly misguided, his attack missed his targets by several feet.

As one, Ryan, Krysty, Doc and Mildred took steady aim and sent the man on the last train west in a volley of bullets.

Then, moving away from the flaming arch, the companions began jogging through the ice-walled tunnel with Nyarla in tow. As they ran, Mildred brought

J.B.'s mini-Uzi out from where she had stuffed it in her satchel.

"J.B., you'll be needing this," she said. "Locked and loaded, I checked before we found you."

"Nice work, Millie," J.B. said as he took the blaster from her, hooking the sling over his shoulder so that it would ride horizontal just below the level of his belt. "You always know the way to a man's heart."

"I have one question," Mildred said as the friends made their way through the ville. Behind them, the hole in the arena wall was spewing flames, ending its use as an exit from the flaming courtyard. "Anyone know where they're keeping Jak and Ricky?"

"They're not here," J.B. explained, bringing his Uzi up to take out a sec man ahead of them. "They made a successful escape while we were out of the ville confines."

Mildred looked at him with obvious surprise. "You were outside?"

J.B. nodded. "Guess we have us some catching up to do," he said. "Mebbe best leave that till we're out of this pesthole, though."

Behind them, the first of the gas lamps that lined the floor were touched by flames and they began to explode, one after another, in a line running down the vast, curving tunnel.

"This way," Nyarla said, directing the group through an arched doorway leading to a short, four-step staircase.

While the ville burned around them, the companions made a swift exit from its icy hollows along with almost fifty ville dwellers. In the confusion, it didn't

take too much stealth for Ryan's group to escape un-
noticed, wounding and chilling just a few enraged ville
men who attempted to get in their way.

Chapter Fifteen

In His Ink Orchard, Jak and Ricky were lost. They had turned back, following the path they had taken to try to get back to the mines, entertaining the idea of freeing their companions in a bloody showdown. Jak could handle himself, and with the right cover he could overcome significant odds. Further, he had seen Ricky in action and knew he could trust the kid to provide that cover. All they would need would be sufficient weaponry to mount an attack, which meant disarming the sec patrol and using their own blasters against them.

But when it came to it, returning to the mines had been more difficult than either friend had expected. Cold mist clung to the earth like a sheet, obscuring their view and making it almost impossible to see more than fifty yards in any direction. Jak's spatial awareness was exceptional, and it granted him the determination to follow their path even where Ricky was admittedly lost. But as they closed in on the area where the invisible barrier lay, beyond which the mine should still be, they found themselves somehow turned around, as if the invisible wall itself was exerting a magnetic repulsion.

"What is it?" Ricky asked after they had found themselves turned around for the third time.

Jak stopped in place, turning on the spot until he was sure that he was facing the mining development. Freez-

ing mist slipped before him in wispy clouds, great blurts
of it wandering slowly across the icy plains.

"Nothing good," Jak stated, shaking his head. "Place
not right. Broken somehow."

Ricky looked at Jak, trusting the albino's keen instincts. "Then what do we do?"

"Can't go backward, got go forward," Jak said. But
he remained in place, his ruby eyes narrowed as he
sought out a sign in the mist. Beyond it, he imagined
he saw figures moving, but they weren't moving the
way that people should move. Instead they moved like
things that had been launched, hurrying across the terrain around the mine with incredible speed, blurring
dots on the horizon. It was like watching people's movements that had been sped up beyond comprehension, as
if they existed at another pace to that of Jak and Ricky.

Touching the barrier—if, indeed, they *could* touch
the barrier—might chill them, Jak concluded as he
watched those figures hurtling past beyond it. If the
people on that side were moving fast, and that would
have included himself and Ricky at their point of entry,
then trying to pass through the barricade at anything
short of top speed would prove deadly, or more likely
impossible. Like trying to grab a moving buzz saw; only
by somehow matching its speed could one ever hope to
do anything other than lose one's fingers.

Above the barricade, Jak saw the sky change, turning darker as if the struggling sun had set once more. It
made him wonder how long they had been here, in the
frozen wilds of His Ink Orchard, beyond all the maps.

"Reason for everything," Jak said, turning away
from the barrier. "Just got find."

Then he began marching away from the hidden wall

that loomed between them and the mine, and Ricky followed. Together the friends made their way across the frozen plain, carefully avoiding the spot where Jak had been attacked by the mouth-in-air.

THE COLD GOT COLDER. Jak and Ricky pulled their jackets tighter and marched with more determination, having run out of options to stave off the cold. Neither one could say how long they had been walking. They seemed to be trapped in a netherworld of mist and snow, a place where time had lost all meaning, where it had become unhinged like in a dream.

Things moved beyond the misty blanket and occasionally the fog would part and they would glimpse great hulking shadows shifting across the snow.

The snow itself continued to fall in flurries, dropping on them erratically.

Eventually, they came to a settlement. Just three buildings in total, the settlement appeared and disappeared between the swirling curtains of mist, dark lines amid the white. It crouched low to the horizon as if cowering from the falling snow, and Jak approached it warily, the stolen pistol raised and ready in his hand. One shot left, he reminded himself. That's all.

Without a word, the two companions approached the little cluster of buildings. It was the first sign of habitation they had come across since they had entered this area hours—*or was it days?*—ago.

Faintly, a road could be seen making its way cross-country toward the buildings, the asphalt old and broken, snow settling on it in powdery white streaks. Once upon a time, Jak realized, this place had been a community, serving either ice fishermen or truckers carting oil and other goods across the bleak backlands of America. Now, it was just three abandoned buildings in a forgotten nightmare, their occupants long since moved on.

On closer inspection, two of the buildings had fallen into terrible disrepair, so much so that it surprised Ricky that they were still able to stand. "They're just shells," he said, keeping his voice low.

Jak shot him a look, commanding the teen to silence. He was listening to the sounds here, the creaking of ancient wood in the furious winds that whipped across the plains.

The third building had metal sidings that had survived the quakes and chem storms that had done so much damage to Alaska. Little more than a two-story shack, it looked structurally sound, and Jak approached it warily. "Somewhere to sleep," he told Ricky as he plodded toward it.

Ricky followed and Jak tried the door. It was unlocked, but it opened only two inches when the albino pushed it. There was something behind that stopped the door opening farther, and Jak stepped back with his blaster raised, calling out for anyone who might be inside.

No answer.

Stepping back to the door, Jak handed Ricky the blaster before placing both hands against the door. Then he shoved, forcing whatever obstruction waited behind the door to move. In a moment, he had the door open and was inside.

It was dark, and Jak took a moment to let his eyes adjust. Ricky handed him back the Colt, bringing the knife up in his other hand.

Jak checked behind the door, saw the rotted remains

of a man lying there with a longblaster lying across his withered knees. The man had been backed against the door, presumably to protect himself. All he'd managed to do was die, cold and alone. Judging by the state of decay, the man hadn't been there that long.

"Dead friend," Jak told Ricky as he indicated the corpse.

Ricky gulped. "A warning to us both," he muttered, shaking his head.

Jak moved on, striding past the little alcove and into the main bulk of the building. Inside lay a general store, its contents looted, shelves upturned. All that remained were empty shelves and the faint smell of rust. They had entered from the rear, and they paced through this storage area checking empty cans and boxes, automatically searching for things of value or simply something to eat. It was a scavenger lifestyle, surviving in the Deathlands. With so little infrastructure, survival often came down to rummaging through places like this that still retained stuff from before the nukecaust.

They checked over the store swiftly. There was a gaping hole in the center of the floor, eight feet across and yawning down into the cellar and beyond that into the earth itself. The hole was so wide it took up almost half of the available floor space, and Ricky, who didn't enjoy Jak's superior night vision, almost stepped into it before Jak pulled him back.

"Watch first step," Jak warned, and Ricky nodded frantically as he caught his breath.

Finding nothing of interest in the store besides a few bullet holes in the walls, Jak led the way upstairs through an enclosed staircase that ran behind the store counter. Ricky trotted along behind him on the dilapidated carpet, their footsteps echoing on the wood that had been exposed there.

It was obvious that the second story had once served as living quarters for the store owner and his family. There were two bedrooms, one just a box room, and a lounge that ran almost the length of the building, windows boarded up with the flimsy sides of old packing crates. A figure was on the bedraggled couch; a boy no older than Ricky, missing his left leg and half of his left arm right up to the elbow. He was dead, his flesh as blue as a day-old bruise.

The boy had probably entered with the man, his father perhaps, in search of shelter, like Ricky and Jak. Now they were both dead, frozen to death, their bodies almost perfectly preserved by the chill air. No insects came to feast on them, not here where daytime temperatures never struggled above zero.

While Ricky checked the corpse for weapons and ammunition, Jak scoured the rest of the apartment. There was a bathroom featuring a blocked-up toilet, the blockage iced over, and a small kitchenette. There was also another door that opened into a cupboard where the water heater was stored; thick lines of calcium carbonate buildup ran down it in faded streaks.

Jak joined Ricky back in the living room where the teenager was just finishing checking over the corpse. "Anything?"

Ricky shook his head. "Three bullets, two of them different gauges, and what looks like the blade from an old razor." He showed Jak his haul, and Jak saw that he had tossed aside a few other items that had been in the corpse's pockets—colored beads, a patterned kerchief and a little figurine of a laughing man carved from wood.

Jak nodded grimly. Nothing of use.

"Rest here," Jak said. "Stay alert, one on, one off."

Ricky agreed, and before long he had wrapped himself in the coat of the boy corpse—after all, he figured it wasn't much use to him anymore—while Jak took the first watch.

JAK WOKE UP, sensing the movement in his sleep. He didn't know how long he had been asleep. He had swapped shifts with Ricky at the ascribed time, difficult to judge since neither of their wrist chrons seemed to be operating, as if they were caught in a strong magnetic field. Still, Jak had guessed when he'd reached the four-hour mark of his shift and went to rouse Ricky, handing the kid his blaster along with the automatic rifle he had procured from the dead man downstairs by the door.

The longblaster was a homemade weapon—with some artistic flourish, no less—on the standard AK-47 design. Jak had checked its magazine, ascertaining that there were at least two dozen rounds still in the blaster, and tried the safety a few times while Ricky slept upstairs. That was hours ago.

Now he awakened to find the building creaking. Outside, a fierce north wind was caroming against the shack like a child throwing a tantrum, tossing snowflakes all about in its fury. That could make an old property like this creak, Jak knew, but he sensed it was something else. A quake maybe? Alaska had suffered earthquakes before now, he recalled.

But no, he felt sure it was something else, something alive.

Jak was sitting in the chair he had fallen asleep in. He dropped the thin cover from his chest, immediately feeling the punishing cold of the apartment, the frigid wind rattling through broken and boarded windows.

In darkness, he scanned the room. The dead boy remained on the couch; nothing looking amiss.

Where was Ricky? The thought came to Jak immediately, fear prodding at the back of his mind. The kid should be on watch, but he wasn't in the room.

Another room then, or downstairs?

As he thought it, Jak felt the vibration run through the building again, making the boards in the windows shake. He was on his feet now, prowling toward the open doorway. He checked the other rooms from the corridor—bedrooms, bathroom, kitchenette—before making his way to the narrow staircase. The staircase had been boxed in on both sides and it ran up through the building at a steep angle, noticeably steeper than most old buildings that Jak had been in.

The building shook again as Jak took the stairs, hurrying down them two at a time, reaching the closed door at the bottom in record time. Ricky's voice called from behind the door, blabbing a prayer or something very much like it.

Jak pushed the door open, saw the thing looming in the darkness as it emerged from the hole in the basement floor. It was huge, its bulk taking up almost half of the store's area as it smashed up through the hole, knocking shelving units aside. It was covered in gray fur, with a great square head, two pointing ears protruding above it, two mighty limbs ripping aside the rotted floorboards as it pulled itself out of the basement.

Jak smelled the creature's breath as it turned to face

him, the stench of fish exuding from its open mouth where an array of impressive, foot-long teeth glimmered in the darkness. Sighting Jak, the creature began to charge.

Chapter Sixteen

The creature charged across the confined space of the dilapidated store, knocking aside shelves and clutter in its hurry to reach its prey. The obstacles slowed it just enough, giving Jak a fraction of a second to think and respond. He turned back, springing into the stairwell and slamming the door closed. A moment later he heard a mighty crash and the door shook behind him as the beast struck against it.

He had seen it only for a moment in the darkened store but he recognized the creature as some kind of mutie polar bear, teeth extended into mighty points designed to rend flesh from living prey. He had seen something similar before, but at a distance. It had to have sniffed out him and Ricky here in the general store, the same way it had most likely found the man and his boy, tearing the boy's limbs from his living body as he struggled to get away.

One thought flashed through Jak's mind then: Ricky.

The resourceful teenager had been left on watch while Jak slept and he had heard the lad's voice coming from behind the door in the storefront—but he hadn't had time to locate him out there in the dark.

Jak cursed as the door shook again under the attack of the mutie polar bear. What the fuck was he supposed to do now?

IN THE STORE, Ricky had hidden within the arch of two collapsed shelving units as soon as he saw the creature emerging from the ground. The shelves acted like an A-frame, leaving a small area with just enough room for his frame. Had he been any larger, blessed with the shoulders of Ryan Cawdor say, then he would never have made it into this enclosed space in time. What a fool he'd been to come down here and check on the noise he'd heard. Why hadn't he just awakened Jak? Was it pride?

He watched from his hiding place as the polar bear pawed at the stout door where Jak had disappeared. The creature was snuffling as it searched for a way in, its breath hanging there in great clouds of mist as it stalked before the closed door.

Ricky had two blasters with him, the stolen revolver and the knockoff AK-47. Maybe he could shoot the wretched creature, either chill it or just scare it away with a faceful of lead. There was just one problem with that—he had tried using the AK as the thing emerged, muttering a prayer to his sainted aunts, only to find the bastard mechanism had jammed, locked in place by the freezing temperature.

He peered at the longblaster in the darkness of the store, struggling to make out the details. He had been brought up around weaponry, his Tío Benito had been his ville's armorer and had shown him how to field-strip and rebuild a blaster, making it run smoother and better in the process. Ricky glared angrily at the auto-rifle in the gloom. If he had to he would strip this thing down to get it working again, if only he could be sure he would have time.

The polar bear was still prowling around the doorway, snuffling at the gap underneath and clawing at the wood there. Over the sounds of the creature's angry growl, Ricky heard Jak's booted feet running back up the wooden stairs and a moment later the floorboards creaked directly above him. Without the obvious prey nearby the creature might leave; it was a desperate hope, but Ricky was running low on options.

The mutie polar bear seemed to sense Jak's disappearance, too. It sniffed at the heavy door again then backed away, its broad head swinging left and right as it scented the air.

In the darkness, Ricky worked his thumb into a groove along the longblaster's casing. There had to be something he could do. If only he could think.

The polar bear stalked through the room, sniffing at the air as it hunted for prey. Ricky didn't know much about polar bears—he figured that maybe he and Jak had entered its hunting ground and it had smelled them out as they crossed the plains, leaving some trail of scent that had awakened the creature from its resting place under the snow.

Midway through the shelves, the creature stopped and turned to face Ricky's hiding place, its nose twitching. The kid watched in the darkness as the creature's black lips pulled back to reveal those hideous knifelike teeth, each one as long as his forearm.

I'm invisible, Ricky thought, not daring to move. *Just ignore me.*

The polar bear had other ideas. With a growl like a battle cry, it began to charge at the fallen shelves where Ricky hid, straining floorboards creaking beneath its weight.

Ricky moved at the very last instant, diving out from cover as the beast slammed against the propped shelves, smashing them to smithereens. Legs pumping, he ran across the store, the useless AK-47 in one hand, the pistol in the other.

Ricky propelled himself across the shop counter as the polar bear turned to face him, batting debris aside. Sweet Maria but that thing could move, Ricky thought as the creature charged across the room.

Ricky was behind the counter by then, scrambling across the debris-strewed floor to where the closed door to the stairwell was located. The beast crashed over the counter, looming behind Ricky with the pungent odor of rotting fish. The door was ahead, still closed. He wouldn't make it, Ricky realized.

He turned then as the polar bear lunged at him. One mighty paw swished through the air, claws extended. Ricky ducked and the claws raked across the wooden panelling at the rear of the counter with a great screech of nails on a blackboard.

Ricky's heart was pounding in his chest like a jackhammer, a mighty *buh-boom, buh-boom* against the wall of his rib cage. The polar bear moved like a storm come to life, batting everything aside as it reached for its prey. Ricky brought the useless AK-47 around and used it like a staff, jabbing the monster in the face with its butt. The creature's jaws clamped down around the rifle, snapping it in two.

Ricky almost fell backward as the creature let go of the longblaster, stumbling against the counter with a gasp of pain. The polar bear's tongue worked the metal from its mouth, spitting it to the floor in a long bead of drool.

Ricky brought up the weapon again, now almost a foot shorter than it had been seconds ago. The beast was six feet away, that shimmering loop of drool hanging from its lip.

UPSTAIRS, JAK HAD gone back to the small cupboard and worked free a metal strut from the rotted water tank. Though discolored with calcium carbonate buildup, the metal seemed solid enough. Jak had been making his own knives for years now. There wasn't time to fashion anything clever up here while that mutie ran riot below, but Jak was satisfied that the hunk of metal would do for the purpose he had in mind.

Moving swiftly through the room, Jak reached for the wooden boards that had been placed across the windows, testing for the weakest before pulling it from its housing. The boards had been put up with little craftsmanship; it wasn't difficult to break them away.

Within ninety seconds he had two boards, enough to expose the busted window and to climb through it. The polar bear had burrowed through the floor of the building, but it didn't have an easy way out again. If Jak could keep moving, and get Ricky out of there in the process, then maybe they would survive this encounter.

Jak shimmied through the gap in the exposed window, brushing aside the last few shards of glass that clung to the broken frame. Then he was outside on a lintel, snow billowing about him on the icy wind. He used the lintel as a stepping stone, dropping to the ground with an agile leap.

INSIDE THE ABANDONED store, Ricky was forced into the corner as the hulking polar bear prowled toward him. There was no way he could get to the back of the store and through the door there.

As the polar bear loomed over him, its mouth wide in victorious roar, Ricky tossed the broken remains of the AK-47 at it, aiming right between those open jaws. The longblaster flew through the air before striking the beast between the teeth. Automatically, the polar bear clamped down with its fearsome jaws, snapping up the remains of the weapon.

Ricky brought up his remaining weapon then, the stolen pistol that Jak had snagged from the sec man in the mine. In the space of a heartbeat he aimed and fired, sending the one remaining bullet from the Colt's chamber into the polar bear's mouth.

The shot was true and the bullet struck the smashed remains of the longblaster, igniting the propellant in a white-hot burst of illumination.

Dazzled, its mouth on fire, the polar bear swayed blindly into the counter, bumping against it before staggering back against the wall.

That was all the opening Ricky could expect and he knew it. In an instant he was over the counter and running across the ruined aisles of the store, giving a wide berth to the hole in the floor.

He reached the front door in five seconds, pulled at the handle with all his strength, but the door wouldn't give—it was locked in place.

Ricky glanced back over his shoulder, to where the storeroom was with its back door leading into the cold. The polar bear was writhing behind the counter, black smoke billowing from its ruined mouth. There was simply no way that Ricky could get past it and reach the back door. The creature was as mad as hell and whatever damage he had done its mouth wouldn't stop its muscular arms delivering a bone-shattering blow to his body, nor its wicked claws carving up his flesh. He was trapped.

"Madre de satanás," Ricky cursed.

Then something smashed through the boarded-up door behind him. Ricky stepped back, fearing it was another of the mutie creatures. He watched in the darkness as something smashed against the middle board, and it began to splinter, breaking up under a relentless attack from outside. Then he saw the glint of metal, and Jak's face appeared in the gap that had been created.

"Jak, what kept you?" Ricky asked. It was a stupid thing to ask, but he was scared and close to panic.

In reply, Jak just gave him that eerie, feral grin he sometimes had, and began working the great strip of metal he had produced to pull at the second board over the door, ripping at it like a jimmy.

Behind them, the mutant polar bear was shaking its head angrily as it recovered itself, trudging drunkenly from behind the ruined counter. Ricky watched over his shoulder, bringing the blaster up for another shot and taking careful aim as Jak ripped out the boards that crossed the door. His finger snapped at the trigger, once, twice, but nothing came out. The weapon was empty, but in his panic Ricky had forgotten that. He looked at the blaster angrily, muttering a curse at it as, deep in the darkness of the store, the wounded polar bear began to charge.

Jak's pale hand reached through the door and shoved a board aside before grabbing Ricky by the back of his jacket and pulling. He wrenched him through the gap as the polar bear hurtled toward them like a runaway steam engine, black smoke still pouring from its burned mouth.

Ricky awoke from whatever daze he had been in and kicked back, wending his body through the narrow gap in the door and almost diving through as Jak pulled him. Behind him, the polar bear continued its charge, battering against the broken door like a rock from a catapult. The door frame shuddered and a cascade of snow tumbled from the roof where the whole building shook. But the door—or what remained of it—held, caging the wild animal within.

Ricky lay faceup in the snow, his breath coming in ragged gasps, Jak standing beside him with the make-shift tool in his hands.

"Okay?" Jak asked.

Still breathing heavily, Ricky nodded. "Damn blaster quit on me," he explained. "Both of them."

"Out of ammo," Jak said and he handed the teenager one of the finds from the corpse upstairs. "Not any-more." It was a single bullet, one of the three and the only one that would fit the Colt blaster. Ricky took it and fumbled with the weapon, reloading it as the polar bear slammed against the other side of the door just a few feet away from them both.

Jak's eyes flicked knowingly to the crumbling store-front as the door shook again. "Best move," he said.

Ricky agreed, pulling himself to his feet and follow-ing Jak in a brisk jog across the snowy plain, getting far away from the cluster of buildings as swiftly as they could, before the mutie bear figured another way out.

As they trudged across the white-blanketed hellscape, the snow swirling across their path in fits and starts, Ricky handed the blaster back to Jak. "You should keep this," he said. "You found it, it's yours."

Without a word, Jak took the blaster and shoved it into his waistband with the safety on.

Already, the clutch of buildings was lost behind them amid the swirling snow, while up ahead all they could see were a few trees dotting the horizon like mourn-ers at a grave site.

"You reckon J.B.'s okay?" Ricky said after a while. "Ryan? The others?"

Jak looked at the kid with knowing eyes, eminently wise in comparison to this newcomer to their group. "Ryan always survives," he said. "J.B., too. We find or they find. We just stay alive."

Ricky nodded. Stay alive. It sounded so easy the way Jak said it.

FROM THIS DISTANCE, looking through the ice-caked windowpane, the vicious, gnashing teeth of the chronovores looked like blades stabbing at the snow. Attacking the ground, snapping at the place where the energies swirled uncontrollably, more and more were appearing with each scissor snap of teeth, the sound like crunching aluminium foil. Symon watched uncomfortably as they all attacked the same spot in the snow, dozens of them materializing from the ether, feasting on time's spilling energies.

"Where did they come from?" he asked.

"Who can say?" Piotr replied. "Something draws them, the same way it stops things or speeds them up, over and over. Sometimes we see ourselves in the mists."

"Or people we knew," Marla interjected.

"I saw myself," Symon admitted thoughtfully. "Out there, when the caribou died. I thought I was hallucinating."

"You weren't," Graz said sullenly. "Time is unchained here, it loops and swirls. Sometimes it's like looking in a mirror, just seconds between you and your other self."

"It's worse when you see what you're about to do," Marla said. "You watch but you can't stop yourself doing it, taking that step, brushing that branch aside."

Standing beside Symon in the patchwork shack, his

daughter Tarelya looked fearfully through the misted window, her breath hanging in the air like fog. "What happens if they see us? Won't they try to eat us, too?" she asked.

Piotr looked at her and nodded. "Stay out of sight."

"Do you have weapons here?" Symon asked, glancing around the claustrophobically disorganized interior of the supermarket.

"Besides what we carry?" Graz challenged. "Very little."

"We've found a few blasters in some of the houses," Piotr admitted, "but there's barely any ammunition. And without ammunition, the weapons are useless."

"Could a blaster put a dent in one of those...things?" Symon asked, indicating the swarming mouths.

"Yes," Piotr told him. "But there are too many to risk it now. At first, we would pick them off, but our ammunition runs low and their numbers are never ending. Now we pick our battles with care and run when we can."

"What if they come to eat this place?" Tarelya asked worriedly.

"Then we shall move," Piotr said.

"Or we shall die," Graz added ominously.

Symon shot him a warning look. "Don't tease my daughter like that, friend."

Graz began to reply but Piotr stopped him. "He meant nothing by it," Piotr reassured the fisherman and his daughter. "Just a joke."

But it wasn't a joke, Symon knew that. It was a reality that these poor wretches had resigned themselves to. No doubt they had been forced to make a hasty exit from other locations. Perhaps they had lost others of their number. It was best not to ask in front of his daughter.

"Does anything eat them?" Symon asked after some consideration. "The crows?"

"Not eat them, no," Graz told him, "but the watchers sometimes hunt them for sport."

"They catch them," Marla added.

"What for?" Symon asked.

Marla shook her head. "They're psychotic. Only a nutcase would do that. The chronovores are relentless. Trust me—you don't want to go near them."

"Or the clockwatchers," Graz added firmly.

Symon and his daughter continued to watch the chronovores as they feasted on the untamed energies amid the snow. Out there, through the window, End Day ran on.

Chapter Seventeen

They had left the ville far behind them now, yet it still shone like a beacon on the gray horizon as the fires burned through it. The place had been lit and heated with gas and oil, highly flammable materials that had caught the fire and spread it. The companions could only hope that the prisoners and those ville dwellers who had some decency in them had escaped the raging inferno that had once been their home. Even now, more than an hour after J.B.'s initial fire, they could hear the occasional explosion as another canister of gas went up, the boom echoing through the snowy landscape in an eerie, muffled kind of way.

Nyarla walked up front with Mildred and Doc, while Ryan spoke with Krysty and J.B.

"Quite a show you put on back there," Ryan told J.B.

The Armorer smiled briefly. "Just survival," he said, downplaying the whole affair. "Any showmanship was strictly accidental."

Snow was falling still, not thick but well-spread, dotting the air with its pretty white specks. To Ryan, his face wrapped in the weighed white scarf he had carried with him longer than he cared to remember, the snow didn't look pretty—it looked like everything else in the Deathlands, just one more way to execute a man, freezing him to death.

The falling snow left no paths visible so the group

approximated the way to the mine as best as they could, sticking to the cross-country route so as to avoid stragglers from the ville. While Jak was often cast in the role of tracker, each of the companions had a strong sense of direction. Such was necessary in the shockscape of the Deathlands, where few of the traditional symbols remained by which a person could navigate, and where so much could change in a single shower of acid rain.

The military site waited as they remembered it, a crater punched into the earth, the missile tail jutting from the ground like some conquering flag placed by the gods. In a way it was, for the missiles had conquered the land once called America, leaving nothing that person could truly call his or her own. Total war had led to near-total annihilation.

As soon as they were within sight of the mine, Ryan halted the group, commanding everyone to find cover. With snow falling and the poor illumination of the struggling sun, it wasn't hard to stay out of sight this far from the base. There had been sec men waiting when Ryan and the others had been taken there yesterday, and he didn't want to run in to any additional problems now.

Crouched behind the bole of a tree, Ryan brought his Steyr Scout up to his eye and peered through its magnification scope. The metal felt ice-cold against his face. Beside him, J.B. produced a pair of binocs from his coat, recovered by Mildred from the haul that had been taken from him by the ice ville dwellers.

"There," Ryan said after a moment. "Two of them, waiting right by the entrance."

"I've got a third," J.B. added. "Up at three o'clock. You see him?"

Ryan moved the rifle's scope around until he had the sec man framed in the crosshairs. The man was taking a slow drag from a hand-rolled cigarette and smoke seemed to pour from within the confines of his fur-lined hood.

"We could take them," J.B. suggested.

Ryan moved the Steyr's scope back to frame the two men at the entrance. "The sounds are sure to bring backup if they have it."

"Bring it," the Armorer replied. "I'd sooner see them chilled now than find them snapping at our backs when we enter *that*." He meant *Temno Bozh'ego Sada,* of course, the edge of the world. It loomed just beyond the complex of mines, a great wall of magnetic distortion turning the air into eerie shades of green and blue, warping the atmosphere in an ever-changing miasma of light.

Agreeing with his friend's logic, Ryan hissed out commands to the other companions, warning them to get in position and get ready. If he could, he would chill these sec men from a distance and that would be the end of it. But if there was backup, like J.B. reckoned, then it would require all of his team to stay alert until the threat was dealt with.

Wrapping the shooting sling over his left arm, Ryan secured the butt of the longblaster in the groove of his shoulder, watching the sec men through the falling cascade of snow. Magnified into great white streaks by the scope, the snow obscured his vision. Ryan took a moment, steadying his breath. A thin trail of mist ballooned from between his parted lips as he prepared himself.

Then he fired. Twin shots rang out across the snowy plains, blasting in quick succession. The first sec man collapsed backward, his face erupting in a spray of blood. The second took a bullet just below the chin and he, too, went down, flopping to the ground like a beached fish.

Ryan was already switching his aim, bringing the Scout around and fixing the third sec man in its sights. The man had heard the shots, and he began sprinting across the snow toward the mine entrance. Ryan tracked him for three seconds, watching as he leaped over a mound of snow, shoving the twigs of a dead bush aside in his haste. He had the man's speed now, and his index finger brushed the trigger of the longblaster again, sending another 7.62 mm slug hurtling from the barrel.

In the crosshairs of the scope, Ryan watched the third sec man drop to the ground, tumbling over himself as he struck the snow. The one-eyed man waited a moment, his breathing coming faster now, to see if the man would move again. A tiny red patch began to emerge beneath the sec man's fur coat, leaking into the snow like spilled paint.

The sound of a bullet cut through the air, and J.B. cursed from beside Ryan's shoulder. "Dark night! More of them coming. Mine entrance and up on your nine."

"Fireblast," Ryan spit, bringing the scope around. Five more were at the mine entrance, he saw. They were using the walls for cover and bringing up long-range blasters as they searched for their attackers.

"You handle the main entrance," J.B. said, drawing himself up from his hiding place, "and we'll deal with the stragglers."

Before Ryan could say anything, J.B., Doc and Krysty were running toward the mine, while Mildred remained with Nyarla.

Ryan swiftly picked off two of the men at the mine entrance, drilling them through the skulls with a bullet each as they tried to locate their attackers. A third man got lucky, pulling up a longblaster and sending a half dozen shots in Ryan's direction on semiauto. Ryan rolled back as the shots peppered the trees and the ground around him.

"Get the girl back," Ryan said to Mildred as he dropped down to his belly.

Behind him, Mildred ushered Nyarla away, her hand on the young woman's head, urging her to stay down.

Ryan had the Scout back in firing position, his eye pressed against the scope. Two of the sec men had broken away from the main entrance of the mine while the third stayed back, using a modified sniper rifle to scour the territory. The man was well-covered, peeking out from cover only briefly, just the muzzle of his rifle visible.

Ryan shifted his focus, searching the snow-covered plain for sign of the other men.

INSIDE THE EXCAVATED redoubt, twelve sec men were readying themselves for the assault. The mine had been attacked before, over the past few years, from the time that Baron Kenojuak and his people had first begun investigating the site. It had been hard work back then, burrowing into the earth, inch by unforgiving inch, reaching into the collapsed base where the missiles had sunk it into the soil. Now, the alarm had been raised and it appeared that the place was under attack again.

"No one gets in but us and our people," the lead sec man commanded. He was a tall, broad-shouldered man called Curt, with a scar down his left cheek and one eye turned blind white. He had fought for the ville for as long as anyone could remember, even served time in the gladiatorial ring for the entertainment of the masses. He had defended the mine from attack more than once before. "They'll try to storm the mine soon, and we need to be ready. Grab a blaster and whatever ammo you can, and if they move against us, chill the prisoners." He was smart enough to know a liability when he saw one—prisoners, miners, slaves, they could be replaced. The weapon stash was the important thing here.

All around Curt, the sec men split up, making their way toward the nearest exits to rain fire down on whoever dared attack their mine.

CLOSE TO THE MINE, J.B., Krysty and Doc were working their way through the sparse cover of dead trees, searching for the enemy. They kept well apart, following a path that J.B. found to bring them around to one of the mine's several side entries.

J.B. spotted movement in the bushes to his right, brought his M-4000 shotgun up to track it. The Armorer didn't want to shoot without being sure. Could be it was Jak or Ricky, making their way back from the edge of beyond.

Then two figures emerged from the scrappy undergrowth, shoving a chain gun mounted on skis ahead of them. J.B. recognized the weapon, a U.S.-built EX34 that used a potentially endless loop of ammunition to deal damage to an enemy. The two men had it prepped, nudging the pipe nose of the weapon through the cover of the bushes. In the split second it took for J.B. to process this information the sec men wedged the skis in place and a stream of 7.62 mm bullets cut through the air toward the Armorer.

BULLETS PELTED THE AIR all around Ryan as he brought the longblaster around in a slow, steady arc, searching for the missing sec men. He found one creeping up the crater bank, his body low to the ground and the familiar black shaft of a shotgun barrel in his right hand.

Ryan fired, sending a shot through the trees. The bullet clipped the creeping sec man in the shoulder, sending him tumbling down the slope of the crater and back toward the mine entrance in a splash of spilled blood and snow.

Mildred's voice rang out behind Ryan. "At your ten!"

Ryan saw the man's shadow cut across his line of fire.

Chapter Eighteen

Ryan rolled, pulling his eye away from the scope and bringing the longblaster around to his ten o'clock, firing automatically. There was another sec man there, just twelve feet away. This one was wrapped in bulky furs and carrying twin handblasters in his gloved hands as he stalked toward the one-eyed man. Ryan's blind shot hit him in the upper flesh of his left leg. The man cursed, bringing up both blasters to chill Ryan.

The sound of a shot echoed from behind Ryan, off to his exposed left, and the sec man went down without firing, tumbling forward to drill the barrels of both blasters into the snow.

Ryan turned to see Mildred kneeling a dozen feet away, the ZKR 551 clasped in a sure, two-handed grip. He dipped his head once in thanks before turning back to the Scout's scope and searching for the man hiding in the mine entry.

IN THE SNOW-PACKED wilds, J.B. was scrambling toward one of the mine's side entries. Bullets zapped through the air toward him as he ran, but the men at the chain gun were too high and they had trouble dipping the weapon's fixed muzzle low enough to snag their target.

The two men stopped firing, and after a momentary discussion they worked together to heft the gun forward, arrowing the skis toward the retreating form of the Armorer. As they did so, Krysty and Doc appeared from opposite sides, bringing their own weapons to bear.

"You gentlemen may wish to reconsider your life choices so far," Doc mocked as he held them both in the sights of his LeMat.

The men spun, looking for an escape route only to come face-to-face with the muzzle of Krysty's Smith & Wesson. Behind it, her emerald eyes were all that could be seen beneath the protective wrappings across her face, a single wisp of red hair flying free from beneath her hood.

"I'd tell you not to move," Krysty warned, "but I figure that's redundant. Besides, I almost want you to give me an excuse."

One of the sec men appeared to take Krysty at her word, and his hand dipped to his belt holster, reaching toward the blaster he wore there. Krysty fired but the man had ducked just out of the bullet's path, bringing his own weapon free from its holster as the bullet careened off toward the mine.

Krysty shot again and the man sagged to the snow, the shot ripping the blaster from his hand and mangling the glove he wore into a blood-soaked mess in an instant. She stepped over him, aiming the barrel of the Smith & Wesson at his frightened face.

His partner, finally seeing the way things were headed, raised his hands in the air in surrender to Doc. "Don't shoot!"

WITH HIS BACK to the outside wall of the sunken redoubt, J.B. looked around, scanning the immediate area. Two mutie caribou were tethered just above the lip of the crater, close to the unexploded missile lodged in the soil. Behind that, the faintly unreal line that marked the so-called edge of the world shimmered in place like a towering wall. What was it the girl had called it? The Tall Wall.

The mines could still be full of chillers, J.B. realized. No doubt some of the refugees from the torched ville had gravitated here, taking a much more direct route than he and his companions had. There was every chance that the mines held another fifty men and women, each one armed ten times over with blasters and ammo and who knew what else. The place was a stockpile of weaponry, and the number of sec men at any one time suggested that they had kept much of the stock there even after recovering it from the collapsed base. It stood to reason—why move it until you needed it?

"We need to shut this pesthole down," J.B. muttered as another clutch of bullets drilled the ground beyond the mine shaft's reach. He placed one hand to the side of his jacket, felt there for the items he had replaced a little over an hour before. These cannies had had the run of this snowbound corner of Hell for too long, terrorizing innocents like Nyarla and her missing father, he thought. It was time to cut off their lines of supply forever.

SEC MEN CONTINUED pouring from the exits of the mine, hauling fiercer weapons with them as they tried to defend their territory. In the trees, Doc and Krysty found themselves under attack from a tag team wielding a rocket launcher and a submachine gun, the latter laying down cover fire while the former reloaded. They raced for cover, leaving the two men who had operated the chain gun to stand or fall as best they could. There was no time to restrain them; it was chill or be chilled out there now. A copse of leafless trees provided scant shelter, the billowing snow blustering all around it.

Krysty gasped as a miniature rocket zipped through the trees. "We should have gone around."

The two of them watched for a moment as the rocket impacted with a far tree in a blossom of flames.

"And have these people at our backs? Following us?" Doc suggested. "No. We burned down their ville and they have nowhere left to go now but into the very place they fear. If we had run, we would be running still, and we would never outdistance coldhearts such as these."

Krysty knew he was right. She hated it, hated the position they had been forced into. But she thought of Kirima, Narja and the other women who had been forced to serve these heartless men, and she made peace with what she had to do.

Doc shouted a warning, and Krysty ducked automatically as another antitank missile cut a path through the leafless trees.

While the rocket launcher was being reloaded, Doc led the way across the drifting snow, blasting his LeMat in the direction of the chillers, with Krysty just a pace behind him.

HEAD TUCKED IN, longblaster in hand, Ryan sprinted across the snow as bullets cut the air around him. The sec man at the mine entrance was getting bolder, and though he wasn't counting the shots—it was hard to do so over the general cacophony of blasterfire—Ryan was pretty certain the man had been joined by a second sharpshooter, the two of them covering the ground in an expanding semicircle.

Ahead of Ryan, a bush poked out of the snow, its twig fingers reaching up from the blanket of white.

It wasn't much in the way of cover, but it would have to suffice. Ryan ran to it, dropping and rolling to tuck himself down behind its fanned branches.

He had the Scout laid out before him instantly, the scope to his eye. He saw both men in profile, facing away from his direction, unaware that he had moved.

Gently, Ryan stroked the trigger with his index finger and let loose two quick shots, watching through the crosshairs as the man with the scoped longblaster went down, his head and chest exploding almost simultaneously.

The second man moved, not back toward the cover of the mine as Ryan might have expected, but forward, out across the snow with his longblaster resting in both hands. Ryan tracked him across the snow, breathing deeply as he lined up his shot, then fired.

The final gunman went down, a bullet wound like a bloody rose in the center of his chest.

THE MEN WITH the rocket launcher saw Doc and Krysty charging toward them through drifting snow flurries, Doc like a scarecrow from a nightmare, Krysty's now untucked hair blowing behind her like a living flame. The submachine gunner slammed a new magazine in the stock and depressed the trigger while his colleague took aim. Bullets sprayed the site, throwing puffs of snow all around them as Doc and Krysty weaved in a zigzag pattern down the slope.

Doc's LeMat blasted again, but this time he had engaged the shotgun barrel, which blurted a great ball of shot at his would-be chillers. The man behind the rocket launcher took the full blast in his face, tipping him over. His finger twitched against the weapon's trigger, discharging a rocket straight up into the air as he keeled to the ground.

His partner continued to spray the air with lead as Krysty ran at him through the trees. With incredible agility, the red-haired woman leaped over the hail of fire, her free hand snagging one dead limb of a tree overhead and swinging her up and outward in an arc perfectly judged to meet with the triggerman. She barreled through the air for a second, plummeting feetfirst into the man's face as he tried desperately to adjust his aim. Krysty's boot heels hit him with bone-jarring finality, the snap of his jawbone audible even over the wild discharge of his weapon.

The man looked up, but the next thing he saw—and also the last thing—was the barrel of Krysty's blaster as she drove it down between his eyes and shot him.

"Get back," J.B. called to them from a little way up the slope. Krysty and Doc turned, saw that J.B. was scrambling toward the half-sunken missile that dominated the crater.

"John Barrymore Dix," Doc called, "what is it you plan to do?"

"Close this pesthole down," J.B. replied, "once and for all."

AT THE TOP OF THE SLOPE, now standing next to the missile, J.B. enjoyed a brief moment of silence. The blasters had stopped firing and the world quieted, the angry wind muffled by the falling snow.

Taking a deep breath, J.B. looked at the missile before him. The workings had been opened at some point, and the metal panel that once hid them was torn away and hung broken. Ice glistened on the exposed insides, snow tumbling from the missile as he brushed one gloved hand across it. The Armorer reached into his jacket and pulled loose the little wad of plastic explosive he had set aside for the task.

Down below, the collapsed redoubt-turned-weapons-mine waited in ominous silence. It broke J.B.'s heart to lose all that weaponry down there, but there it was. Chipping ice away with the end of his shotgun, J.B. placed the explosive against the exposed workings and gritted his teeth as he primed it.

The little charge slapped in place, J.B. slammed the broken remains of the panel closed on the missile housing and began to run, shouting to Doc and Krysty to do the same. The timer had a short fuse—twenty seconds maybe?—and J.B. knew he simply had to generate as much distance as he damn well could before it went off, triggering the far bigger payload inside the missile. Buried the way it was, the missile's effect would be dulled, but that wouldn't matter. Just so long as it took this pesthole, with its psychopathic mining op, out for good, that's all that he cared about.

He was almost level with the side entrance now, about a quarter turn around the mine and well up from the base of the sunken crater. It had to be far enough, just had to be. The count in J.B.'s head had reached fifteen and he threw himself to the ground, his arms over his head protectively, his face down in the snow. Another second of ominous silence...two...and then the charge went off. It sounded loud as it echoed across the plain, like a cosmic anvil being struck by a hammer.

But the sound was nothing in comparison to what came next. J.B.'s tiny charge ignited the long-dormant works of the missile, setting the payload off in an explosion that turned the whole place into daylight-flash for a second and a half, the accompanying noise deafening in its magnificence.

The explosion ripped across his closed eyelids in a cough of brilliance, visible even through them. And it did a magnificent job of sending the left-hand line of the crater deeper into the earth, driving a punishing stake through the heart of the mine and turning its foundations to dust, collapsing the scratch-built mine shafts.

Chapter Nineteen

The only place to go was onward, Jak knew. To turn back was to reach the barrier again, which had proved impossible to penetrate. To keep moving meant to stay alive, the same basic equation that had guided Jak and his companions through the Deathlands.

He trekked across the dead land with Ricky at his side. The kid was tired and cold, Jak knew, but he didn't complain. The incident with the polar bear had shaken him up badly, and he would peer over his shoulder every now and then as if certain that the hulking creature had found a way out of the store and was following them.

There were roads drawn in the snow, and one time they heard voices echoing from somewhere nearby. They looked, but the voices went silent and there was no clue where they might have been coming from. Through the snow and the fog, Jak could see a line of buildings, but they were at least a half mile away, and a great chasm yawned between here and there. If the voices came from there, then they would have to stay there. The only real path to take was forward, into the onrushing storm.

Lightning strikes rocked through the sky in the middle distance, a fearsome play of electricity. Jak and Ricky stopped, watching the fiery display shoot across the skies. For a moment, the atmosphere felt charged as a mighty lightning bolt shot up into the air from the ground.

"What would do that?" Ricky asked.

Jak narrowed his eyes, watching the fearsome bolt rocket into the sky before breaking apart with a trident fork of illumination. "Weapon, could be," he said.

"Damn big blaster if it is one," Ricky observed worriedly. "No one could survive against something of that size."

Despite that, the two companions agreed to head toward the lightning's source. Any other destination seemed pointless.

THEY ENCOUNTERED a cluster of the eerie bodiless mouths as they paced close to the epicenter of that lightning storm. The mouths had gathered around a smoldering pool where eerie lights flickered. From the distance they looked as if they were grazing.

Crouched on the summit of a snowdrift, Jak and Ricky watched as the disembodied mouths flocked around the pool. It looked like a tear in the earth itself, as if something warm was located beneath the snow, melting it before it could settle. The mouths gave no voice, but Jak's ears tingled, as if something was vibrating the bones there, just beyond the range of human hearing.

"I don't like it," Ricky whispered beside Jak. "They're creepy and shouldn't exist."

Jak said nothing, waiting for the bodiless creatures to move on. The locustlike mouths continued to drink from the spilled liquid, gorging themselves on the deposit of whatever it was. After a while, they seemed satiated and they finally began to drift away in ones and twos, floating sets of teeth swimming through the air.

Warily, Jak watched them part, waiting until they had
moved well away from himself and Ricky.

"Come on," Jak instructed then, pushing himself up
from the ridge. He and Ricky made their way down to
the strange pool.

Jak stopped before it and leaned down to get a closer
look at the pool. It seemed alive with color, and he
watched images cast across the water's surface. For a
moment, he thought he saw his father's face in the pool.

Beside Jak, Ricky cinched forward on elbows and
knees, gazing into the mirrored surface. "That doesn't
look like water to me," he said, keeping his voice low.

"No," Jak agreed. "Looks like mem'ries."

Ricky gave him a sidelong glance, wondering what
he meant. Then, staring back at the heart of the misting pool, he also thought he saw the face of someone
he knew, reflected in the waters—Yami, his older sister, her shy smile materializing across her face. When
he looked again she had gone, nothing but a trick of
the light.

Nearby, the mouths were moving with apparent aim-
lessness, taking wide circular paths across the ground.
Their circuit would bring them back here soon enough,
Jak reasoned, which meant it was time to move on.

Unseen by the mouths, Jak urged Ricky back and together they located a new path that took them into the
heart of *Yego Kraski Sada,* where the lightning touched
the sky. It seemed normal enough, but as they walked
past a cluster of snow-laden trees, something strange
happened. Jak noticed it first, his preternatural senses
ever alert. He spun on his heel, drawing the stolen Colt
Anaconda and thrusting it toward the highest branches
of a tree. The tree looked like a skeleton, its bark turned
charcoal-black with the damp, its reedy branches speck-

led with snow. Jak scanned the tree, carefully eyeing those skeletal branches. One of the upper branches near to the top of the tree was broken, and Jak watched as it started falling. But its descent was impossibly slow, slower even than a feather dropping in the breeze.

Jak watched, his blaster redundantly pointing at the branch.

"What is it, Jak?" Ricky asked. The olive-skinned teen had skipped back a few steps to rejoin Jak, standing ten feet from him while light snow flurries dotted his hair with white.

"Not sure," Jak replied. "Something not right. See?" Jak indicated the snapped branch.

Ricky narrowed his eyes, peering at the dangling branch. The branch had broken clean off and appeared now to be hanging there in midair.

"How is it doing that?" Ricky asked, tilting his head in both directions to try to see if there was some trick to it, perhaps some strings holding the broken branch in place. He couldn't see any.

Then, without warning, the branch tore away from the tree, shooting toward the ground like a launched rocket. Jak and Ricky leaped back as the branch drilled point-first into the ground, driving two inches beneath the snow. It had moved with a blur.

"What—?" Ricky began, but Jak was already moving toward him and shoving him aside.

Ricky rolled to the ground as the rest of the tree began to blur. He watched in amazement as leaves appeared on the once-dead branches, blossoms budded and grew and fell away, the leaves turned brown. The air around shimmered with waves of color.

"What is it?" Ricky asked. "What's happening?"

"Not the tree," Jak said. "All around."

Ricky remembered the bullet he had seen earlier, the way it had waited in the air before surging suddenly forward and into the tree trunk. He turned his eyes from the tree as it hurried through its seasonal cycles again, racing past fall into winter, then spring and summer again. Around them, the snow seemed to melt and straggly blades of grass popped through the melt, then ice appeared in layers before washing away as water, seeping into the ground. It was like time-lapse photography, showing the rush of the seasons in the blink of an eye.

Looming over the two companions, the tree began to shake, faster and faster as if in the grip of an earthquake. It moved so swiftly that neither Jak nor Ricky could see the details of the branches any longer. Behind, the sky seemed to lighten then darken, over and over. The tree fell, its now-dead branches tumbling through the air like bones, crashing to the ground in a heap, leaving nothing more than a twisted stump where the tree had stood just seconds before.

"Hell!" Jak spit, scrambling out of its way.

Ricky shifted himself away from the remains of the tree, stolen knife in hand. Beside him, Jak was back on his haunches, drawing himself up from the frozen ground.

"Something's really wrong here," Ricky said, his breath coming fast. "Bad juju, my uncle would have called it."

Jak shook his head. "Not that." He had grown up in the fetid swamps of Louisiana, where voodoo ritual and mysticism played a pivotal role among the terrified locals. Whatever was going on here, he felt sure, it was something that could be explained. They just needed to figure out how.

Unconsciously, they felt the rippling waves of energy

lashing against their bodies. It was an energy neither of them could possibly recognize, yet it was a pressure that had been on their bodies ever since they had come here to His Ink Orchard. It was the pressure of time breaking apart, piece by tiny piece while the chronovores feasted on excess chronal energies.

Chapter Twenty

It was like the world was turning the wrong way here, that was the only parallel that Ryan could come up with as he stood at the barrier. The sense of wrongness was so intense, and so unlike anything he had ever felt before.

"This is it?" he asked, addressing Nyarla. "His Ink Orchard?"

Nyarla nodded. *"Da."*

"Feels wrong, Ryan," J.B. opined. "Like walking with fever. It feels sick."

Ryan kept his own counsel on the matter, but silently he agreed. J.B. had nailed in a handful of words exactly what it felt like. Like trying to shoot a blaster while hopped up on jolt.

Absently, Doc rubbed a hand through his hair, casting it in further disarray. "I am inclined to agree with the esteemed John Barrymore," Doc announced, "and yet I feel, too, something calling to us. Which is to say—to me, leastways. How I imagine a magnet must feel when faced with an opposing pole."

Mildred shook her head while Krysty stood back, as far from the invisible wall as she was able without leaving the group entirely.

"I don't feel anything," Mildred told the old man, "except a little nausea. Something isn't sitting right out there. I wish we knew what."

Krysty's hair had begun to curl in on itself, making it look as if she had a head full of writhing snakes. "I feel it, too," she admitted. "The earth here is…broken in some way." She looked hopefully at Ryan as she said it.

"Lot of this ground is broken," J.B. reminded the woman. "Nukes hit all around."

"No, J.B." Krysty shook her head. "It's more than that. It's as though something deeper has gone askew."

Ryan remained silent, watching the area and judging its feel. His skin was cold, but not in the way that the cool air would make it. This was the kind of cold that accompanied dread. Ryan was tough, but he was no fool and he surely hadn't survived this long in the Deathlands by making rash decisions. He had walked away from situations before now, when the odds proved too much or the rewards too slim.

The area loomed before Ryan like a monster of myth. He estimated that it ran eight miles square, and whatever lay at its center was likely responsible for whatever the hell it was.

Now, as he looked out across that stretch of land, the atmosphere sparkling as if alight with fireworks, Ryan wondered if this might be another of those situations that he should just walk away from. He feared he was chilling his own people here, handing them a death sentence, leading them to a place from which they could never escape.

J.B.'s voice interrupted Ryan's silence, breaking his train of thought. "We're going in?" the Armorer asked, his eyes scanning the flecks of half-seen light that buzzed through the heavens above the area.

"I don't see as we have much choice," Ryan told him. "Doc would go in without us. I know he would. We can't leave him to find out what's in there alone."

"No," J.B. agreed, "we can't."

Ryan looked out into the area of land known as His Ink Orchard. The hairs on the backs of his arms were upright, his skin prickling all over. Nyarla, Ryan could take or leave. But Doc had been a companion—and a friend—for a long time. He wouldn't turn his back on that. And then there was Jak and Ricky, one a companion for almost as long as Doc, the other a new ally but a loyal one. *"The ones we leave behind are the ones that are dead"*—wasn't that what Trader had always bragged when they were moving into unknown territory?

Ryan took a step closer to the invisible barrier that appeared as nothing more than a film across the air, yet that he could sense as a buzz in the back of his mind. Wordlessly, his companions followed, stepping closer to that hidden barricade that cut the land and air. Whatever His Ink Orchard contained, Ryan reasoned, it had better be worth it. Jak and Ricky had better be alive.

Beside Doc, Nyarla was yearning to step through the invisible barricade and enter the area. Yet something stopped her. She stood there, her body tensed, her fists clenched. "My father..." she muttered.

Doc leaned close to console her. "There, there, my dear, it's all right now. We'll find him and your missing sibling soon enough. You mark my words."

Nyarla looked up at Doc and offered him a brilliant smile. "You are good men," she said in her heavily accented English. "You help me much already."

Doc inclined his head demurely to show he was embarrassed but wouldn't argue the point. Then he turned to Ryan and the others. "Well, gentlemen, ladies," he announced. "Shall we enter this dark orchard of God?"

Ryan dipped his head once. "We shall." He reloaded his SIG-Sauer before addressing his companions in a firm voice, a natural leader. "Everyone stay alert. None of us like what we're feeling here, and that's generally a good indicator that something is royally fucked up. Keep your eyes open and trust your instincts. If you see anything that don't sit right—"

"*Doesn't* sit right," Krysty corrected him quietly.

"—you sound an alert, you chill it or you wait for help," Ryan finished. "Or all three."

With that, the companions moved forward in step, their weapons held ready as they entered His Ink Orchard. A road waited before them, its asphalt gray peeking through the snow that patterned across it like sawdust on a workshop floor. Walking through the barrier felt like stepping into the path of strong fan, a momentary blast of rippling air lashing across their flesh before disappearing as suddenly as it had begun.

J.B. looked back, eyeing the desolate track they had just been on. "Nothing's changed," he said, confused.

"And yet it feels as though everything has," Doc told him. "Whatever this place is, it bewitches the instincts in ways unimaginable."

J.B. nodded at that comment. It seemed a reasonable enough description of something he could likely never truly comprehend.

The snow clung to their soles as they brushed through it, while the trees remained dreadfully still. There was wind here, mean howling wind that cut against the face like a knife. Yet there came no other sounds of life, no bird calls or animal howls, nothing to suggest that the place held anything living other than the companions and Nyarla. It was eerie.

Lights popped and fizzled in the distance, blurting from the air in random patterns, their existence measured in the fractions of a second. What it meant, Ryan didn't know.

"You have any idea where your father is?" Ryan asked Nyarla as they trekked across the snowy wastes.

Nyarla shook her head and said something in Russian.

The only direction worth taking was downslope, to follow the road.

THE HOUSE WAITED in the wasteland, a ghost from another time. It looked like an old air-raid shelter, a slash of metal and concrete that hugged the ground in a depression, lightning playing across its metal roof. Beside it stood a second structure, much larger with its purpose clear from a single glance. Four long lines of upright cylinders stood like eggs in an egg carton, twenty-four in all, joined together by thick cords of insulated metal. They were storage capacitors, each one standing twenty-five feet high and ten feet across, the hum of the energies they contained audible even here, a quarter mile away from them. The rumbling snake of an icy river churned behind the power plant, cutting across the frozen terrain with its mirrored ripple. The river was wide enough to incorporate the full wing-span of the crashed passenger jet that poked out of its depths like the skeleton of some great leviathan. Besides the jet, the river contained great chunks of ice, some as large as automobiles or small buildings, wending their way along its unknowable depths. Great gullies ran down to the river, carved rents in the ground as if a laser beam had been used on it. Jak wondered if that might truly be the case, lying so close to the bunkerlike redoubt as it did.

Jak looked at the buildings with narrowed eyes, piecing together the picture presented before him. The network of capacitors fed straight into the low building, incongruous in their enormity compared to the little hut that they powered. As they got closer, Jak realized that the hut was much larger than he had first estimated, a single story covering an area the size of a predark field. The building had slit windows running in a line along its facade, set horizontally like old-fashioned letter slots. Some of the windows emitted a faint green-tinted glow as luminous as cats' eyes.

It was a crooked house, Jak thought, set here in a crooked patch of the world, protected from the rest of the planet by its invisible wall.

"You figure someone's inside?" Ricky asked.

Jak nodded. They hadn't come this far to find an empty shack.

Pulling the stolen Colt Anaconda from his waistband, Jak hurried toward the old structure with Ricky at his side, and together they scrambled down the slope. There was a smattering of snow all about, marking the area indifferently like flies on a wound. There, half-buried in the snow, jutted the remains of an old wire fence, its struts sticking out from the ground like spokes. The fence made a noise like dropped coins as they stepped over it, and Jak saw a sign there on the its bent face. The sign showed a lightning bolt beside bold lettering exclaiming this to be a private area. Another block of lettering warned that the fence was electrified—which was to say it had been a hundred years before—with Danger of Death in bold type beneath that. Now, the fence was as dead as the trees they had seen on the slopes above, providing no protection for the building or its occupants.

Jak and Ricky continued their march toward the shack, pacing around the vast cage of generator capacitors. The snow petered out here, giving them a wide berth where it was unable to settle on the power generators. Even twenty feet from a protective wall, the capacitors emanated incredible warmth, and Jak pulled at his jacket sleeve, feeling the heat burning against it. It was like standing beside a fire.

The two companions traipsed past the field of capacitors, moving toward the low building itself. It was the work of a few moments to locate a door, nuzzled in the shadows of the wall facing the power plant. Jak approached first, the blaster raised high in one hand. He expected trouble, but couldn't say why. An active power plant out in the middle of Alaska like this—it didn't add up.

Ordering Ricky to stay well behind him, Jak placed his free hand gently on the knob and tried the door. This close they could feel the crushing heat from the generators. It burned against them with the ferocity of a forest blaze.

The door opened without force; it had been left unlocked. Jak's lips pulled back in a grimace. He had wanted the door to be locked, the whole building locked, so that he could walk away without investigating it.

With the blaster poised before him, Jak stepped into the building. It seemed bright in here after the overcast twilight outside, a series of fluorescent lights running from one end of the short corridor to the other. The corridor was painted a sort of putrid yellow color, with four square metal plates riveted along the walls at regular spaces, each one running through a gamut of safety procedures in thick, black type. The safety procedures concerned the generator housings, but the detail meant nothing to Jak.

Besides the metal warning plates, the corridor was

bare, just a single box left propped against one wall close to the far end where a door waited. The box was made of cardboard, and its top had been torn away to reveal its contents. Jak paced warily forward and peered within, but the box appeared to be empty now other than a handful of screws, each no longer than Jak's little fingernail.

Jak took another step forward, checking the door at the far end of the abbreviated corridor. The corridor reminded him of an air lock; he'd once been in just a little space between the main building and the generator plant that could be locked when not in use. The door was painted a pinkish red and had a small square window in its center a short way above the handle. The window was made from thick doubled glass and featured the familiar crisscross pattern of black lines where strengthening wire ran through it.

Jak peered through, eyeing the area beyond. It showed another corridor, this one wider with gray walls that featured two colored stripes. The stripes had peeled and faded over time, leaving an eczema-like pattern across the walls where they had once been. Like the first, this corridor appeared empty. Jak tested the door and was unsurprised to find that it, too, was unlocked.

Jak and Ricky hurried down the corridor, checking the rooms that flared from it before making their way into the next corridor. There were signs guiding one to the visitor's desk, inquiries, control center and other esoteric names that meant nothing to either of them. The atmosphere was charged, an unseen energy rippling through the whole complex.

As they turned a corner in the latest of the brightly lit corridors, they came to a manhole set in the floor. The manhole was open, its cover propped against the wall beside it, a key-tool resting there on the floor. Jak halted, peering down into the manhole. There appeared to be a second complex below, lit in muted colors, a red tint washing through what he could see of the space there. A similar set of corridors seemed to run through the subterranean level, but these were more like tunnels, with low ceilings and pipe work running along their walls in thick lines.

As Jak peered into the red-lit space, he heard a noise coming from farther down the corridor, a brutal clanking of metal against metal. Ricky turned at the noise, which was coming from ground level.

Jak looked at him before peering down the corridor. A set of double doors stood there, yellow and black stripes running diagonally across their center. The friends paced toward the doors, their weapons at the ready. A sign on the wall featured arrows and directions: For Operations Center follow Green Stripe.

Ricky looked at the peeling paint on the walls, spotted the stripe of green leading to double doors.

"Operations center," Ricky read in a quiet voice. "Straight ahead."

Once again, the noise came from behind the double doors, a clanging of metal striking metal, loud enough to be heard even through the closed doors. Ricky flinched but Jak remained calm, the blaster held rigidly in his hand.

"Come," Jak whispered, trotting briskly down the gray-walled corridor to the yellow-striped doors.

Close up, they saw that the doors featured two metal handles that stood out like bars. Evidently, the metal had once been wrapped in some kind of rubberized material to insulate it, but it had largely rotted away and in its place blue strips of insulating tape had been wound over and over. The doors were hinged to open either way, like saloon doors. Jak placed one hand on the left handle and pushed. The heavy door swung open without a sound, revealing a well-lit area within.

Jak stepped swiftly through the gap with Ricky following an instant later. Inside, the room was loud with the regular sound of mechanical movements. They stood on a railed catwalk overlooking a vast control area full of machinery and comp systems. Arrayed along three walls in an incomplete square, the machinery glowed with vibrant colors and computer screens flashed with information. A figure stood at the center of the network, wearing a thick radiation suit made of a bright yellow rubberlike fabric. The suit incorporated a wide helmet that sunk down over the shoulders with a view plate in its center and twin filters placed to either side of where the wearer's mouth would be. The suit was linked to the central machine by way of a vast umbilical cord, its flexible metal-link tube running across the floor and then back up into a feeder unit buried snugly amidst the flashing machinery.

For a moment, Jak and Ricky watched as the figure manipulated the dials on several machines, flipping switches and testing the gauges. Beside the figure stood a flat, wheeled cart on which was spread a selection of tools, including a wrench, a hammer and three different sizes of screwdrivers. A toolbox was open on the lower tier of the cart, and the man in the protective suit leaned down to pull something from it. He emerged a moment later with a rivet gun, glancing up through the glassy visor of his headgear to where the two companions stood by the doors of the room.

"You can't come in here," the man in the radiation suit announced. He had a rich voice that, although muffled, carried with ease across the room, despite the chuntering of the machinery.

Warily, Jak walked across the catwalk, toward a feeder ramp that led down into the sunken workstation area. "Where here?" Jak asked in a loud voice.

"Your weapon," the man in the suit replied, indicating the blaster. "You can't have that in here. It's too dangerous. You must put it away."

"Must and will—not same," Jak warned the man, still holding the blaster high. He was standing at the midpoint of the incline now, a line of metal plates that led down to the work area where the figure in the protective suit stood. "Now," Jak repeated, "where here?"

Without warning, the man in the radiation suit thrust his right arm forward as if punching the air. Jak didn't even see what it was he threw, he just felt the object strike him full in the chest, knocking him from his feet. Jak crashed back into the railings that lined the catwalk, and Ricky watched as he flipped over the side in a sprawl of limbs.

Without hesitation, Ricky leaped over the railing after Jak, plummeting straight to the floor of the control room. He lay slumped on the floor, the Colt Anaconda hanging loosely in his right hand. He was unconscious—or worse.

Already the figure in the protective gear was tracking Ricky across the room. The kid glanced up, seeing his own face reflected dully in the plastic faceplate on the man's suit. The yellow man raised his right arm again, sending another pulse across the room. Ricky rolled out of its path, his body spinning across the plastic-coated deck. Behind him, something struck one of the machines and for a moment it seemed to sing as its dials went wild.

Knife in hand, Ricky pounded across the deck toward the mysterious figure, slashing at the air with his stolen blade. The man in the protective suit sidestepped with impossible swiftness, his body shimmering from one position to the next, faster than Ricky's eye could follow.

Sure you're fast, Ricky thought irritably, *but can you outrace a bullet?*

Still low to the floor, Ricky sprung to Jak's side, snatching up the blaster he held limply in his right hand. Ricky raised the weapon without effort, its sleek lines becoming an extension of his hand, the eight-inch barrel an accusing finger.

"Don't move," Ricky ordered, a slight tremor in his voice.

The figure in the radiation suit eyed him through his protective visor, anonymous beneath its dark tint. He was twelve feet away, attached by the metal-link umbilical to the room's machinery. He said nothing, instead waiting for Ricky's next move. He outmatched this intruder ten times over, his experience stretching back further than the kid could even hope to guess.

"Now," Ricky said, catching his breath, "you're going to tell me exactly where we are. Then—"

The figure in the protective suit moved in a blur, knocking Ricky backward into the wall with such speed that he hadn't even seen the move. Ricky sagged down to the deck, bringing the Colt around to fire on his attacker. His head seemed to sing with pain from the impact with the wall.

"No..." Ricky spit, his mouth filling with blood. "You're not going to—"

The figure in the protective suit moved again, limbs blurring, sending another blast into Ricky's chest with the power of a hurricane. The kid was thrown back, his feet giving way under him, his whole body rising off the floor and dancing backward through the air until he struck the wall once more. The blaster fell from his hand and crashed to the deck, followed a moment later by Ricky and the knife. He was no longer moving, no longer conscious.

Satisfied, the figure in the protective radiation suit turned back to his work at the vast complex of machinery that crammed the room. And for just a moment, one of his shadows seemed to flicker.

Chapter Twenty-One

They walked for a time that felt close to an hour, six figures huddled against the cold, the chill wind returning with a vengeance as they got a little closer to the clutch of buildings hidden by the fog. Ryan wondered if this was all a big mistake, but Doc seemed in high spirits, regaling the others with stories of his youth back in the 1800s. Listening to the tales, Ryan and the others were reminded of how much Doc had lost, transported to the Deathlands via a time trawl activated by the cruel whitecoats of the twentieth century, treated with all the dignity of a lab rat. If Doc cared, he refused to dwell on the fact.

As they moved farther through the dead zone, the wind around them began to pick up, howling through the clumps of trees as they trekked past them. There was still a significant distance to go until they reached the first of the buildings. J.B. calculated that the nearest was still an hour's walk away, and that assumed that the weather didn't worsen.

A clutch of trees lay in the road ahead, dead things with black bark and a smattering of moss and snow running across them. One of the trees had fallen across the road itself, forcing the companions to move around and past it. Ryan assessed the route in a moment. To the left, a banked ridge of snow rose eight feet above the road. To the right, a trench had been scooped out where the tree's roots had been yanked free. Just past that, a crevasse cut through the land, its jagged rent twenty feet across.

"Anyone else feel that?" Mildred gasped, clutching Nyarla's arm.

"Quake," J.B. stated.

Around them, the snow rippled and began to tumble from the high-banked slope, bumping down it in a powdery cascade. In a moment it had turned into a full-blown avalanche, bounding down the slope in great gouts of dislodged snow.

"Get moving, people," Ryan shouted, "before we get buried."

They needed no further prompting. Ryan and his companions began running away from the rushing snow as it hurtled down the slope toward them, smothering what was left of the asphalt strip of road in a matter of seconds. All around, the trees shuddered in place and the ground shook as if being struck repeatedly with a giant mallet.

"Keep moving," Ryan commanded. No blaster could fight this enemy. The only chance they had was outdistancing the avalanche before it reached them.

Ryan ran ahead, with Krysty keeping pace with her long-legged stride. A pace or two behind, Doc made swift progress as the snow tumbled down from the slope in a great wave, using his lion's-head swordstick to propel himself over the unstable ground. J.B. kept up with Doc, his shorter legs and lower center of gravity helping him remain upright as the world all around him violently shook from the earthquake. At the rear, Mildred was hurrying Nyarla along. The young woman was cold and exhausted from her journey to this place, and her every step seemed to be a struggle.

"Someone's going to have to carry her, Millie," J.B. said, turning back to join the physician and her charge.

"I can manage," Nyarla insisted, pushing J.B. away. "You don't need to treat me like child."

"I'm not arguing with you, girl," J.B. told her, scooping her up in his arms. "Once we've survived this, then you can bitch at me all you please."

While the teenager may have wanted to argue, her limbs were too exhausted to fight back. She sunk into J.B.'s grasp, lolling there like a ragdoll, her heavy coats making her look more like a bundle of rags than a human.

J.B. trekked on through the snow, keeping his head down as debris from the wave front of the avalanche slapped against his back and licked at his shoulders. Two paces ahead, Mildred turned and saw how close the front of the avalanche was.

"Keep going," Mildred shouted.

"How close is it?" J.B. asked.

Before Mildred could answer, the three of them were swallowed into the earth as the ground crumbled beneath them.

Chapter Twenty-Two

Everything turned white in an instant. J.B. felt something crack against the sole of his shoe and then he was falling, still clinging to Nyarla's body.

"Oh—shit!"

He tumbled downward, feeling as though his stomach was still six feet above him as the ground gave way and his feet cycled for purchase. For a moment there was nothing beneath him. J.B. clung tighter to Nyarla as she screamed in his ear.

A moment later they hit something. J.B. let his knees go limp, springing with the impact as he struck solid ground again. Freezing cold slapped behind him, striking his back and rushing over his head from behind. There was snow in his mouth now, turning to ice water before he could spit it out, so cold it numbed his tongue and made his teeth ache.

"Hang on, girl," J.B. shouted over the sounds of tumbling snow. Automatically, her hands had grabbed around his neck as they began to fall, and he felt her grab tighter.

J.B. let go with one hand, holding Nyarla close to him with the other as he reached out and slapped the ground, trying desperately to slow their descent.

Then they struck something hard, solid unforgiving ground, struck it with such force that J.B. swore that he felt his brain jar against his skull.

"WHERE THE FUCK did they go?" Ryan asked irritably.

He was standing with Krysty and Doc amid the swirling aftermath of the avalanche. Great swathes of powdery snow hung in the air like dust, obscuring everything beyond a few feet like a raging sandstorm in white.

"I can't see them," Krysty said. "Should we go back?"

Ryan looked uncertain. The earth was no longer in the grip of the quake. The avalanche had petered out. The worst of the damage was done, leaving a whole new mess of snow where the companions had stood just moments before. Disturbed snow swirled through the air on the harsh wind, churning over and over like flour in water, swilling in space. He took a wary step into the cloud of settling snow and felt his foot slip as the ground fell away.

"Ryan, are you—?" Krysty began as Ryan leaped backward.

"Ground's gone," he replied.

The mists parted and for the first time Krysty and Doc saw what Ryan had almost stepped into. A great chasm cut across the ground where they had walked just minutes before, sweeping out beyond them like a gaping mouth. The chasm stretched as far as they could see, its width almost a half mile across and dropping to a depth of hundreds of feet. The walls of the chasm showed gray rock and already the snow was settling there, burying them beneath its white blanket.

"By the Three Kennedys!" Doc snapped. "J.B., Mildred and Nyarla… They must be…"

Ryan nodded, his lone eye fixed on the chasm that had appeared in the ground.

EVERYTHING TURNED black for an instant. J.B. lay on the ground, his body hunkered over Nyarla as loosened snow tumbled all around them. He had lost consciousness, and awakened to her still screaming right up against his ear.

"Shut up, will you?" J.B. said, the words coming out slurred.

Beneath him, Nyarla continued to shriek in Russian, peppering the words with what sounded a lot like curses. "You're lying on my leg, you're lying on my leg," she screeched.

J.B. pushed himself up, felt the wave of nausea run over him and instantly regretted the move. No matter. He forced himself up as the last of the compact snow dotted the ground around them like debris from a meteor shower. "Are you all right?" he asked, wiping a snowy drool from his lips.

Nyarla had lost her scarf and she was breathing heavily, the breath pluming before her in great white clouds. "*Da*—yes, I am…aches and needles."

J.B. looked past her, scanning the territory they had landed in. "Nothing broken?" he asked absently. "Can you walk?"

They appeared to be in a valley, characterless thanks in part to the new tumult of loosened snow. J.B. looked overhead, using one hand to shield his eyes from the tumbling snow. They had come down a long way; it had to be 150 feet to the summit. Thank goodness snow's soft, J.B. thought, though not so damn soft he wouldn't have bruises in the morning.

Beside him, Nyarla had pushed herself to a standing position and was brushing snow from her clothing, clapping her hands together. "I stand, I walk," she told J.B. "I'm alive. You're alive."

The Armorer was still scanning the area. "Where's Ryan?" he muttered. A moment later he repeated the question, louder this time, letting his voice carry around the chasm.

"J.B.?" It was Mildred's voice, muffled but close by.

"Millie?" J.B. called. "I can hear you but I can't see you. Where are you?"

"J.B.? Is that you?" Her voice was still muffled.

"Yeah, it's me," J.B. confirmed. "Where are you?"

There was a pause and J.B. wondered if Mildred had heard him. For a brief moment, irrationally, he wondered if she was dead.

"It's dark," Mildred's voice answered. "I can't see anything. And it's cold. Real cold."

"Yeah," J.B. said irritably, "cold. That narrows it down." Then, in a louder voice he called Mildred's name again. "Keep talking," he told her when she had answered. "I'll pinpoint you by your voice."

J.B. and Nyarla listened to Mildred as she sang an old nonsense song, something about a red-nosed reindeer that J.B. could only assume was some mutie critter Mildred had once known in her own time. It took thirty seconds to figure out that the singing was coming from a little way downslope and, once they reached it, from below their feet. J.B. began digging and Nyarla kneeled and helped.

It took precious seconds to locate Mildred, buried beneath the snow. She had fallen with the cave-in, become buried by the falling snow. J.B. felt relief when he touched her hand, putting a sudden end to her song.

"You got a good singing voice," J.B. told her as he

scooped more snow from her body. "Don't stop on my account."

J.B. listened to Mildred's voice as he pulled the loose snow from around her buried body.

"J.B.?" Doc CALLED. "Mildred? You down there?" He stood at the misty edge of the new-formed chasm, leaning on his swordstick as he stared into the abyss.

Beside him, Ryan had unstrapped his Steyr longblaster from his back and was using the scope to peer down into the yawning gap, searching for his friends. Loose snow was still toppling down the walls of the chasm, and there was so much mist it was hard to make out much of anything. For a moment Ryan thought he saw J.B. and Mildred. He halted the scope on the figures only to see them wink out of sight behind a smudge of falling snow. "They have to be down there," Ryan said. "There's nowhere else for them to go."

"Ryan, look!" Krysty blurted in shock.

Pulling the scope from his eye, Ryan turned to where she indicated. She was pointing to the place where they had just run from. There, trudging through the mist came three familiar figures—but it wasn't J.B.'s party, it was themselves.

"What in the name of heaven…?" Doc whispered.

MILDRED EMERGED from the snow shivering like a leaf in the wind. She had been buried for about five minutes, but it was enough to send her core temperature plummeting. "I—I n-n-need t-t-to g-get-g-get w-w-warm," she told J.B.

J.B. had weapons and fire-lighting equipment, but there was nothing to blow up and nothing to set light to. So instead he leaned against Mildred, pulling her close and wrapping her coat around her while she hugged herself, trying to warm up. After a moment, Nyarla leaned close, wrapping her arms around the woman, too.

"I used to do this to keep my little sister Elya warm when the nights were too cold," she said. "We would share a bed on those nights and tell each other stories along with my brother Evan. He always told best stories."

After a while, Mildred stopped trembling so violently.

"No use us staying here," he said. "Ryan won't be able to follow us. The ground's sheared away like someone took a knife to it. We need to keep moving, find a way back up top to where Ryan and the others are. Or find some shelter and get warmed up. Whichever we find first."

Mildred nodded, her teeth still chattering. "Agreed."

RYAN, KRYSTY AND Doc watched in stunned silence as the three eerily familiar figures rushed toward them from the swirling mists. The figures were Ryan, Krysty and Doc, running for their very lives as the tumult of the avalanche caromed after them. Behind them, three more figures could be seen—Mildred and J.B. with the latter carrying Nyarla in his arms.

Ryan reached out, calling to his friends. But even as he did so, the ground beneath J.B. seemed to shudder and then it fell away. J.B., Mildred and their charge disappeared amid a cascade of collapsing snow.

"What are we watching?" Ryan snarled as the flickering images of himself, Krysty and Doc came running ahead, now just a few steps away.

"The past," Doc decided firmly, his eyes narrowed as the ghost of his past self came running by.

"That's impossible," Ryan growled, looking around for some projector or other similar equipment. It had to be a trick. Had to be.

"Something has been happening ever since we left that redoubt," Doc insisted. "I have felt it even if none of the rest of you have."

"I felt it, too," Krysty admitted, stepping between the two men. Behind her, the other figures of Ryan, Doc and Krysty faded to nothingness. "Gaia is unsettled here, as if something has poisoned the Earth, something integral. I can't explain it."

"Nyarla said that time was broken here," Doc said with deliberation. "Many years ago I was a young man with a wife and children. The calendar on the wall told me it was 1896. I came through a hole in time's flow to be here, was dragged against my will and shunted from one era to another. Twice over, in fact. Time is a far more fragile commodity than we credit. To see this place with its time echoes and its broken weather patterns makes me suspect that something is pulling time contrariwise, a direction it was never meant to go."

Ryan looked from the old man to Krysty, his beautiful lover. "Krysty?" he encouraged.

"I understand what Doc is saying," she said slowly. "I feel it differently, my connection to the Earth—to Gaia—is so intuitive it's hard to put it into words. But I believe that Doc is right, that something is corrupting the laws that govern the world."

Ryan nodded. "Then we should go find out what it is—and stop it before this Ink Orchard place expands further."

Together, the three companions made their way from the edge of the chasm. They could come back for J.B.

and the others if they succeeded. And if they didn't, then no one was coming back for anything—ever.

MACHINERY RATTLED all about him as Don Nectar stood in the control area. Two free-standing cylinders reached toward the ceiling with prongs atop them like tuning forks. The prongs were glowing now as the energies flitted through them, drawing more and more power from the generators that fed the building. The two intruders hadn't stopped that, hadn't even slowed him.

Overhead the lights dimmed. Within his radiation suit, Nectar watched as the power needles flickered back and forth, trying to register the swiftly changing currents as the time window charged. This place had been built to accommodate this process, he knew, but it still rattled uncomfortably when he sent full power through the channeling rods that opened the chrono window. There was a leak somewhere, had been so for as long as Nectar could remember. He had tried doing this all before. Tried and failed.

Was that yesterday?

Had he been married then?

Between the towering cylinders, the coalescing chronal energies began to take shape once more, opening a doorway into the past.

To one side of the room, Jak and Ricky shook against the wall where they had been tied to keep them out of the way. Neither of them awakened as the wanton energies of time exploded from the chronal doorway and danced through the room. And Don Nectar, in his radiation suit, watched impassively, his face hidden behind the dark glass of the suit. He could feel it deep down, the sense that one part of the equation was still missing, one final piece of the puzzle that yet needed to be slotted into place.

But that puzzle piece was close now, closer than it had ever been before. The time-lost traveler was nearly here. Once he arrived, the window into the past could be stabilized and Don Nectar could finally travel home to his wife and children, a whole man again.

Chapter Twenty-Three

The wind was howling. Snow was swirling through the air, clogging their view. Mildred, J.B. and Nyarla had been walking a long time in the cold. They didn't know how long. Perhaps appropriately, they had lost track of time. The sun had sunk, giving up on what little effort it had made to rise, leaving the whole terrain in a sort of bleak grayness, as if filtered through old film stock that had been left too long to develop, its colors expired. The cold was biting at them, too, like a living thing that kept trying to take chunks out of their faces.

At first they had been speaking, buoying one another's spirits with anecdotes and jokes, remembrances of shared times in days gone. Nyarla had been more dour, of course, worried about her father and sister, about how anyone could survive in this deranged plot of real estate. But the cold worked its magic on them all after a while, freezing the conversations before they could take hold, turning them into unstructured sentences spit from broken keyboards.

In silence then, they moved on, mutually agreeing that they would keep going, stay in one direction with J.B. taking the lead. There was no way to reach Ryan's group. The quake had drawn such a valley behind them that they would never be able to climb it. Instead they followed the incline of the newly formed valley, work-

ing their way up toward what they perceived as ground
level, miles from where they had begun.

The weather became worse and icy mist washed over
them in clouds, each one cold enough to make one's
bones ache.

The Armorer hunkered down, trudging forward, one
foot after the other, looking up only occasionally to see
where they were headed. The snow clung to the shoulders and sleeves of his jacket, webbed across his boots
and the cuffs of his pants. The cold bit at his face.

There was something wrong about the way the snow
fell. It seemed abrupt. Yet when Mildred watched it, it
fell languidly, as if it had all the time in the world—as if
it knew that she was on to it, that it was being watched.
It was disquieting somehow.

How long they walked, none of them could say. The
cold made it seem like an eternity, one without a start.
It felt as if they had been walking forever, clock hands
returning to twelve-noon, twelve-midnight, caught on
the endless rotation of the clock's face.

The landscape was simply snow with trees. Some
of the snow was patchy and thin, showing the frozen
ground that hid cowering beneath it. In other places it
reached up almost to their knees, making them wetter
and colder without respite. They knew they needed to
find shelter, someplace to warm up, and find it soon.

"Makes no sense," J.B. said through chattering teeth.

"What doesn't?" Mildred prompted. It had been so
long since she had spoken that her mouth ached from
the cold air as she opened it.

"Snow falls thick then thin," J.B. said as he kicked
through another clump of the frozen white carpet. "Yet
snow falls evenly. We know it does."

"Maybe it's what it's landing on that's making the

differences," Mildred said. "Different rates of melting, like the way snow settles on grass before it settles on stone."

J.B. shook his head, unconvinced. "Weather like this." He sighed. "It's not natural, Millie. I tell you it isn't."

The snow continued to swirl around them, catching in the howling winds. Without warning, J.B. stopped. He stopped so abruptly that Mildred almost walked into him while Nyarla just seemed to flag and halt, the collar of her coat frozen stiff in an upright position by her ears.

"What is it?" Mildred asked, doing nothing to hide the irritation in her tone.

J.B. pointed, and through the swirling miasma of snow Mildred saw the dark shape that clung to the horizon like a snail shell on a garden path. It was a building, boxy in shape, and even at this distance it was unquestionably man-made, its straight lines and incongruousness in the landscape a tribute to man's battle against the elements.

The building sat in the middle of the wastes, a dark box on the blank horizon. J.B. looked at it, looked at Mildred, then looked back to the building. More buildings were materializing behind it, peeking shyly through the billowing snow like a bride though her veil.

The snow was swirling in the air, stabbing at their skin like a handful of tossed quills. It didn't feel like snow, it felt harder than that, more like ice in the air. Its patterns were visible if you took the time to stop and watch, the flecks of snow falling too slow here for the drag of gravity, then too fast there, as if a speeded-up recording on an old video cassette.

"Weather's shot," J.B. said, his eyes fixed on the

building up ahead. "We need to get inside, warm ourselves up. Warm up you—the girl, too."

"I don't know, J.B.," Mildred disagreed. "This place
doesn't feel right."

J.B. looked at Mildred then, his mouth a grim line.
"If we stay out here much longer, we're going to freeze
to death. We're no use to Ryan dead. And even if we
survive, Nyarla there is just skin and bones—she's prac-
tically an ice block even now." He didn't say what he
was really thinking—that Mildred had been under the
snow long enough to get hypothermia before any of
them. She'd turn down his concern, he knew, try to
bullshit him with medical speak. She wasn't thinking
straight out here; maybe none of them were.

Reluctantly, Mildred agreed, nodding. She couldn't
let Nyarla die. They trekked across the ice-flecked path
to the low buildings.

The nearest building looked to be just one story, but
as they neared it they saw that it had two floors, but
they had become buried in the piling snow. The exterior walls were painted a drab olive color, with stenciled yellow lettering at the doorway that indicated it
had been constructed for military use. J.B. reached into
his jacket, placing his hand on the butt of his mini-Uzi.

"Army hole," J.B. said.

Beside him, Mildred nodded and plucked the ZKR
551 from where it was holstered at her hip. Behind her,
Nyarla cowered in the lee of the building, keeping out of
the biting wind. She didn't offer to pull her own blaster
out; she was simply too cold to do that now.

"Still feels wrong," Mildred muttered.

"It's dry," the Armorer replied. "That's enough for
me."

There were other buildings close by, a little cluster

of them meeting in a junction. The mess hall was the nearest, but the others were just a little way from them now, appearing and disappearing through the flickering snow.

All around them, the snow seemed to billow then wait, billow then wait. For a moment, Mildred could have sworn she saw it stop dead in the air, held there as if in a photograph; a frozen image of frozen water. She almost laughed at that, despite the way it worried her. Natural reaction, laughing at what scares us, Mildred reminded herself. Maybe J.B. was right, maybe she was delirious.

The building had a curved roof with a corrugated pattern across it, and it stretched back sixty feet. Wide-spaced windows ran along its sides, but the ones they could see had blinds drawn over them, likely to keep the heat in. Behind the building, J.B. eyed the other buildings, dotted around a central hub, materializing through the falling snow like a stalker's shadow.

J.B. stopped at the doors, reading the words that had been stenciled there. "Mess hall," he read aloud. The name was followed by a serial number that he figured meant nothing to anyone not a part of the army base.

After checking a few of the windows, Mildred hurried back to where J.B. waited at the main set of doors with Nyarla. Once she was within hearing range, she raised a concern in a quiet voice. "Are you sure this is a good idea, J.B.? Can't see shit inside and it's awful quiet. Gives me the heebie-jeebies."

"Me, too," J.B. agreed, "like snakes running up and down my spine. But the weather out here is seriously harsh. I haven't ever seen its like. And I've seen toxic rains that could strip a man to his bones quicker than a stream full of hungry mutie fish."

Nyarla balked at that, her eyes going wide.

"It's okay, sweetheart," Mildred reassured. "That's not going to happen out here."

Then Mildred turned to look behind her, eyeing the falling snow and the way it seemed to stutter and stop in the air for a moment every few seconds. J.B. was right—there was something seriously wrong with this place. "Guess we won't find out anything out here," she agreed after a moment's consideration.

J.B. nodded, pleased. "That's my girl."

He pressed his hand to the doorknob and pushed. It took a moment—the ice had frozen to the edges of the door—and J.B. had to shove against it to break the light film of ice that had sealed it in place.

"One thing's for sure," J.B. said. "No one's been in or out of here in a while. Guess we take what comfort we can from that."

Comfort, perhaps, but J.B. still entered the building with the Uzi extended in a ready grip before him.

Inside, the building was dark, and it took the companions a moment for their eyes to adjust. The place smelled of burning dust. The smell wasn't coming from anywhere in particular, as far as J.B. could tell—it simply *was,* the smell all around them, the smell of the air. They were standing in a lobby, just an anteroom that held a desk and an area presumably for storing coats and bags. The area was empty and J.B., Mildred and Nyarla stepped inside, kicking snow and ice from their boot treads as Mildred pushed the door closed. It was warmer maybe than outside—they were too numb to really say right then—but still cool enough that they could see their breath in the air.

J.B. crept forward, his movements appreciably silent. Mildred aimed the blaster over J.B.'s right shoulder as he prowled into the next room. This room was larger, taking over maybe two-thirds of the floor space. Canvas shutters had been pulled down over the windows, he saw now, but from inside enough light peeked around their edges that J.B. could see in the gloom. Long tables were arrayed in rows that stretched four tables to the length of the room, and three across; twelve in all. There were seventy, eighty, maybe a hundred soldiers sitting at the tables, poised over their food trays, cutlery in hand.

RYAN, KRYSTY AND Doc traveled across the white blanket of snow for several miles, leaving a trail of footprints that slowly filled in with fresh snow. It was bitterly cold and they couldn't help wondering about J.B. and the others, whether they were doing the right thing to leave them in the crevasse.

Early on, Ryan made a decision to find the highest ground. Perhaps from there they would be able to see what was going on here, and maybe get a better idea of how to stop it. He led them up a slope where no path existed other than the one Ryan made with his footsteps. It was slow, laborious walking, but over time they found themselves high enough to get a clearer idea of *His Ink Orchard*.

With the sun—what little they had seen of it—dipped below the horizon, the world was turned into a pale blue blanket of moonlit snow. The moon looked cold, a silver coin flicked into the air in some cosmic heads-or-tails wager.

There was something else, too, visible even through the falling snow. "Look," Ryan said, pointing to the thing his keen eye had spotted.

In the distance, all but masked by the falling snow,

a lightning storm seemed to be in progress. But as they watched, Doc and Krysty realized that there was something odd about the storm.

"The lightning is traveling upward," Doc said. "Which means it is being launched by something on the ground."

"Exactly," Ryan confirmed. "And I figure if we locate the source, we'll be a step closer to figuring out just what the hell it is we've walked into here."

Agreed, the group moved onward, pacing slowly down the slope as the wind whipped all around them, heading toward a wide, icy river that could be seen in the far distance wending its course through the land.

J.B. GASPED before he could stop himself, halting in place with the Uzi ready. The air, the smell, the dust; J.B. didn't like it.

Inside the dining hall, no one moved. For a moment, J.B. stood there, watching the diners as they sat poised over their meals. Like the anteroom, the mess hall had that same distinctive smell of burning dust, the dead smell of dried-up insects left on sunny windowsills.

J.B. paced warily into the room. The diners were all soldiers, dressed in olive drab fatigues with peaked, soft caps on their heads. But there was something strange about them, J.B. realized as he walked up to the first table in the half light filtering through the shuttered windows. They were all in various stages of decomposition, like corpses torn from the ground. And whatever had once been served on their trays, the meals had turned to dust, grease spots and dried residue all that remained.

J.B. stared at the occupants of the nearest table for a few seconds, trying to figure out what had happened.

Could a weapon do this? The result of the Megachill, mebbe?

"J.B.?" Mildred called from the antechamber of the mess hall, where she stood with Nyarla. "Everything okay in there?"

J.B. swivelled his head back to address Mildred. "It's fine—" He stopped himself. From the corner of his eye, one of the figures at the closest table had moved. J.B. was sure of it.

As he turned back, the diners began to rise, each one a desiccated corpse coming horrifically to life.

Chapter Twenty-Four

"Run!" J.B. shouted, scampering back from the nearest table.

At the lobby entrance, Mildred watched J.B. race across the room, shadowy figures rising from their seats behind him.

"Wh-what are they?" Nyarla asked, peering into the gloom.

Mildred saw J.B. spin back, bringing up the mini-Uzi and unleashing a rapid burst of blastfire at the nearest figure. "Nothing good," she assured Nyarla, bringing up her own weapon to target another soldier-corpse.

Within the vast mess hall, J.B. watched as the lead corpse crumbled to the ground, his face a wound of dried flesh cut to ribbons by 9 mm slugs from the Uzi. The next corpse was moving across the room at a frightening clip, bringing up rotted, talonlike hands to reach for J.B.'s face. The Armorer swung his compact weapon around on its strap, sent a burst of fire into the dead thing's belly.

How the hell they were alive, he couldn't even begin to guess. What J.B. did know, however, was that they sensed him as an enemy, and whatever they planned to do once they caught him he'd bet shells to sand was nothing he'd appreciate.

There were ninety dead figures standing in the room, and they were surrounding J.B. in a swift pattern. The

Armorer looked from one to the next, seeing their ruined faces, white eyes sunken deep into deteriorated sockets. Even as he watched, the first figure he had shot drew itself back up from the floor, rising in a wavering, unsteady fashion on rotted legs.

The dead soldiers swarmed at J.B., leaving him no time to pick targets. He sent another burst of bullets in a low arc, cutting the animated corpses at chest level, commanding Mildred to duck even as he squeezed the trigger.

At the lobby doorway, Mildred targeted one of the rear-most corpses and sent a flat-tipped wad-cutter bullet into the back of its head. It impacted with the corpse's skull in a spreading circle of debris, sending shards of bone and leathery flesh across the room.

Mildred ducked back as J.B. brought his own attack around in a rapid arc, cutting down the corpses in powdery bursts of dead skin and flesh. Behind her, Nyarla crouched against the farthest wall, her hands cupped over her ears to drown out the cacophony of flying bullets.

They weren't zombies, J.B. realized as he sidestepped the reaching arms of one of the soldiers. They were dead things, pure and simple—people who hadn't realized that they were dead yet, who remained obstinately animated despite their senses and their consciousness having long since rotted away.

He kneed the nearest soldier in the gut, driving his leg up with such force that the figure in the olive fatigues jumped up off the floor.

They had to have died here, J.B. knew. When time began going askew, these poor bastards had either been caught in the time bubble or drawn up into it from whatever era that they had started at, trapped in static place as time held them in its unforgiving grip, squeezing the life out of them as they struggled to resist.

Whatever had triggered them to move now, J.B. couldn't guess. If the snow outside was any indication, time was running in fits and starts, moving forward like a stuttering wag engine with dirt in the fuel line.

Why it hadn't affected himself, Mildred and Nyarla was anyone's guess. Maybe things from outside the bubble of broken time weren't affected in the same way. Or maybe they were and they just couldn't see it because their perception was so altered by the rogue chronal energies that surrounded the area.

One thing J.B. did know was that he had to get out of there before they were all killed.

He drove the Uzi into the next corpse as it reached for him, drilling the weapon's muzzle into the dead man's gut and pulling the trigger. Dried chunks of intestines burst loose from the dead soldier's back, spraying across its colleagues with a sound like rocks striking glass. Now gutless, the soldier's corpse sagged in on itself, its torso lurching to the left and down as it keeled to the floor.

J.B. turned away from it, batting away the grasping hand of another corpse, sending a short burst of fire at another attacker. As he did so he spotted Mildred and Nyarla still crouched in the lobby. "Move," J.B. shouted. "Get her out of here."

Mildred glanced back at the door. J.B. was right—they had promised to protect the young woman. But Mildred was reluctant to leave J.B. behind.

"No way. We're doing this together, cowboy," Mildred shouted as she darted into the room, her Czech-made ZKR 551 pistol spitting bullets at the deathly soldiers.

J.B. had no time to react. He was already disappearing beneath a mob of long-dead people.

SYMON TURNED to Piotr and the others in the hovel they shared. "I heard a blaster," he said.

Outside, the chronovores had dissipated, leaving a great chasm where they had eaten displaced chronal energy from the very atmosphere.

"I heard it, too," Marla said. She was playing solitaire with a deck of cards, teaching the simple game to Symon's daughter.

Piotr grabbed his climbing gear, cinching the rope around his middle and looping it over his shoulder while Graz checked their blasters. "We'll check it out," he said. "You stay here, where it's safe."

"No." Symon shook his head. "My other daughter could be out there. She would follow us if she could."

Piotr nodded. "Then pray she is not the one being shot at."

RYAN, KRYSTY AND Doc continued downslope toward the icy river and the distant lightning storm. The snow was falling in spots, swimming through the air like a shoal of fish.

As they descended the gentle slope, Krysty's foot snagged on something and she dropped to her knees.

"Krysty?" Ryan asked, turning back.

"I'm okay," Krysty began. "I must have—"

But when she looked back, Krysty saw something reaching through the ground, grasping for her foot where she kneeled. Snow fell from the creature's limbs as it emerged from the icy soil—its twin arms a hideous blue like a long-dead corpse.

"Get back," Ryan shouted, whipping his SIG-Sauer

blaster from its holster in an instant. Beside him, Doc was reaching for his own weapon.

Krysty scrambled across the snow on hands and knees, urging herself out of the path of the grasping thing. Ryan stepped forward, bringing his weapon to bear as the thing emerged from the ground, its head and chest following the hands in a tumble of caked snow. It looked human—or at least semihuman—naked with bloated blue skin. Utterly hairless, the creature had wide-set, bloodshot eyes in a flat face. From a pace away, Ryan stroked the SIG-Sauer's trigger, sending a single Parabellum bullet through the thing's forehead, right between those blood-red eyes.

Caught in the tunnel it had channeled through the snow, the creature just swayed in place, its head lolling on its shoulders, a single black hole marking the kill shot.

Ryan didn't know what it was; it reminded him mostly of corpses left too long above the ground.

"Looks rather like it was already dead," Doc said helpfully.

Ryan nodded. "Dead but alive," he said. "Whatever's going on here, it's—"

"Beyond reasoning?" Doc suggested as Krysty wiped the snow from her clothes.

Ryan nodded his agreement. "Let's keep moving. And keep our eyes open. There could be more of these things under the surface."

There were. As the companions jogged down the slope, the ground beneath them burst open and another blue-gray figure emerged, followed by another. A whole community of the molelike things appeared drawn by the movement above their home.

Ryan watched as another creature burst from the

ground a dozen yards ahead of them like some demented jack-in-the-box, snow falling from its naked body. Without slowing, Ryan aimed and fired, shooting the thing on the run. Beside him, Krysty and Doc were picking off the creatures even as they emerged, the crack of their gunshots echoing across the snowy ground.

IN THE MESS HALL, Mildred scrambled across a table and dived toward the scrum that had descended on J.B. Her blaster fired shot after shot, each bullet taking chunks out of the skulls of the nearest corpses. One corpse turned as Mildred's latest bullet ripped a wound across the left-hand half of its skull, peering at her with its remaining sunken white eyeball, its lips peeled back in a sneer.

Mildred squeezed the trigger again, sending another bullet into the dead thing's face, leaving little more than a stump of neck and a jawbone in its wake. The man-thing toppled back, doing a spastic death dance as it crashed into a table. Plates and cutlery careened from the table, spilling their dried-up contents to the floor in a clatter.

The animated corpses were beginning to react to Mildred's presence now, a whole gaggle of them turning to face her, striding down the aisles between the tables, knocking chairs over in their wake.

"Okay," Mildred told herself as she pumped the trigger of the ZKR, "bad move."

A moment later, like J.B. before her, Mildred felt herself fall beneath the weight of the animated corpses.

Nyarla watched helplessly as Mildred and J.B. disappeared beneath the mob of living death. She had a blaster on her and a knife but she knew it wouldn't be enough, knew there was no sense in getting herself chilled, too.

She turned, shoved the freezing door open and stepped back out into the falling snow. Wasn't that what Mildred had told her to do?

THE SNOW-COVERED slope was coming apart as more of the blue-skinned figures emerged from their hiding places beneath the ground. Ryan, Krysty and Doc kept running, their legs pumping as they hurried down the slope at breakneck speed. Up ahead, Ryan saw another blue-fleshed hand reaching up through a parting in the snow and he leapt over it, shouting out an alert to the others.

Behind Ryan, Krysty swerved to avoid the reaching hand while Doc ran straight for it, driving the end of his swordstick down into the wriggling fingers. Something cried beneath the snow and the hand went limp.

Doc ran on, hurrying after his two companions. They were already obscured by the falling snow and mists that clouded the area. Doc stepped up his pace.

Up ahead, Ryan came to an abrupt halt as his ankles caught against something, sending him head over heels before crashing down hard in the snow. A few paces behind him, Krysty slowed, looking for what it was that had tripped her lover. As she did so, she heard the whiz of displaced air and something cinched around her neck—a bolo, two weights at opposite ends of a cord. She, too, went down in a tumble of limbs, the .38 Smith & Wesson spiraling out of her grasp.

"Doc?" Ryan called, pushing himself up from where he was sprawled on the ground. A thin white wire had been stretched taut between two tree stumps, he saw now, wide-spaced and perfectly camouflaged in the snow. It was this that had tripped him and sent him flying, a trap that could have been left weeks before by the hibernating blue things.

He turned, calling again for Doc. As he did so he saw the figures emerging from the curtain of falling snow, five in total, each with the blue flesh of a frozen corpse. Some wore loincloths and had carved tattoos across their flesh, bloodshot eyes peering from their ugly, hairless faces. They were some version of human, Ryan saw, but had become so far removed from humanity that they were barely recognizable. Muties.

Ryan raised his blaster, but as he did so a sixth figure appeared, blue-fleshed like the others...and this one held Doc in a death grip, a curved blade held against the old man's throat.

"I am sorry, Ryan," Doc gasped. "They came at me from all sides at once."

Chapter Twenty-Five

Nyarla had taken only a few steps from the mess hall when she spotted the figures moving toward her. There were five of them trekking across the snow, bundled up in material and furs, each one wielding a firearm. Snow fell all about them, billowing in the icy wind.

"We heard blasterfire," the lead figure called. His voice was heavily accented, like Nyarla's own.

"My friends—" she said breathlessly. "We were trying to shelter from the storm and—"

"Nyarla?" another of the figures called. "You made it?"

"Papa?" Nyarla asked timidly. Her gaze swept across the mismatched group, searching for a familiar face. They were so bundled up it was hard to even tell who had spoken.

One of the well-wrapped figures hurried the last few paces in the snow, rushing to take Nyarla in his arms. A shorter figure traipsed through the snow beside him, and Nyarla realized it was her sister Tarelya.

"You're alive," Symon Vrack cried. "My goodness, child—you made it!"

Nyarla looked from her father to the others. They had halted at the lip of the slope that led down to the mess hall doors.

"You must help my friends," Nyarla hastily explained. "We tried to shelter, but there were dead people inside and they came back to life. My friends are still in there."

"Wakers," Graz said, spitting the word out like a curse.

Piotr and his allies didn't hesitate. They scrambled down the slope and through the doors of the mess hall. They slammed open the doors and surveyed the scene within.

Over forty figures in drab olive uniforms were piling around the center of the mess hall amid the strewed remains of tables and chairs. Mildred and J.B. struggled beneath them, but it was like swimming against a strong tide—for each corpse they shifted another took its place.

Piotr, Graz and Marla charged into the room, pulling a rope from the possessions they wore strapped about their thick clothing. "Surround and drag them," Piotr instructed. "Swift as air now."

Graz had one end of the rope and he whipped it over the heads of three moving corpses from behind. The corpses seemed only now to become aware of the newcomers and they turned to face Graz and the others. With Piotr securing the far end of the rope, Graz yanked the other, snapping the rope like a whip and dropping the three corpses to the floor. Nearby, Marla was using her own climbing gear to similar effect.

From somewhere amid the pile of moving figures a blaster rang out, its death song echoing around the mess hall. A second later, J.B. was standing, gasping as corpses were dragged away by Piotr and his team. "Need air," he muttered. "Need to breathe."

Mildred emerged a moment later as more of the corpses were snagged by the ropes and drawn away.

"You people alive? Need help, yeah?" Piotr called across the room.

J.B. nodded. Now just who the hell was this guy? he thought.

"Get to the doors," Piotr commanded. "Run and don't look back. We'll hold them off until you're safe."

"You need help?" J.B. asked as he sent another burst of semiauto fire into his nearest opponents.

"We have this one, friend," Piotr told him. "Go. Git."

Living corpses plunging to the floor all about them, J.B. and Mildred ran for the doors.

"THERE WAS NOTHING I could do," Doc explained. Along with Ryan and Krysty, he had been disarmed and taken to one of the tumbledown buildings down the slope, close to the river where great chunks of ice shuddered on the current.

Standing next to him, Ryan shook his head once in understanding. "Ambushed twice in almost as many days," he stated. "We're getting soft."

"No, we're tired," Krysty said, correcting Ryan's assumption. "We've been running too long."

The three companions were marched under armed guard into the main room of a vast old church dating back to predark times. The church was simple inside, with wooden walls and a large stained-glass window showing an abstract, modernist design. The design was of a large white circle like the sun, around which someone had carved numerals, like the numbers on a clock dial. Close up, the window appeared to have been patched together from two or more. There had been other windows once, but they were now covered with metal sheeting. Ryan and his companions eyed the sheeting and the remaining window warily, alert for possible exits. There were several doors, including the main one—a double door—through which they had entered.

The walls of the church dripped clear water and when the companions looked overhead they saw stalactites had formed in the rafters, great pointing struts like sharks' teeth aimed down toward the church's congregation. The air felt sullen with the cold, each breath expelled in a great plume of misty water vapor.

The blue-fleshed muties who had captured them had been joined by a dozen or so more figures, and all of them went shuffling to their places in the pews while Ryan, Doc and Krysty were led to the front of the church. Two figures stood behind the companions, brutal-looking knives in their blue hands, their bare flesh looking like something that had died too soon. The companions' own weaponry had been laid out across the church font at the rear of the room, like some strange offering to the gods of war.

The captives were made to wait in silence until a figure wearing a hooded white robe emerged from one of the side doors. Beneath the robe he had pale skin like the others, but his flesh was more of a gray-white than the dramatic blue that so many of the congregation sported.

"You are honored, brothers and sister," the hooded figure said as he strode up the steps toward Ryan and his companions. His voice was accented with a lisp that made him hiss like a snake. "You have come at the ideal time."

"Do tell," Ryan growled in a tone dripping with sarcasm.

The robed figure pushed back his hood to reveal a pale, bald head carved with intricate designs that turned his features into those of the dial of an old-fashioned timepiece, his eyes become the three and nine of the clock's face. Though his skin was whiter than the others', his eyes displayed that same red-ringed ferocity, as if he had been in the cold for too long. "Time is loose here," the man explained, "freed from the bonds of Swiss precision, left to idle its own path.

"Once time tamed man," the pale figure continued, addressing his eager congregation, "but now we have been freed from its cloying grip. We, the clockwatchers, shall instead tame time."

At the front of the church, Krysty leaned over and whispered to Doc and Ryan, "What the hell is he talking about?"

"Beats me," Ryan admitted, "but he wouldn't be the first whacko we've had to chill."

"Once, time followed a straight path," the minister continued, "circling the same points of sunrise and sunset. But after the great change, once End Day came, we were left to shape time in new ways. With our mastery shall come dominion of all of history—past, present and future. We need only become one with the chronal energies in flux, imbibe them and so become beings who sit outside time's stream."

The congregation was warming to its leader's words. They were the only things that were warming in the great church space—the minister's breath could be seen clouding the air with every word, and slowly melting ice dripped like some awful rhythm section to his speech.

"But the chronovores amass to consume our bounty," the minister cried, "and their numbers double at every turn. The crows must be appeased."

The congregation took up this chant, cheering and

applauding. "Appease the crows! Appease the crows!" they howled.

Ryan spoke to Krysty from the corner of his mouth. "I'm not liking where this is going."

"I'm guessing this is the part where we get sacrificed," Krysty replied.

Four more blue-fleshed muties strode through the same side door where the minister had appeared, balancing a large cage between them. The boxy cage had wire mesh sides and was obviously used to contain an animal. Something was moving inside, bashing against the cage walls with such fury that the bearers were having trouble keeping it upright.

The minister turned back to the three figures on stage, a wicked glint in his eye. "You shall be fed to the chronovores," he commanded, "and in the aftermath we shall absorb their expulsions and become time's arrows, the promised children of Old Father Time."

Ryan gave Krysty a sideways look.

"Nailed it," she told him.

PIOTR AND HIS ALLIES had locked the mess hall doors. "They won't follow," Marla explained. "The force that animates them won't reach far enough."

J.B. accepted that on faith. These people seemed competent and experienced, and they had dealt with the creatures swiftly and decisively. It seemed the trick was not to try to kill them—how did a person kill the dead, anyway? No, the secret was to restrain them.

"You know what those things were?" Mildred asked.

"Yes," Piotr told her. "End Day produces a lot of… curiosities. They take strategy to stop. We've had some practice. You couldn't have known."

J.B. and Mildred were relieved to see Nyarla had

been reunited with her family. They had entered His Ink Orchard to find Symon Vrack and his other daughter, but it seemed that Symon had instead found them, along with the group of survivors, drawn by the gunshots.

"Piotr kept us alive," Symon told J.B. and Mildred after he had been introduced. "But I understand I have you to thank for doing the same for my dear Nyarla."

"Little of both, really," J.B. said, downplaying his role. "Your daughter's smart, thinks quick when her ass is backed against the wall."

They trekked across the unforgiving landscape to the clutch of buildings where Piotr and his allies had made their home. The disconcerting mouths of the chronovores snapped at unleashed energies in the distance, the noise of their feast like a swamp cricket rubbing its legs. J.B. checked over his shoulder, watching for the corpses and the things that Piotr and his team referred to as crows.

"You'll be safe here," Marla assured J.B. and Mildred, leading them inside the supermarket building that they had made into their base.

"Those things out there—" J.B. indicated the feasting chronovores "—they look hungry."

"We're all hungry," Marla told him. "No way to change that on End Day."

Within the building was cold and dark, but at least the walls kept the wind at bay. That was something, J.B. concluded. Together, the group sat around a pockmarked wooden garden set and introduced themselves. Symon explained how he and Tarelya, his younger daughter, had been caught in the snows beyond the barrier of the Tall Wall, and how this team had rescued them.

"When was that?" Mildred asked. She sat wrapped in a blanket now, the color coming back to her cheeks.

The rugged ex-fisherman shook his head. "It's so hard to tell," he admitted. "Time here has no meaning."

As he oiled his blaster, J.B. asked about the moving corpses they had discovered in the mess hall.

"We call them Wakers," Graz told him. "Dead people. We avoid them."

"Where do they come from?" J.B. asked.

"Time's in flux here," Piotr told him, "in case you didn't notice. We figure the Wakers get caught up in time's dilation and bounced from wherever they were to here. Like echoes."

"Are the Wakers always dead like that?" Mildred asked him.

"We've never seen a live one," Piotr confirmed.

"And we've seen a lot of them," Marla added. "End Day throws up a lot of repetition."

Mildred looked pensive. "End Day," she said. "What does it mean?"

"It's a day without end," Marla said. "Time's glitching and twitching here but it never seems to go forward."

"Time travel experiments…?" J.B. mused.

"I didn't say that," Marla corrected.

"You didn't have to," J.B. told her. "But this kind of hubbub could very likely be the result of someone experimenting with forces they oughtn't to. Time travel and shit."

"And Doc's been acting weird ever since we got here," Mildred said in realization. "J.B., you don't think…?"

J.B. nodded solemnly. "Someone's jazzing with the time stream. Whatever they've done, it's going way off course. This place is evidence of that. I'm figuring this whole pesthole is the fallout of an experiment gone wrong."

"It's still going wrong," Graz said miserably. "The bubble expands and the crows' numbers are getting higher. They're feeding off every iota of displaced time."

"You ever seen what these crows of yours do to a person?" J.B. asked.

"Once," Graz told him. "They strip a man to his essence, leaving nothing but a trailing spume of soul."

PLACING THE ANIMAL CAGE before Ryan, Doc and Krysty, its four bearers stepped back, taking up positions at the four corners of the raised dais. Each man had a knife strapped to the belt of his loincloth. Ryan looked from one to the other. They were rugged men with flat faces and wide brows, their flesh blue from cold. Whatever this environment had done to them was inexplicable, but it had left them able to survive the cold to some extent. Their flesh looked thick and blubbery, like the flesh of a seal. They were some kind of muties, Ryan reasoned, who had developed a primitive culture based around the one driving force in their lives—the unchained chronal energies that plagued this tiny region of Alaska.

The pale-faced minister took a step forward and bent toward the catch on the cage, keeping himself at the same side as the hinges so that the door would swing back to cover him. "The chronovores choose their victims," he explained. "Once you have been consumed, we are left with your immortal souls, the one thing that cannot be corrupted by time's influence."

"Sounds great," Ryan told him, "but I think we'll pass." With that, the one-eyed man pounced forward, batting aside the thrusting knife blade of his nearest guardian as he reached for the minister's throat.

The minister moved fast, too, yanking back the cage door even as Ryan leaped at him. The two men went down in a tangle of limbs, Ryan's fingers closing around the pale man's throat as the cage door swung open.

Behind Ryan, the creature in the cage emerged, leaping at Doc in a clatter of gnashing teeth. And gnashing teeth was all it was. The rest of its body remained bizarrely unseen.

Chapter Twenty-Six

The chronovore rushed through the air in a rage of snapping fangs. Though Doc had been disarmed he still had his swordstick. He drove the ebony cane at the beast, knocking its lower jaw upward in a swift motion. The chronovore's jaws clashed together with a loud crack, and it seemed to dance in the air for several seconds as it tried to recover.

Beside Doc, Krysty closed her eyes and began to summon her Gaia power.

All around them, the surprised congregation was reacting, drawing weapons—knives and clubs—and hurrying to the raised area of the church. To see the sacrifices fight back was sacrilege!

His hands fixed around the minister's throat, Ryan saw the congregation rushing toward him. With a grunt of effort, he hefted the minister up and launched him headfirst at the closest of his would-be attackers. The minister shrieked as the crown of his skull slammed into the chest of his blue-fleshed colleague, and both men tumbled to the floor with a crash.

"Time to move," Ryan shouted to Doc and Krysty as he got back to his feet. Ahead, the first of the blue-fleshed figures had just reached the stage. Ryan kicked out, driving his boot into the mutie's face and forcing him back.

From the back of the stage, the minister's assistants

had drawn their knives and were rushing the strangers. While Doc parried with the chronovore, Krysty turned her attention on the armed assistants. Her red hair crackled around her head and her emerald eyes seemed almost to glow as she channelled the Gaia power, tapping the Earth itself to grant her a brief burst of incredible strength. She slammed into her nearest opponent, driving the heel of her right hand into his face with such force that the mutie's jaw shattered. But Krysty was already moving on, bringing her elbow up and around in a harsh blow to the next figure's windpipe. He sagged to the floor, gasping for breath.

The third guardsman slashed his knife through the air at Krysty's face. She sidestepped it with ease, bringing her left hand up and striking the mutie's forearm where he held the knife. The mutie's arm snapped, forearm bending to an acute angle as he staggered away.

The power surged through Krysty in enormous waves. It was as if the force was unrestrained now, no longer held back to the constraints of time.

RYAN HAD DEALT with several of the blue-fleshed muties, but it was taking too long. He leaped to the nearest pew and, with long-legged strides, began running across its back, his feet glancing across their crossbars as he swiftly made his way to the rear of the church, avoiding most of his potential attackers.

Two muties remained in the pews as Ryan hurried past. The first he stepped on, using the head as a springboard to launch himself across the room. The second one Ryan simply kicked hard in the face, driving his boot with such power that the blue man was knocked back into his seat even as he endeavored to stand.

A moment later, Ryan was at the rear of the church,

reaching for his weapons atop the unguarded font. "Sacrifice this," he snarled, grabbing his SIG-Sauer.

THE CHRONOVORE WEAVED through the air as if sizing Doc up. With a long-practiced move, Doc slipped the sword from its hidden sheath in his walking cane, brandishing the blade with a flourish. The chronovore's double set of teeth snapped at the air again, foot-long incisors clipping down in a blur of cruel motion. But the out-of-time beast seemed unable to fully focus on Doc, it snapped where he had been or, stranger still, where he would be, Doc realized. As long as he kept moving without retracing his steps, Doc figured he could avoid the strange creature—or, at least, what he could make out of it.

He stepped aside again and the disembodied mouth swirled in place, bumping back into the wall with the stained-glass window. Doc powered the point of his sword into the creature's mouth—the only part he could see—forcing it between the thing's snapping teeth.

EMILY, JOLYON AND RACHEL were already in their chairs. Rachel had made a ribbon for her dolly's hair, and she was showing it to Doc. "Look, Daddy. Becca's dressed for church," Rachel said with childlike glee.

Doc looked at the doll, the pink ribbon drawn into a bow through her hair. Then he looked at Rachel—beautiful at three years old, having thankfully taken after her mother—and he smiled. "I agree. She looks splendid," Doc said.

From the doorway of their dining room, Emily Tanner, with her lustrous hair pulled back from her face to reveal her beautiful eyes, entered the room with a fresh-cooked chicken on a covered plate. "Come now, Rachel," *she said,* "no toys at the dinner table."

Rachel began to whine in complaint, so Doc shot his daughter a conspiratorial wink. "You must do as your mother says," *he told her gently.* "There will be ample time to play after dinner." *Then he sniffed the air.* "Which smells wonderful."

Emily smiled, resplendent even in her apron with her hair tied back from her face for cooking. "Mmm, someone is hoping for seconds," *she said,* "before he has even had his firsts."

Doc laughed. The roasted chicken did indeed smell wonderful. But there was another smell mixed in with it. One he remembered from a journey he had taken...

FOR A MOMENT, the chronovore swayed there, shimmering in place as Doc's blade pierced it. And in the center of the church's raised dais, Doc's body seemed to glow as he held his sword in the monster's mouth, swirling energies misting from his form like smoke. He could smell his wife's roast chicken, the way only she could make. And something else, too—the smell of that terrible journey he had taken through time.

All around, the blue-skinned clockwatchers had stopped fighting, pausing to admire the spectacle of Doc's glowing form.

AT THE REAR OF CHURCH, Ryan raised his SIG-Sauer pistol and fired a single shot into the rafters, blasting a great chunk out of one of the stalactites that depended from the ceiling.

"Nobody move!" he ordered.

But there was no need. The whole melee had stopped moments before. Rubbing at his bruised head, the white-robed minister led the members of his weird congregation toward where Doc stood over the shimmering remains of the chronovore, his body racked with multicolored energies. For a moment the minister stood and watched the spectacle, an astonished look on his flat face.

Doc could still see Emily and the dinner table in their home, could still smell the roast. But the church was re-forming before him with the ice-pale figure at the forefront of the congregation, watching Doc with something akin to awe or reverence. At the end of Doc's sword, the chronovore was dying, its body finally materializing, a ridged wormlike form the color of an overcast sky. Then, to Doc's surprise, the thing spit forth a rising gout of energy that crackled through the air in a purple-and-blue array like a budding violet. And finally, Doc recognized the smell of the dying chronovore. It was the same smell he had scented before, when he had been shunted through time by the whitecoats of Operation Chronos. It was a smell he had almost forgotten.

"You chilled it," the minister said, smiling broadly. "You chilled it, dead."

Doc looked up at the pale-faced man, seeing the wonder in his eyes. "I do believe I did," he remarked. Its dying energies had passed through Doc, toying with the fixed points of time.

Behind Doc, Krysty had stopped battling with the guards. Only two remained standing, and one of those was clutching the snapped remains of his blade in his blood-drenched hand. Krysty's bright hair still stood out around her head like a halo of flame, and her body tensed as she tried to hold back the incredible power surging through it.

"You have done the impossible," the minister said

before bowing before Doc on one bended knee. "You are a man without time."

From the font at the back of the church, Ryan could only stand in wonder at what he saw. Somehow, Doc had outmaneuvered something these people considered impossible to outmaneuver. And in so doing he had become something akin to their savior. But what was happening to Krysty?

THE CLOCKWATCHERS let Doc and his friends go, accompanying them to the edge of the icy river. They would find the source of the disruption there, the minister told Doc, where the great bird had died in the ice.

Utterly bemused, Doc thanked them for their aid and he, Ryan and Krysty watched as the blue-skinned muties returned to their hiding places beneath the snow, back to hibernation until their next unwary prey awakened them.

"What in the nuking hell did we walk into?" Ryan asked when the last of the figures was finally out of earshot.

"A self-contained area with its own ecology and social systems," Doc said, watching the blue figures depart. "Everything here is new and different. But I will tell you this—whatever is happening here, I have grave suspicions it involves experimentation with the forces of time."

"You were glowing like a radzone, Doc," Ryan said. "You all right now?"

Doc nodded. "I…have a lot to consider." Things had been moving so fast he had yet to really process what it was he had experienced when he stabbed the time eater.

"Stay alert. We aren't out of the woods yet," Ryan said, glancing over to Krysty. The red-haired woman stood a few paces from the men, her prehensile hair still poised about her head as if she were being jolted with electricity.

"Krysty, are you okay?" Ryan asked.

"The power of the Earth is still churning inside me," Krysty explained. "It's never been like this before. It won't subside."

"Is that so bad?" Ryan asked.

"Not now," Krysty said, "but what happens when it does fade? A burst of power like this could chill me, Ryan."

Ryan reached forward, placing both his hands very gently over Krysty's. "I'll be here for you."

Doc stepped away, granting the two some privacy while he pondered what had happened in the church. He was a time traveler, although that term suggested he had done so of his own volition or that he could do so again at will, and that certainly wasn't the case. But for an instant there, while the chronovore's energies raced along the metal of his swordstick, Doc had leaped back in time to a meal he couldn't even remember. How many times had Rachel brought one of her dolls to the table? How many times had he eaten Emily's roasted chicken? No man could be expected to recall every meal, every familial conversation.

But there had been something about the vision, if that indeed was what it was. Doc had the distinct impression that the chronovore's energies had sent him back through time, albeit just for a moment. *When you open up the belly of a beast, you'll smell part-digested food.* In piercing the chronovore, could it be that Doc had smelled the scent of that creature's last meal—the smell of fractured time?

He was a man displaced in time and this region

seemed somehow unhinged from time, too. Could there be a connection? Doc stood beside the icy water's edge at the riverbank and wondered if, somehow, this place held the key to his return home to the 1800s and the family that loved him.

"My dear Emily," Doc said, shaking his head, "please let this be the miracle we've hoped for."

Without a sound, something emerged from the icy water, whipping around Doc's ankle in a second. "What the deuce—?" Doc gasped, and then the thing pulled him down. Ryan and Krysty turned as Doc disappeared beneath the surface.

Chapter Twenty-Seven

"Doc!" Ryan shouted. "Doc!" He was hurrying along the edge of the icy stream, his SIG-Sauer poised to shoot anything that emerged from the water, his Steyr longblaster slapping angrily against his back like the Grim Reaper's scythe.

The water churned for a moment before settling. There was no sign of Doc in its fast-flowing depths, as thick chunks of ice bobbed along the surface obscuring almost everything.

"Fireblast!" Ryan cursed, bringing up his blaster. "It's moving too quick. Doc could be anywhere by now."

"Did you see what it was?" Krysty asked. She, too, had her blaster in her hand. She scoured the water with narrowed eyes.

"Saw it for less than a second," Ryan admitted. "Looked like a tentacle, gray and rubbery."

"Octopus?" Krysty suggested. "Squid? Kraken? What could live down there, amid the ice?"

Ryan shook his head, his eye still fixed on the churning river of ice. "I don't know, but if Doc doesn't reappear quick he'll freeze to death."

BENEATH THE WATER, Doc felt a cold so intense that it was like the wrong side of the grave. His eyes burned when he opened them—he had closed them automatically when he had first struck the water—the temperature of the water was so low.

He was moving. Everything around him was churning, great white slabs of ice rushing past him as he was dragged along the riverbed. The water itself was clear and cold. He was spinning so violently that it was hard to gather his thoughts, hard to make sense of anything. The stones of the riverbed loomed into view for a moment before rushing away, like some manic fairground ride.

Automatically, Doc's hand reached for the LeMat blaster he wore at his hip, yanking it free of its holster.

For scant seconds, Doc's mind raced, hurrying to piece everything together.

This much he knew for certain: he was dragging behind something, being pulled feetfirst. Or footfirst, more accurately, for the thing had snatched him by his left ankle, leaving one leg wavering in the freezing waters as he was dragged deeper into the river. Doc spun as he was pulled ahead, the LeMat almost slipping from his grasp as he tried desperately to bring it up to target this predator.

The thing was swimming beneath the great floes of ice like a guided missile, pulling Doc along in its wake as it plunged toward its unknowable destination.

Momentarily, Doc caught sight of the creature's bulk, a dark shape in the water above—was it above?—him. He snatched at the LeMat's trigger, sending a .44 slug into the belly of the creature, whatever the hell it was.

In the freezing water, the blaster's report sounded like an undersea quake, the sound carrying in a muffled kind of echo. All around him, blisterlike bubbles blurted to the surface as the shell was expelled.

Doc flipped and spun, trying to keep sight of the bullet as it disappeared. Below him, he saw the telltale kick of riverbed where the bullet impacted uselessly; his aim had been thrown by the movement and he had wasted the shot.

He had been under the water for almost thirty seconds now, barrelling beneath the freezing waves as the creature hurtled onward. It was moving at a decent clip, Doc surmised, difficult to tell with the light-dark flash of sunlight through water. His chest cried out for air, his eyes ached from the water pressure and its punishing temperature. He needed to get out of the water, and get out fast.

He brought the blaster around again as he spiraled through the water, timed more carefully to try to snag the creature. It loomed ahead of him, pushing through the water, one thick tentacle wrapped around his ankle as it hurried through the ice, a dark shape at the edge of his vision. It had a rounded body and moved with a kick of limbs, propelling itself with a sort of thrust-brake, thrust-brake movement. Some kind of mutie, Doc guessed, didn't matter what. The thing wanted him for lunch; that's all that really mattered right now.

Gritting his teeth, Doc fired the LeMat again, sending another .44-caliber slug through the water. He heard it dreamily, muffled by the cool medium, then watched as something began to leak from the creature's flank.

The creature's grip slipped fractionally. He fired again, feeling the pressure rising in his lungs, seeing the dark spots before his eyes that either meant the sunlight was being obscured by ice, or he was running out of oxygen. The bullet hit home, slamming again into the creature's body somewhere among that cluster of writhing tentacles.

WOUNDED AND LEAKING dark, inky blood, the creature surfaced, batting great chunks of ice aside. At the river's edge, Ryan and Krysty spotted it—fifty yards downstream—and brought their weapons to bear without a second's hesitation.

The side of the river erupted with the sounds of blasterfire, the grim cough of Ryan's SIG-Sauer sending four 9 mm slugs at the creature in a flash, Krysty's .38 driving two rounds into the creature's side. They chased along the river, sending more shots into the wounded creature as it thrashed in the icy waters. It looked massive. Limbs seemed to spew from everywhere, trailing behind the beast like great swirling snakes, their flesh as gray and shiny as a seal's pelt.

The thing was pinned against the bank, struggling among great hunks of ice where it had been forced to surface by the wound Doc's blast had dealt it. Ryan rammed his SIG-Sauer into his waistband, bringing the more powerful Steyr Scout to bear. He had the weapon up to his shoulder in a matter of seconds, centered the mutant creature in the center of the crosshairs. Beside him, Krysty reloaded her blaster and sent another burst of fire at the horrendous beast.

Ryan aimed and fired, feeling the familiar kick of the Steyr as it pumped against his body. A 7.62 mm slug drilled into the creature's face where one milky black eye was sunken in place, staring out at the sky and the riverbank. The shot turned the eye into so much jelly, spurting gunk and mist into the air.

Doc emerged from the water a moment later, Krysty's bullets spitting great gobs of water all about him as he thrashed amid the ice. He had his own blaster in hand, the replica LeMat, and he brought it around even as he heaved for breath, squeezing the trigger and sending another blast at the creature's writhing form.

The mutie squid-thing hissed like a burst tire, sending a jet of dark inky liquid up into the air.

Icy water poured from Doc's hair as he struggled to take another breath before the mutie submerged him again. His shoulders struck against the water as the creature thrashed, flipping him up and back. The water felt hard, striking Doc with the forgiveness of brick.

On the riverbank, Ryan calmly reloaded and aimed the Steyr at the creature's other eye. Before he could fire, the mutie disappeared under the surface, dragging Doc with it.

"No!" Ryan shouted as his colleague disappeared under the ice once more.

Beside him, Krysty was a blur of hair and rushing limbs. She had removed her fur coat and she threw it and her Smith & Wesson aside as she leaped into the water in a graceful dive. Ryan watched her go, all too aware of how bitterly cold that freezing water was.

ADRENALINE PUMPING, Doc switched barrels as the creature dragged him beneath the water again. He didn't think about it, just brought the LeMat around to where he was certain the beast was. Then he pulled the second trigger, which activated the 18-gauge shotgun barrel. Even beneath the water, the weapon sounded like a thunderclap as it sent its deadly cargo through the waves and into the creature's body.

The mutie squid rocked as a huge chunk of its flesh was torn from it by Doc's blast. A great gout of inky blood filled the waters around it, and the monster began to sink.

Doc gazed up his spinning body, trying to see what it was that was pulling him through the water. The dark shape loomed lower now, dragging him by his foot toward the bottom of the river.

Blaster still in hand, Doc reached down to snatch his foot away. His boot slipped back and forth against his ankle but he couldn't pull free. Once again his chest was aching, burning with pressure as the need to breathe threatened to overwhelm him.

Then, suddenly, something pulled Doc away, dragging him by his shoulders and yanking him out of the mutie's grip. For a moment, the world seemed to spin, flashes of light and dark—*and heaven help him, was that Emily?*—as he swam away from the plummeting creature in the river.

Doc surfaced a second later, gulping down a single great breath as soon as he saw the sunlight. Beside him, Krysty was gripping his waist, holding him up above the shimmering surface of the water, bobbing there with swishing feet. Her hair was soaked through and it trailed about her in jagged lines. Her Gaia power was still with her, Doc realized, turning her into a human weapon, a fantastical capacitor filled to brimming with the power of the Earth Mother.

He thanked his lucky stars. "So good to have

friends," Doc muttered as Krysty coasted with him back to the shore, where Ryan was still watching the water through the rifle's scope.

Momentarily, Ryan spotted the beast surface amid a spume of ink, its black tentacles thrashing in the water. He squeezed the trigger again, sending another 7.62 mm slug into what he assumed was the creature's head. The bullet struck in a great burst of exploding flesh and Ryan sent a second bullet that hit home a moment later. The creature reared from the water before diving back beneath and disappearing from view.

At the side of the river, Krysty had recovered her coat and wrapped it around Doc's shivering body. She had to be cold, too, Doc realized, and he offered her the coat.

"Just get yourself warmed up," Krysty said. "I don't feel cold at all."

Doc pulled the coat over his shoulders, staving off the freezing temperature that had dug into his core like a burrowing dog.

How much time had he been down there, under the water with that thing?

Minutes?

Hours?

It was so hard to tell. Time, that great cosmic joke, seemed so fluid, so unreal here.

"You're losing it, Theo," Doc chastised himself, mumbling the words.

He looked up, confirming that no one had heard him. Krysty was standing with Ryan, looking powerful and determined, her body displaying none of its usual signs of post-Gaia fatigue. Was it still coursing through her, that incredible power? Could it be that

Krysty had tapped a wellspring so deep that she could remain superstrong for hours—or perhaps even longer?

And Emily. What was she doing, watching over him, whispering in his ear all the while? "I hear you, my darling," Doc whispered, shaking his head. He wanted her to go, yet he feared she might never come back if she went this time. It was all in his head—wasn't it? All some grand delusion, played out because of the cold, the mat-trans jump scrambling his mind so badly he was still suffering its aftereffects the way Ricky had suffered the stomach cramps.

Reason it away all you like, Doc told himself, she was still there. The smell of her perfume, the sound of her voice. He might be able to apply cold logic, but it didn't change the reality he felt.

His dear Emily was there, more now than ever, as if she was closer—perhaps not geographically, but chronally, the ages reaching out for her, pulling her to him.

The eras folded and unfolded like origami, making new patterns, new days of the old.

RYAN LOOKED AT Krysty now, the worry clear on his face. "You've been channeling Gaia too long," he said. "No question."

Krysty looked strong, her hair still crackling around her head. "It won't stop," she explained. "I've never really had a way to shut it off. It wasn't a problem before n—" She stopped, her eyes flicking from Ryan's face to something behind him. "Ryan, look!"

He turned, saw the disembodied mouths—the things that the minister had called chronovores—moving in a pack across the fields of ice. Not just one this time, but a hundred of them, with more emerging from the ether even as he watched. Doc was still huddled in Krysty's coat, shivering as he tried to warm up from his impromptu dip.

"Doc," Ryan called, "we have to move."

Looking up, Doc nodded. "Time is coming for us," he said. "Sending everything it has to force this aberration out of existence. And us with it."

Chapter Twenty-Eight

A noise drew J.B. to the window of the shack and he peered through it, wiping away the dirt with his sleeve. Something was massing out there, a great cloud of teeth flashing through the air. "What the hell is that?" he asked.

Marla was beside him instantly, staring at the dark cloud of teeth that loomed above the abandoned settlement. "Crows," she said. "More than I've ever seen in one place my whole life."

"And they're coming this way," J.B. observed, his hand automatically reaching for his blaster.

"They can't come here," Tarelya insisted. "You promised."

Piotr shot her father a look. "We've hidden from them for all of End Day. But it seems that we've hidden for as long as we can. Now all we can do is fight."

Grimly, Piotr led his companions out into the snow-racked plain where the chronovores were swarming. J.B. followed, turning back to Mildred.

"Come on, Millie. You wouldn't want to miss the end of the world, would you? You slept through the last one," he added with grim humor.

Pulling the ZKR-551 from its holster, Mildred followed the Armorer into the freezing air outside.

RYAN, KRYSTY AND Doc raced along the winding path of the river toward where the lightning shot up at the sky. There was a passenger jet in the frozen water up ahead: the minister's fabled giant bird.

The chronovores were moving, swirling around as they searched for prey. Ryan hurried the group on, checking on the insatiable creatures every few steps, assuring himself that the chronovores weren't following. The river waited before them, a great, wide line of churning water littered with thick hunks of ice. The ice sat low to the water, which made Ryan fairly certain that the water itself had to be deep. There were what looked like gullies running around the edges of the river, thick rips in the ground that seemed abrupt in their start and end. Some didn't even reach the river, and Ryan wondered what could have caused them. If he didn't know better, he would guess a military laser had been used here, but then he remembered the lightning sparking from the bent building and figured that to be the source.

They crossed the river on the aircraft's wing, using it like a bridge to climb over the freezing water. Doc stopped and peered over the sloping edge of the wing for a moment, using his swordstick to steady himself.

The port-side wing of the crashed airplane veered down into the river, where it dipped below the icy surface just a few feet from the shore. In the lead, Ryan scrambled across to the gap then sprang, jumping the last remaining space in a graceful leap. He turned back, reaching his arms out to catch first Krysty and then Doc. The old man seemed rejuvenated somehow.

On the far side of the jet's wing stood the crooked building, with concrete walls and the power plant attached to its side like a cyst. The plant hummed, the generators buzzing angrily, and lightning played havoc across the surface of the main building itself. It was old military, Ryan saw, recognizing the style from long experience with redoubts and other army facilities. Yet another hangover from the days before the nukecaust, when the U.S. Army seemed to expand into every corner of the country. Ryan wondered what it had been like a century earlier. It was impossible to guess, of no more practical help to him than trying to imagine himself a pharaoh in ancient Egypt. Just a lot of dead people living dead lives.

Uncontrolled electricity played across the concrete walls of the building, arcing up into the air in forked lines. Doc, Ryan and Krysty balked as a great streak shot out from the building, snapping at the locustlike chronovore swarm and blasting two of their number to a grisly ash.

"We're not safe out here," Krysty said, and Ryan agreed. The chronovores were snuffling around again, a whole swarm of them blipping in and out of sight through the falling snow, just their rows of teeth hanging in the air.

The sky above them was charged with electricity and color, a great prismatic wash visible through the falling snow. The companions watched as another streak of lightning, twenty feet wide like a laser beam, blasted from the building in a crackling arc before striking the ground. Where it struck, the lightning left a chasm as wide as the blast and at least ten feet deep, a great trench that ran across the land like a scar. There were other similar rents all around, pits in the ground where the lightning had struck before.

"Inside," Ryan ordered.

The companions sprinted across the snow-smeared plain toward the building, ducking their heads as another out-of-control burst of electricity zapped from the roof, reaching out in a trident fork of white against the night sky.

The main doors sat in a thick housing at the front of the building. There were two doors constructed from thick metal that met in the center in a striped yellow-and-black line. Reaching them first, Ryan shoved the point of his panga into the gap and twisted. The doors parted easily, their locks long since disengaged. If someone was inside, Ryan thought, why would they bother to lock a place like this? The whole area of His Ink Orchard was so inhospitable that he and his companions had only gotten there by chance.

Inside, the companions found themselves standing in a wide corridor with bland gray walls. The tunnel-like corridor stretched a long way into the building, the only sign of color a faded yellow stripe painted along the floor. A desk waited to one side of the entry behind a thick plate of what appeared to be armaglass. The desk featured a comp and a telecommunications setup, but it was unmanned. Ryan tried to peer through the glass for a moment before moving on, leading them deeper into the building.

Behind them, the winds billowed and the lightning crackled, snow smattering the floor as it was blown in through the open doors.

Doc stopped in his tracks. "I recognize this place."

Chapter Twenty-Nine

Ryan and Krysty stopped, too, staring at the old man.

"You've been here before?" Krysty asked.

Doc shook his head. "Not here, but a place very like this."

"We've been through a lot of redoubts and military bases in our time, Doc," Ryan reminded him. "They all blend into one after a while."

"No," Doc insisted, pawing at the nearest wall. "This is familiar. It's a facility for Operation Chronos."

"The people who plucked you out of your own time and dumped you in Deathlands?" Krysty asked.

"Yes. I have not been to this facility, but I have been to one very like it," Doc insisted. "It is not the design, it is the smell. Unchained energies, chronal energies. Time travel has a smell about it, the facilities that operate it—well, it is something I could never forget."

Ryan and Krysty sniffed the air, but to them there was nothing. It simply smelled dry after their breakneck passage across the ice.

Ryan started to ask Doc a question. "You sure you're not—?"

"Imagining it?" Doc finished. "No. Trust me, my dear Ryan. This place has something to do with Operation Chronos. And it is not a dead facility—it is alive."

Ryan nodded. The generators outside had told him

that much, though whether there was a human hand at the center of it all he could only speculate.

Doc stepped forward then, marching down the corridor with newfound determination. Ryan and Krysty hurried to keep up.

"I have been getting flashes from the past," Doc explained. "They began almost as soon as we arrived here, and they have been getting steadily stronger. I felt the last one when I was plunged under the ice water by that beast."

"You've had episodes before," Krysty said gently. "Mat-trans nightmares, things like that."

"I assure you that these are not the dreams I have had before, Krysty," Doc insisted. "They are not memories that I am reliving. They are something different, a sense of being close to home."

"It's your imagination," Ryan insisted. "Nothing could possibly set that off."

"Do not be so sure," Doc told him as they stopped at a closed doorway. He peered through the glass panel in its right-hand side above the doorknob, checking the corridor ahead. It was empty.

"Animals mark their territory," Doc continued as he pushed through the door. "They come back and they recognize their own musk. And we humans are just animals by another name. Perhaps we, too, lay down trails we recognize, the things we call memories."

"But you said yourself," Ryan reminded him. "This isn't the facility you were held in."

"True, but this place is rife with chronal energy in flux," Doc replied. "An old way station perhaps for Operation Chronos, a backup facility to experiment here in Alaska, well away from the hustle and bustle of other, more populous regions."

A set of double doors waited at the end of the corridor, painted in yellow and black stripes with a red plaque at their center. Noises issued from beyond the doors, the crackling sounds of sparking electricity. Doc stopped before the doors, turning back to face Ryan and Krysty, his face taut with determination.

"I can sense my Emily as if she were waiting around the very next corner," Doc told them. "What if the Chronos people brought her here? What if she has been waiting for me all this time?"

Ryan looked at his friend, feeling his dilemma as if it was his own. He had been with Doc for several years now, and in that time he had lost other friends, even lost his own son, Dean. To prevent the old man finding out what lay behind the door would be cruel.

"Keep your blaster ready," Ryan said, turning from Doc to Krysty. "Both of you." He raised the SIG-Sauer in his own hands, taking a step back from the doors and targeting them over Doc's shoulder. "Go ahead, Doc. We'll follow."

Warily, Doc pushed at the double doors, slipping between them with Krysty and Ryan a step behind him, their blasters poised. They found themselves on a railed catwalk overlooking a vast control area filled with sparking machinery and flashing comp screens. The machinery of the operations center was arranged along three walls of the room in the middle of which stood the figure garbed in a thick radiation suit made of bright yellow fabric. The figure's protective hood hid his features behind a plate of tinted plastic.

"Who—?" Doc began and stopped himself.

The lone figure on the deck below turned to face them. "Come in," he said, "fellow traveler."

Gingerly, Doc strode down the metal steps of the room with his companions just a few paces behind him. Reaching the floor below, the team saw two familiar people—Jak and Ricky—bound hand and foot against the jutting machinery that lined the wall beneath the stairs.

"Those are my friends," Doc said without hesitation. "We are here to—"

"Rescue them?" the hooded figure suggested. "No, perhaps these others came for that, but you came here for something else. You heard my call, didn't you—brother?"

J.B. AND MILDRED joined Piotr, Marla and Graz as they stormed outside to face the swarming cloud of chronovores.

"Looks like your End Day is finally coming to its end," J.B. remarked as the dark swarm oozed toward them across the darkened sky.

The swarm was made up of hundreds upon hundreds of shining teeth, each one a foot long and as sharp as a knife. Behind those gnashing teeth, the chronovores were beginning to take shape, great snaking bodies that wound in and out of existence, curling through time itself.

"We can't fight these things, John," Mildred insisted. "Look at them."

J.B. eyed the approaching cloud as the locustlike creatures began to eat through the rogue energies of the Operation Chronos facility. "Then we'll die the way we lived," he told Mildred, "fighting for our lives every step of the way."

Mildred and J.B. hunkered down as the cloud of

time-eating monsters swarmed toward the buildings, chomping great swathes of reality out of existence, leaving nothing but the bubbling wounds of shattered time in their wake.

"BROTHER?" DOC SHOT back. "What are you talking about?"

"They dragged us through time," the yellow-suited figure replied angrily. "Placed us here in the desolate future against our will. When I stepped out of the time window, I couldn't even remember my name—can you believe that?"

Doc nodded. His own journey through time had been so traumatic that he had physically aged more than thirty years, and his mind had been almost broken, his memories like a jigsaw puzzle that he had slowly pieced back together. "Who are you?" Doc asked.

"My name was Don Nectar," the man in the radiation suit said. "That was the best I could remember of it.

"The men in white lab coats launched me here like a firework, blasting me through time," Nectar continued. "I staggered from this facility into the cold out there and I could barely stand, so much of me had broken away in the time stream."

"You lost bits of yourself?"

While Doc kept Nectar's attention, Ryan and Krysty took the opportunity to check on Jak and Ricky where they had been affixed to the wall by insulation tape. They were unconscious but still breathing. "Jak?" Ryan whispered. "Come on, snap out of it."

Jak's eyelids flickered for a moment. Beneath them, Ryan saw the albino's familiar ruby orbs but he seemed unable to focus. Whatever had happened here, he had taken a punishing blow to the skull.

A few steps away Krysty was reaching the same conclusion with Ricky. Her own body still rocked with the Gaia power, her hair tangling and untangling with phantom energy.

"I have strived all these years to find the way back home," Nectar told Doc.

"I…" Doc began uncertainly. "I don't understand."

Nectar took a step away from his equipment, his tether line swaying as it spooled out from the machinery. "This place is a backup facility for Operation Chronos. You remember Operation Chronos, don't you?"

Doc nodded. "I suspected as much as soon as I entered," he admitted.

"We came through time together, but while you lived your life I was stuck, tethered here like a shade, unable to function," the man in the hood said.

Doc took another step forward, peering at the man's features through the darkened pane of his suit. "Who are you? I cannot see."

"I told you—my name is Don Nectar," the man told him. "We were—we *are*—friends."

Doc shook his head. "No, I know of no one of that name."

But Nectar ignored him. "If you could only know the struggles I had been through to open the tunnel through time," he said. "If only you could feel the agony I have felt."

Behind him, the machinery was flickering with light as some function reached its crescendo.

"It's taken years," Nectar said with bitterness. "There was a part of the equation missing, you see. No matter what I did, one piece of the puzzle remained tantalisingly unreachable. *You.*"

Doc took a step back. "I'm not responsible for—"

"Yes, you are," Nectar snarled. "You always were. Without you, I'd still be at home with my wife and children. I was dragged in your wake, caught up in the chronal energies that sent *you* through time."

"I played no part in that experiment," Doc told him. "I am as much a victim as you are, Mr. Nectar."

"I lost everything," Nectar growled. "Even myself. I am a man who barely exists. I cannot step outside of this facility. Once I go beyond the reach of the time equipment my body begins to break down. I have been trapped here for years, trying to fix things, trying to reset the equipment so that I can go home."

"You're destroying this whole area," Ryan growled, reappearing from beneath the stairs, blaster in hand. "Your experiments in time travel have created a sinkhole in the very fabric of time itself. It's slowly consuming everything."

Nectar's head moved beneath the hood as he identified Ryan and Krysty. "You think this place matters to *him?*" he asked, indicating Doc. "You think he wouldn't leave you in an instant if he had the chance to?"

Ryan and Krysty turned to Doc. "Doc?" Krysty asked.

The old man's face was screwed up as he wrestled with his conscience.

"No one could blame you if you found a way home," Krysty said.

"No, not at this cost," Doc insisted. "This whole bubble of broken time will only expand, consuming everything. And if not, then those awful chronovores—"

"Don't be so naive," Nectar growled. "You want… I have dedicated my whole existence to this."

"To what?" Doc snarled.

"To be home," Nectar replied, slamming his fist

against the control toggle that powered up the machinery, sending it into overdrive. "To be with your…with my…my wife…"

"Her name is Emily," Doc said through clenched teeth, realization finally dawning on him.

"Yes," Nectar said. "Emily. My darling Emily."

J.B. WATCHED IN HORROR as the cloud of grinding teeth hurtled through the air toward the buildings. They had already destroyed the landscape behind them, ripped through it like it was soggy paper, turning the snow and trees into fiery ruins, alive with unrestrained energy.

The cloud front was almost upon them now, and Piotr ordered his people to stick close as he began firing, sending bullet after bullet into the creatures' gleaming teeth. Their bodies popped and fizzed as they winked in and out of time, guzzling at every piece of matter they touched now as chronal energies poured from the distant building.

From their hiding place in the supermarket, Symon, Nyarla and Tarelya watched terrified through the dirt-smeared windows, wondering if anything could possibly stop these monsters. They watched as J.B. tossed a compact charge into a swarm of the impossible creatures, saw it explode and turn a dozen chronovores into flaming forms that crisscrossed in and out of time. It wasn't enough. Their numbers were endless.

"SHE IS NOT YOURS," Doc said, feeling suddenly sick. "She was never yours."

"Ours then," Nectar said.

"No," Doc stated. "Emily is her own woman, and that was why I loved her. And why I love her still. You—an abomination, a murmur from the time stream—couldn't understand."

Nectar stepped closer, cupping Doc's chin in his hand. "I am you," he said. "We are one, you and I. Alpha and Omega, twin sides of the same equation, balanced perfectly. Brothers fighting for the same woman."

"Not brothers," Doc told him. "You are me. A broken sliver of me that those irresponsible lab jockeys managed to foul up into existence when they tossed me so carelessly into the time hole. That's it, isn't it, *Don Nectar?* I should have realized the very moment I heard your name. Don Nectar—it's an amnesiac's remembrance of 'Doc Tanner,' is it not? Of *my* name. You should not exist, foul curse from my heart. That is why you could never—can never—go home. You never existed."

"And yet, I stand before you, a man complete," Nectar said.

"No, you do not!" Doc growled, lunging forward and grabbing Nectar by the mask. In one swift movement, the old man pulled the radiation hood away, revealing Nectar's face for the first time. It was his own face, but insubstantial, like a reflection in dark glass. He was a shade of Doc, a shadow come to life. "You are a ghost who has not even died."

Nectar bared his teeth at Doc, but in his face they were as black as night. "Together we can depart this Hell and return home, return to Emily. We have suffered enough. You out there and me trapped here, unable to leave the time machinery or I'll cease to be. Come with me, brother."

"Learn your place, shadow man," Doc replied, driving his balled fist into Nectar's chin.

Nectar swayed in place, his faint eyes narrowing in his indistinct face. "I hit me," he muttered. "You... I..."

"Your life is forfeit," Doc told him. "You are nothing but a dream thing brought fleetingly to life while the dreamer tried to awaken. But this, all you are doing here—all you have done—is destroying everything. Destroying the world."

"A world neither of us belong in," Nectar replied angrily. "The chronovores, those things out there, are attracted to the time dilation. The only way to halt their progress is to shut down the experiment, close the time window."

"Then shut it down," Doc insisted. "Cease these experiments."

"And what then?" Nectar growled, his hands grasping the comp equipment, sending a final command to open the time window. "Leave both of me stranded here, leading a hand-to-mouth existence in this Hell on Earth? I...we are meant for better than that, Doc Tanner."

Doc watched as Nectar wrenched free his umbilical cord. Behind him, a green button pulsed with illumination. "We're live," Nectar growled. "There's no turning back now. One of us shall return home."

"Don Nectar," Doc growled, shaking his head. "Am I really so selfish? I do not think you know you at all."

Before Nectar could respond, Doc leaped forward, grasping his swordstick and snapping the hidden blade from its sheath. In a moment, he had the blade free, turning on his heel and lunging at his shadow counterpart.

Nectar stepped back, pulling himself just fractionally out of reach of the sword's tip. It was as if he had anticipated the move, could judge the sword's path to the nth degree.

Doc issued an angry noise, sweeping the blade in a broad arc, drawing it through the air toward his agile foe. Nectar stepped back then forward, wobbling on his heels just barely out of the path of the swishing blade.

Behind them, Ryan and Krysty watched, weapons raised but mystified as to what to do. To them, Doc and his foe were talking in riddles.

As Nectar came back toward him, Doc saw him clasp his hands as though gripping something, right thumb to left knuckle. Then he pulled his right hand up…in an eerily familiar move. Doc recognized it as the same move that *he* had performed himself to pull the hidden sword from his walking cane. Something was forming between Nectar's hands, a blade like Doc's own, but this one was made of something insubstantial. It looked to Doc like a ripple in the air and everything behind it seemed to be seen as though through rushing water.

"Though unsuccessful, my experiments have generated certain interesting by-products," Nectar stated as he brought the blade up toward Doc's face.

Doc parried, his own sword clashing with the strange nonblade with a low tolling clang. "Do tell," Doc said as he forced Nectar to retreat a step.

A sinister smile appeared on Nectar's ghostly face. "My blade is made from solid time," he told Doc. "You feel its passage with every stroke, cutting at the eras, hacking at your days."

Doc's gaze flicked to the shimmering blade and he saw things in its depths: grass and trees and the bombs that set the world on the path to wrongness. Something else was there, too—a face, beautiful and all too familiar. Doc gasped. "Emily," he said.

"My Emily," Nectar corrected. "The blade cuts so

much from us. So much we might never retrieve." He lunged again at Doc, slashing with the blade of time.

Ryan prepared to shoot the man in the radiation suit but Krysty stopped him. "Ryan, look."

Behind them, the machines were toiling, a window forming in the air like an opening mouth.

With a grunt of effort, Doc brought his own blade to meet Nectar's, barely holding it away from his face. "You have…discovered something here," Doc said with effort. "You have…tapped into…something…that could be…great."

"Yes," Nectar hissed. "A way home. For one of us."

"And leave the other here, while the chronovores you have unleashed destroy the world?" Doc asked, parrying another clash of the blades. "Is that your plan?"

"No," Nectar snarled, kicking out with his right foot and knocking Doc to the floor. Doc lay there, gasping for breath, his hair clinging to his face with sweat. Nectar strode toward him, bringing the shimmering blade of solid time down toward his throat. "Only one of us can exist. You were right. The other is a disembodied shadow, detached from the whole. Reassembled, we shall travel back to Emily."

Behind Nectar, between the twin pylonlike structures, the time window had taken form. Its edges were insubstantial, wavering in the air like a mirage. Between them it looked like a great tunnel reaching through space, its ripples running back toward a distant street as if seen through the wrong end of a telescope. Doc recognized the street. It was a street he had walked a thousand times before, the place where he had been walking with his family when the Eye had taken him, wrenching him through the time stream. It had been the last place he had ever been with his family.

Doc felt the blade of time pushing at his throat, pricking against his skin. He comprehended Nectar's plan in its entirety now—the blade would knit himself and Nectar, the rogue facets of time, back together. Once fixed they could hopefully survive the chrono jump where Nectar alone had failed. He was a splinter of Doc come detached from him during the original time trawl. The time machinery had spit him out here, at this way station for Operation Chronos, but he was nothing more than false data blurted from the machine. But still, that false data could take Doc home, to see Emily again....

And leave his friends, his companions, here to die in a world consumed by predators who ate time itself. No, Doc could never do that. He could never doom a world, even one as ruined and broken as this one. Not at the expense of his friends.

Who was to say that the chronovores wouldn't follow them—the joined being of himself and Nectar—through the time hole and into 1896, his world, his home? Who was to say that in dooming one world he wouldn't have doomed it through eternity, present and past? There were too many variables, too many unknowns, too many risks. It was an uncertainty he simply couldn't ignore.

This much he knew for certain: whatever Don Nectar was, whatever he had started life as, be it a blip in the data or something more significant, he was no longer Theophilus Algernon Tanner. He was Doc without a moral compass, left with nothing but the vaguest memory of what he had once desired. Don Nectar was Doc Tanner freed from all of the things that made him Doc, a tiny slice of Tanner cut so thin it no longer resembled Tanner at all.

I am facing the darkest aspect of my own soul, Doc

realized as the time blade cut deeper into his neck, *and I am losing. And that is quite simply something that I cannot suffer to endure.*

OUTSIDE THE REDOUBT, the lightning storm had become a full-blown meltdown, sheets of electricity blasting across the ground like a marching army. Each time Doc and Nectar touched, the lightning had fired out with more intensity than ever before. The area known as *Yego Kraski Sada* had suffered terribly at the hands of the time manipulation, generating the ever-expanding bubble of broken time. But now, that self-contained disaster zone was becoming worse as time contorted beyond human comprehension.

NECTAR GRABBED Doc's wrist as the sword streaked by, yanking him toward the widening portal that had appeared behind him, a portal that led into the time stream.

"Prepare yourselves for full emersion into the time flow," Nectar growled, stepping back and pulling Doc with him.

Almost forgotten beneath the stairs where Krysty had been working Jak and Ricky's bonds, Ryan had unslipped his Steyr Scout and brought its scope up to his eye. He was a remarkable shot, with unprecedented aim and speed. But right now he stood there, wondering what—or whom—to shoot. Doc had slipped into the fiery window that had appeared in the center of the machinery, a ceaseless and nonsensical tunnel that burrowed beyond the limits of space and into time's hidden dimensions. Don Nectar had his hands around Doc's throat, pulling him forward as chronal energies massed all around them, the sword he held becoming a surging flame that threatened to engulf them both.

The flux of chronal energy rippled through the room, tearing at the walls and blasting through Ryan's body as he took the shot. Down the scope he could see, magnified and centered in the crosshairs, all of time laid out before him, a spiral of seconds turned minutes turned hours turned days, a lifetime of lifetimes. Doc and his corrupted opposite, the man known as Don Nectar, were caught in pitched struggle, Nectar's hands reaching around Doc's throat, the old man struggling to push him away amid the flames of time. Behind them, 1896 pulsed and bloomed, expanding to take one of them, time opening like the petals of a flower.

Squeezing the trigger, Ryan sent a single bullet through the open rent in time.

Chapter Thirty

Ryan felt the longblaster buck against his shoulder, watched as his bullet raced time itself to strike the grasping hands of Nectar as he tried to chill the source from which he had budded, a parasite come to murder its host. The bullet drilled through Nectar's hands, cutting through the tendons in his left then out through his left palm and into the right palm, continuing onward in a spurt of blood. Wounded, Don let go of Doc's neck for a moment, but it was enough. Krysty was standing ready, her feet anchored to the spot, reaching for Doc's hand with the Gaia power still channeling through her with the fury of the sun.

"I've got you," she breathed.

Doc leaped from the fracture in the time stream, his feet skipping across the decking of the floor as he found himself, once more, on solid ground. Standing there, as chronal energies danced all about them, Doc turned back to the rip in time, saw Emily, Rachel and Jolyon for a fraction of a second. Don Nectar was hurtling through the churning tunnel of time toward them, racing past the ages in a sprawl of limbs.

"Finish him, Ryan," Doc urged, "before it's too late."

Ryan stroked the trigger again, sending another bullet down the fracture of time. But Nectar was moving too fast now; the bullet would never catch up to him. "Fireblast!" Ryan cursed. "He's out of range."

Doc didn't hesitate. Plucking up the discarded sword-stick, he angled it at the heart of the machinery and thrust it into the metal plating with all his might. A great cascade of energy blasted through the swordstick, channeling up its length like electricity through a lightning rod, pouring into the air in a shower of chronal fury.

Thrown back, Doc crashed into the wall beneath the stairs as the unleashed stream of time rushed up the sword.

Ryan felt himself being dragged into the collapsing portal as it began to suck the untamed energies from the air, sealing the far end of the tunnel in a rapid blur of force. His feet slipped out from under him and suddenly he was in the air, still holding his longblaster as he plummeted into the gaping wound in time.

Krysty lunged, grabbed Ryan by his ankle and pulled him back. The full force of Gaia raked through her body, and when Ryan looked back he saw her hair arrayed around her head in jagged lines, like some stylized rendition of the sun. "Hold on, lover," Krysty said, her eyes glowing a fierce green, sparking like fireworks.

Caught up there, with Krysty clinging to his ankle, there was nothing Ryan could do other than trust her. And despite all hell breaking apart around them, that was a trust that—as ever—came easy.

Before Ryan's eyes, the gaping portal into the past flickered, energies cascading through its depths. It was sealing even as he watched, the far end—the one that touched Doc's past—already scabbed over like a bloody wound. Amid it all, Don Nectar seemed to be disintegrating, slivers of his body unraveling as the radiation suit burned away. He had been a shadow of Doc Tanner, an echo taken substance, no more its own life than a heart murmur.

As Ryan watched, a great burst of energy exploded from Don Nectar's form as it broke apart, firing out of the rip in time in a shadow-dark swirl. The darkness touched everyone in the room, tearing through Ryan and Krysty, striking Doc where he lay slumped by the steps, and Jak and Ricky, who were still bound by the wall.

Perhaps a hundred years hence, those echoes would emerge in the swamps of Louisiana, where five shades of long-forgotten companions would rise and take life for a moment, just pale ghosts of what they had once been. For each person had a Don Nectar within him or her, waiting to be plucked from his soul in some bloody, scarlet dream.

OUTSIDE THE BUILDING where Nyarla and her family hid, J.B. was running from a swarm of hungry time-eaters, launching a grenade at them from just ten feet away. The charge struck the nearby wall of a building and exploded, turning another cluster of the disembodied mouths into ashes. All around, his allies were engaged in similar guerrilla strikes. But as J.B. watched, the remaining cloud of chronovores winked out of existence. He halted, breathless, as cries of surprise echoed from all about the abandoned ville. They had been ready to give their lives, but now the chronovores were no more, sucked into the closing rent of the time portal.

Above the distant military base, the lightning ceased, the time window closed at last.

"What just happened?" Marla asked breathlessly, her blaster poised in trembling hands.

Mildred shook her head. "Wish I knew," she admitted. "Just stay ready, okay?"

The other people on the snow-covered streets were

waiting for what would happen next. But nothing did. Without any warning, the chronovores' plague through time had ended.

IN THE OPERATIONS ROOM of the Operation Chronos facility, the crackling aftermath of the closing portal vibrated the air like a low bass note.

"I think this whole place is going to blow," Ryan stated as he looked furtively around the room.

Doc stood exhausted at the edge of the humming machinery and so did Krysty. Her Gaia power had finally abated, having lasted much longer than she had ever known before. As ever, its passing had left her weak as tissue paper, and she stood there hunched over and disoriented. Beneath the metal stairs, Jak and Ricky were just now waking up, their bonds half removed by Krysty and Ryan before the battle between Doc and Nectar had kicked off.

"You two okay?" Ryan asked, swiping the sharp edge of his panga across Jak's remaining bonds.

"Okay," Jak admitted. "Tired, like I awake for weeks."

"Mebbe you have been," Ryan said, handing his panga to Jak. The albino could free Ricky. Ryan wanted to check on Krysty.

Ricky was only just waking up, struggling to remember what he had seen. "That guy in the rad suit...?" he began.

"He is gone," Doc told him, leaning unsteadily on his swordstick, its blade back in the hidden sheath. "As if he was never here at all."

The old man was staring at the smoldering ruins of the time machinery, wondering if this had been his last chance to return home.

"We should get going," Ryan told him. Krysty was in his arms with her arms around his shoulders. She looked limp, as if she had no strength left in her.

Doc nodded. "He was me, was he not? A little sliver of me, like a reflection in a mirror."

"We'll discuss it outside, Doc," Ryan said, urging his exhausted companions back up the staircase.

Before long they had trekked through the military building and made their way to the doors that Ryan and his team had entered by. The lock remained broken, and when they stepped through the doors they were surprised to find that the building had sunk almost ten feet, leaving them to clamber out of the mess that remained. There was no more lightning in the sky above. The generators were burned out, their metal shells black with smoke where they had expelled their last iota of power.

"The whole place looks dead," Doc said as he clambered up the slope.

"It's melting through the snow," Ryan said. "By this time tomorrow it'll probably be gone entirely."

"And there goes my gateway home." Doc sighed.

Ryan looked at the old man, unable to express what he felt. They had all left their homes behind, one way or another, trading them for the endless roads of the Deathlands. The fact remained that they were alive, and that was a fact worth clinging on to.

"Time and tide wait for no man," Doc said sadly.

"Where there's life, there's hope," Ryan reminded him as they walked away from the sinking remains of the military facility.

Epilogue

This much Don Nectar knew for certain: Tanner had been right. He was a shade, a shadow, a heart murmur mistaken for life.

Whatever the time scoop technology had done to Doc Tanner, it had glitched in a way that had created an afterimage, and it was that image that had been spit out in the hidden facility in Alaska, far away from the great workings of Operation Chronos. The facility had been nothing more than a B unit, a place to check data, out of the way of the Washington politicos.

Who knew how time trawling worked? Who could say what rogue data was created when a person's form was shunted into the time stream? What had happened to Doc Tanner had happened against his will, and it had generated a sliver of rogue data that had mistakenly thought itself a man. A glitch in time called Don Nectar.

Now, as Nectar was wrenched apart, absorbed once more by the time flow, he wondered how many other Don Nectars had been created, how much rogue data still existed, searching for the host body that would join with it to make it whole and let it go home. A legion of shadows, each one a tiny sliver of what Doc Tanner could have been.

Nectar closed his eyes as time's river washed over him, buzzing through his body with all the power of the chronal waves.

This much he knew for certain: traveling through time always came with a cost.

THEY MET in the snow-dusted plains of His Ink Orchard, close to the ruined mines. Ryan spotted J.B. and Mildred by the fire they had set to keep warm. The sun was rising once again, making its slow trek over the horizon where it would wait ponderously for the rest of the day.

"We were under attack by crazy things," J.B. told Ryan. "Thought we were going to die when suddenly the bastards winked out of existence as if they'd never been. That was your doing, right?"

Ryan nodded. "We had a little something to do with it, yeah."

Beside him, Krysty was brushing snow from her red-gold hair. Her strength had returned, her normal strength that was, but she would ask Mildred to check her over before they returned to the redoubt and its mat-trans, there to locate a new destination and perhaps a new destiny.

Ricky was annoyed he hadn't seen J.B. in action in the gladiatorial ring. He idolized the weaponsmith, even if he wouldn't come right out and say it.

Searching through her voluminous bag, Mildred produced his and Jak's blasters and other weapons, easing the DeLisle off her shoulder. "You have to learn to pick up your toys after playing," she chided Ricky.

Ricky knew she was kidding and he laughed.

The area that had once seemed to be beyond the edge of the world was returning to normal. Snow fell in its usual pattern, straight down without stopping; and the barricade that Nyarla and her father referred to as the Tall Wall had come down without so much as a hint that it had ever been. The bubble of ruined time—the chrono spasm—had healed, the untamed energies returned to wherever they had come from, the chronovores disappeared. Doubtless, the muties remained, but that was the twisted nature of the Deathlands.

Doc turned to his companions, a look of concern on his lined face. "I am famished," he said. "Wherever we wind up next, let us stay long enough to find ourselves a decent meal. Mayhap, roast chicken, so delicious you can smell it a room away."

Ryan smiled. The man had lost almost everything and yet still—somehow—he carried on. He was an inspiration to them all.

Gradually, the seven companions returned to the redoubt and made their way back to the mat-trans and whatever lay beyond. Whatever it was, they would face it as they always had—together.

* * * * *